JAWBREAKER!

Pulp Fiction in the Classic Mode

Donald F. Glut

STRANGE PARTICLE PRESS
FIRST TIME IN PRINT2021

ISBN: 9798703286166

Copyright 2021 Donald F. Glut

Strange Particle Press is an imprint of PageTurner Editions LLC.

DEDICATION

To "Jaunty" Jim Steranko,

the *real* Mr. Miracle, who, late one night,

told me how to break out of a locked vault.

OTHER THRILLERS BY DONALD F. GLUT

Bugged! (forthcoming from Strange Particle Press)
Spawn (forthcoming from Strange Particle Press)
Brother Blood

JAWBREAKER!

CHAPTER ONE: AGENTS OF DESTRUCTION

The sturdily built man in the blue uniform reacted furtively to the roar of the approaching vehicle. A security guard for more than two decades—he had been employed here since 1944—he was trained to recognize the sometimes subtly different sounds made by a wide range of vehicular motors. What he was hearing now was clearly the deep roar of a finely tuned truck engine.

Turning his body, his sharp eyes focused upon the vehicle approaching under the light of the full moon—a big canvass-topped truck, its headlights cutting through the nighttime fog, roaring towards the big factory he was employed to guard. It was almost midnight, he knew, much too late for any delivery or pickup. And even if this truck did, for some reason, have business here tonight, he would have been informed of it.

Something was wrong here, the guard knew, something that, at least for the present, demanded watching.

Moving quickly, the guard stepped into the shadows, hoping that his dark uniform would be absorbed into that patch of blackness. So far, it seemed, the occupants of that vehicle were not yet aware of his presence. He watched from his place of concealment as the mechanical monster rumbled to a stop, its hulk silhouetted in the moonlight and its idling motor purring, just outside the building.

The security guard's eyes flashed. His right hand mechanically flew to the holster strapped to his side and snapped open the flap. In all his years working this job he had never been called upon to draw his weapon. But now, with the appearance of this truck, he was taking no chances. In a blur of movement the long-barreled .38 revolver was in his hand, his index finger firmly braced against the cold trigger, his thumb resting atop the hammer.

Until now the only time he had fired his weapon was on the target range, where he had never struck a bull's eye. How would he fare tonight, he wondered, if called to put his modest skills with a gun to use? Could he, in fact, really fire upon another human being, even if his own survival depended upon it?

He decided to wait for a while, hoping to take in more information before acting rashly and doing something he would later regret. What if this truck did have business at the factory tonight, and he was simply not informed of it? He took a step forward, careful to remain within the concealment of the shadows.

No, something was definitely amiss here. The vehicle was definitely not a company truck. This one was more like the trucks used largely ten or more years ago. All the company trucks he had ever seen, anyway, were paneled, not covered in canvass. And they were all identifiable by their bold, silver logos boasting the company name: ACME CHEMICAL COMPANY. This vehicle bore no ACME identification, or any other markings.

"Who's there?" he finally said with a slight waver in his otherwise deeply authoritative voice.

Cautiously, the revolver heaving in his hand, the guard slowly began to make his way along the wall of the building. His middle-aged heart raced as the import of the danger struck him. For all his years on this job he had had it fairly easy—a boring job, to be certain, but one that had never yet challenged the safety of his life. Tonight that might all change.

Within seconds he was standing just over a hundred feet away from the waiting truck.

His eyes focused through the darkness upon the massive vehicle. In his nostrils were the smells of the thing, the gasoline, the odors typical of a finely tuned engine. "Who's in there?" he

2

repeated.

But no response to his query came from the truck other than the low sound of its idling engine. "One last time," the guard said, this time in a much sterner voice, "who's in there and what do you want?"

Again, only silence.

Then the doors opened, and a trio of dark-suited men silently—surreptitiously, it seemed—exited the truck, their faces obscured by the night and also the brims of their hats. Whether or not these men were aware of the guard's presence, they gave no indication. Quite plainly, however, they were not here to do business, at least of the legal kind.

The moment of truth had come, the guard told himself. There was no backing down if he was to retain his job along with his self-respect. Taking a deep breath of Los Angeles' cool night air, he rushed forward, then abruptly stopped, his company-issued weapon trained on the suspicious trio. His heart pounded fiercely as he realized the slightest provocation would prompt him to squeeze that trigger.

"Okay, hold it right there!" he ordered. "Don't move, any of you! This isn't a toy and I'm not afraid to use it!" Upon hearing his shouted threat, the three men froze in their steps, giving no reply. "Now get those hands up—and I mean *high!*" the guard warned, feeling a sense of power in the way the three men did as they were commanded.

Indeed, the trio obeyed without question or hesitation. Their eyes, staring from shadowed faces, gazed at the ebony revolver, the gun-metal barrel of which glinted in the moonlight. This made the guard feel good, even powerful, as he realized that he was in control of the situation. And, thus far at least, he had not been required to discharge a single shot. Now, if he could just hold these characters at bay long enough–somehow–to get word to the authorities. . . .

For the moment, however, there was still time to enjoy his feelings of triumph. "All right then," he said, brandishing his revolver boldly, "before I call the police, you're going to tell me what the hell's going on here." But the men in the dark suits continued to remain silent. They just stood there, staring towards his weapon with a kind of arrogant confidence that sent a thrill of terror coursing through the security guard's body. Even more unnerving, their faces, partially seen in the light of the moon, were smiling. "What do you three find so amusing?" he asked.

Again there was no reply, and the reactions of these three men were beginning to tear at his nerves. Obviously these characters knew something that he did not. His finger tightened against the trigger of his service weapon. "I'm warning you again," he said. "You're tempting me to use this."

At last there came a reply, not in words, but in a quiet and confident laughter that emanated eerily from all three of them men — becoming louder, more boisterous, by the moment. The laughter must have had its desired effect, for the guard's hand began to vibrate fearfully, and then shake. He knew that his moment of truth had arrived. They and not he was in control of this situation. His only choice was to shoot now — kill this trio in cold blood — or risk whatever fate they were intending for him. There was no time to hesitate, if he were to live through this night. He had to fire three times and each bullet had to strike its mark, before. . . .

But there was no longer any time to deliberate. No more time even to act. Just then did he notice more movement inside the truck, a dark shape betraying the presence of a fourth body emerging from the opening in the canvass at the rear of the vehicle. The guard jerked to one side, aiming his gun at this new intruder. Yet his movement was not swift enough. For even as his finger began to squeeze back the trigger, a yellow spike exploded in the night and a hot pain tore through his chest.

Instinctively he looked down at the origin of that pain, saw the growing crimson stain spread across his uniform blouse, felt his hand go limp and heard the clink of his gun as it struck the pavement. Those were the guard's final sensations as his knees collapsed and he dropped to the ground in an engulfing sea of blackness.

* * *

The four dark-suited men faced no more opposition to

completing their nocturnal mission.

One of the men—the leader, a stern-looking character with red hair—motioned to the others, giving them a silent command. Two of them, moving efficiently and with rehearsed precision, silently rushed back to the truck. From within its canvass canopy they produced a weirdly shaped metal device about the size of a portable television set. The men strained as they carried the heavy gadget away from the truck and towards the factory. Over the door, emblazoned in bold silver lettering, were the words:

ACME CHEMICAL COMPANY

The windows were barred with crossing rods of thick steel.

Again the red-haired man motioned a hand signal. Without saying a word, another member of this band produced a blowtorch from the truck, and then promptly went to work on the bars of one window. In less than a minute, amid a spray of hot sparks, pieces of the bars fell away—at least enough for the four men to proceed to the next phase of their mission.

One of the men smashed the glass of the window, immediately setting off an alarm. Another man adjusted a timing mechanism on the metal device, setting it for five minutes, at the same time beginning a series of ticking sounds, each one slightly higher in pitch. Then the leader nodded to the others.

Again without speaking, the four men hurried back into the truck. Moments later, engine roaring like some great primordial monster, the vehicle sped away from the building and into the night. Less than five minutes later, the timing device whining to a peak pitch as it reached its mark, the ACME Chemical Company exploded in a cataclysmic ball of flame and debris!

* * *

The figure of a lone man was revealed in the automobile headlights. He stood in the middle of the road, flanked on both sides by the hills through which the road curved. He was waving his arms, frantically, trying to flag down the vehicle speeding towards him.

Almost striking him, the squealing car swerved to the side of the road and screeched to a halt. The 1965 Plymouth Fury stood out in the moonlight, its black and white two-tone coloring instantly recognizable. Atop the vehicle a red light broke through the darkness of the night, revolving continuously and rhythmically.

Instantly the man rushed towards the stopped automobile, as the front passenger-seat window rolled down and a blinding flashlight beam assaulted his eyes. "All right, buddy," stated a voice from inside the car, coldly, "let's hold it right there."

The man stopped in his tracks, apparently knowing that the slightest wrong move on his part could be his last. Throwing one hand over his eyes as a shield against the beams, he raised the other hand in submission. Then he waited, until two men in Los Angeles Police Department uniforms stepped cautiously from the car, service revolvers drawn. "Now," said the first policeman to exit the patrol car, "you want to calm down and show us some ID?"

"But be careful about it," said the other police officer.

Doing as he was instructed, the man regained his composure, then gingerly removed his wallet, opened it to his driver's license and then handed it over to the first of the two officers.

"I'm sorry if I startled you, officers," he said, "but I've just been through a most grueling ordeal."

The policeman who accepted the wallet studied the license, enclosed in a clear-plastic sleeve, as he responded, "Is that a fact?" Apparently satisfied with the license, he flipped through additional see-through sleeves, noting the man's draft classification, then several credit cards. "Dennis Richter," he read from the wallet.

"Everything in order?" the other policeman asked.

"Seems to be," he said, closing the wallet and handing it back to its owner. "All right then, Mr. Richter, what's this 'grueling' experience that's got you standing out in the middle of the road at this time of night, behaving like a lunatic?" For several moments the man identified as Dennis Richter only stared at the policeman's badge, as if its mere presence had the power to bolster his courage.

"It was terrible," he said at last, shaking his head as he

spoke, "just awful. He just . . . *appeared*, like out of nowhere!" The two officers looked at one another, one of them raising his eyebrows. "You think he's high?" asked the first. "Hallucinating?"

"That's easy enough to check," said the other. "But first let's hear him out. Okay, Mr. Richter, simmer down. Who's this 'he' you're raving about and just what did he do?"

Breathing deeply and then exhaling, Richter explained. "I was driving down this road." His words were coming out more slowly now, more deliberately, as he gradually reclaimed his composure. "As you can see, officers, it's pretty dark out here. There's a stop sign back there, at that last intersection. . . ." He nodded off in that direction.

"Yes, we know all that. Please, get to the point."

"And, being the law-abiding citizen that I am, I, of course, stopped."

"The point, sir."

"So, as I was saying, I stopped. Not seeing any other cars around, I proceeded across the intersection. That's when, without warning, like all of a sudden and before I even had a chance to press down on my gas pedal, I heard this . . . *thunk*."

"A . . . *thunk*?" the second policeman repeated.

The man nodded in reply. "Behind me . . . like something had landed in my back seat. I own a convertible—a red 1960 Impala, you see." Motioning with his hands as he spoke, he was becoming more excited again. "Five years old, but in near-mint condition."

"You said . . . *landed* . . .?"

The man paused to breathe deeply again and try to calm down. "I turned around to see what it was—almost a reflex action, you know—and saw this man sitting in the back seat glaring at me. He must have leaped from one of those hills. That's the only way to explain how he got into my car."

"Must have been some athlete to jump from way up there and hit his mark in a moving vehicle," commented the first policemen. "Even a slow-moving one, as you said."

"Uh, what did this . . . man . . . look like?" asked the second officer.

Hesitating, as if embarrassed to go on, Richter replied, "I . . .

don't know, really."

"It was dark."

"No, that's not the reason."

"Then, what *is* the reason?" asked the first officer, his growing impatience obvious.

"He was...*masked*."

"Masked?" replied the other policeman with a chuckle. "You mean like the Lone Ranger?"

"I guess *hooded* would be a more accurate description," he explained. "He wore a hood that covered most of his face, except for the eyes, ears, and the area from the bridge of the nose on down."

"Oh, more like Captain America, that patriotic guy in the comic books." This time he laughed—mockingly—instead of merely chuckling. "And just what color was this...this hood. Blue...with a white letter 'A' on the front and little white wings over the ears?"

Richter shook his head. "I guess it was black. It was hard to tell, even in the moonlight. But, please . . . I'm really serious about this." The two patrolmen exchanged incredulous glances.

"He was wearing gloves, too. Also black, if I remember."

"Then," asked the first policeman, "after he landed in your car, of course, what did he do that was so . . . terrible?"

"Then he said something like . . .'Sorry, pal, but I need this car more than you.' That's all he said."

"Nothing more?"

"No," the man replied. "Then there was this blur of movement, as his fist shot towards my skull. The next thing I knew, I was waking up over there along the side of the road—in a clump of bushes. I saw the moon and the stars. Then, slowly and painfully, I got back to my feet. When I looked around to get my bearings, I was still seeing those stars." The policemen grunted.

"What was worst of all," Richter continued, waving his arms as he spoke, "was that my car was gone. That bum in the hood stole it and left me out here in the middle of nowhere. I was already on my way back into town when I spotted you."

"Hmmm," answered the first policeman, "so this is really all about a stolen car. Okay, come over to our vehicle and you can fill out some paperwork. But I think it'd be best for all of us to leave out that part about the black hood. Let's just say it was too dark for you to make a positive ID of the thief."

"You don't believe me?"

"You've got to admit that your story is pretty far-fetched. Pretty far-fetched indeed."

"But," interjected the other officer, "it's not impossible that some clown out there has finally done it—you know, imitated some character he read about in a comic book or in some ancient pulp magazine, or maybe saw in some old movie serial."

"Forget the hood, I said. Stolen cars fall under our jurisdiction. So does assault, as shown by that nasty bruise on Mr. Richter's face. Hooded mystery men fall under the jurisdiction of the fiction writers." All three men walked back to the squad car. One of the policemen shut off the revolving light, while the other opened the back-seat door.

"Get in," he said. "We'll drive you back to the station, where you can fill out a full report. Then, once we have all the pertinent information—make, year, serial number and so forth—we'll do our best to get your car back. In the meantime, you can tell your story to your insurance company and hope they buy it."

* * *

A pair of high-powered headlights followed those of the canvass-topped truck, so that four shining orbs cut through the darkness of the road. For at least five minutes now the red Impala had been pursuing the larger vehicle along the winding roads that weaved through the Hollywood Hills. The metal monster rattled and rumbled as it struggled to make the curves in the road, the slightest miscalculation of its driver possibly sending it plunging off the edge and into the canyon below.

Inside the truck, four men were fleeing from a scene of disaster—one that they had created. Two of the perpetrators of the ACME explosion were riding inside the cab, one of them doing his best to keep the vehicle on its course.

The other two—including the one who had given the silent

orders during their mission—were hidden beneath the truck's canvass covering. It was clear by now that the truck was being followed, for the Impala mimicked every movement of their own escaping vehicle.

"It's after us, all right," said the red-haired leader, his shoulder rubbing against the canvass canopy.

"Who do you think it is?" asked the other man. "Cops?"

The leader shook his head. "If it was cops, they'd have the sirens going by now."

"Then, if not the fuzz, *who*?"

"How the hell should I know?" the leader barked. "But whoever it is, it looks like he's gaining on us. Better be ready for him in case he catches up." He reached under his dark suit coat and withdrew a shining .45 semi-automatic pistol from its hidden shoulder holster. Checking the clip and making sure that it was loaded, he flicked off the weapon's safety. A look of grim determination showed in his eyes.

The other man also produced a weapon—a long-barreled .38 revolver. The driver of the truck needed no orders or prompting to know what to do. He and the man riding beside him had also detected the lights of the pursuing Impala—initially in the side mirrors—and deduced what was happening.

"If we can't outrun them," said the driver, "at least we might outgun them.

"But we don't know how many guys might be stuffed inside that car," said the other man. The distance between the Impala and the truck was gradually narrowing. All four men in the truck could now hear the other vehicle as its motor purred and its wheels shrieked along the road in its relentless pursuit.

The driver of the truck slammed his foot hard against the accelerator, pushing it to the floor. With its maximum speed, the truck bolted forward. But that burst of speed was not enough. The pursuing automobile was too lightly built . . . too sleek and too powerful. . . . Too fast!

The smaller vehicle was now close enough to be identified by the men riding beneath the canvass. The shiny scarlet hull of the convertible shown magnificently in the moonlight. But what most impressed the two criminals was not the car but the man behind the wheel.

"What the—?" was all that the man with the .38 could say. He pointed with one hand, his other hand gripping tightly his revolver. The red-haired leader of this foursome also stared out the back of the truck in astonishment. He could clearly make out the figure in the open-topped Impala. Moonlight bathed the convertible, revealing its driver in all his improbable splendor.

The driver was indeed a bizarre apparition, for his features were mostly concealed by a hood or mask, a tight-fitting, jet-black hood exposing only the ears and lower face, with the eyes staring ahead through slanting openings cut into the ebony cloth. And the driver's hands . . . the hands that were so expertly in command of the steering wheel . . . they were wearing black gloves.

"I never seen a guy drive like that!" said the man with the revolver. Indeed, the driver of the pursuit car was a master at the wheel. For the slightest miscalculation on his part—or that of the truck's driver—could send either or both vehicles to their doom. There were drop-offs of at least a thousand feet off to one side, and vision was difficult enough in these hills even during the day.

But the driver of the truck, though obviously not possessing the skills of that of the pursuit car, was no novice to the chase. He continued to pilot his tank-like vehicle almost with the skill of a professional limousine driver. Yet no matter the skills of the truck's driver, those of the man in the Impala were far superior.

"It's like that guy knows every inch of the road," exclaimed the man in the back of the truck possessing the .38, "like he's some kind of pro racecar driver or something."

"I'm not surprised," stated the leader, struggling to retain his footing as the truck continued to lurch about.

"How so?" said the other, also being bounced around.

"Don't you know who that joker is? Oh, yeah. You weren't there last night."

"You mean . . . that's . . . *Jawbreaker*? He's for real? I thought he was just some character you made up. A joke. . . ."

"You won't be laughing if that hooded creep catches up to us."

"Why's he called Jawbreaker?"

"If he catches up to us, you'll know." Nodding, the man with the automatic handgun then yelled a command: "Now quit wasting time jabberin' and kill that sucker!" Almost simultaneously, two weapons spoke loudly from the rear of the truck, deadly missiles erupting brightly from polished gun barrels. An instant later the Impala swerved, bullets ricocheting off its shiny surface. Again the men beneath the canvass fired, once more missing their intended target.

Taking aim again, they saw a black-gloved hand leave the convertible's steering wheel. Dip into a trouser pocket. Moments later, produce his own .38 snub-nosed pistol. Then, driving with his left hand, the masked man whom the red-haired man had called "Jawbreaker" raised his revolver, aimed it up towards the rear of the truck, and fired.

The gunman with the revolver buckled forward as a .38 slug cut through his throat. Gurgling incoherently, a hand reaching up in a futile gesture to stop the blood flowing from his neck, he tumbled out of the truck directly in front of the pursuing automobile.

The leader watched in grim fascination as the pursuit car, with no time to swerve away, bounced over his underling's bleeding corpse and continued in the chase. Then, a look of horror twisting his coarse features, he fled into the darkness of the truck, finding concealment behind a large wooden packing crate. Again the man in the hood took aim.

Once more the night air exploded with the firing of a gun. But his target had all but vanished into the darkness of the truck. Hiding behind the crate, the hooded man's quarry was virtually invisible. The hooded man could not see his target!

But the man behind the crate, no longer hampered by being in full view, had the time to take more careful aim. Peering out from behind the wooden box, once again he fired his semi-automatic gun, this time missing the man in the convertible by mere inches.

Three bullets remained in his gun, three more opportunities to miss his erratically moving target. Then, with an empty weapon and probably no time to reload, he would be at the mercy of the man in the black mask. Thinking fast, he considered his options, almost instantly settling on another — easier to hit, from a moving truck and at that distance — target.

A fifth time the red-haired man fired, then in rapid succession a sixth and a seventh — this time not at the man at the steering wheel, but at the Impala's windshield. The leader saw the windshield glass erupt in an explosion of flying shards.

Saw the hooded man suddenly react, instinctively, releasing his hand from the steering wheel to shield himself from the cascade of sharply cutting particles. Saw him lose control of his vehicle, if only for several crucial moments . . . heard the squeal of brakes and the skidding of wheels against pavement, as the Impala swerved to one side of the road and shot off into space.

As the truck continued on its way, the leader saw the crimson Impala arc, its polished surface briefly reflecting the moonlight, then disappear behind the edge of the embankment. Heard the car as it struck the canyon below, then, its gas tank igniting, explode.

A grim smile appeared on the face of man with the red hair, as smoke arose from the canyon while the truck continued on its way.

CHAPTER TWO: ORIGIN STORY

Many times has it been said that, during the act of dying, a person relives his or her entire life. However, none of Dave Andrews' past experiences flashed through his mind as his "borrowed" automobile shot off the road and through the air on its plunge to imminent destruction. If Andrews had remembered anything of his life it might have been of its most recent events. A series of events leading directly to this moment where death seemed inevitable.

Dave Andrews had not always hidden his identity behind the black mask of Jawbreaker. There was a time—only days ago—that Dave Andrews possessed but one identity. Yet those rapidly passing days had been witness to some unusual and rather spectacular events—events that culminated in a more remarkable and definitely fateful metamorphosis.

It was just days ago that the hot, noonday sun of Southern California beat down upon the expansive estate of multimillionaire Aaron Van Aaron. The Van Aaron mansion was a well known home in Beverly Hills; yes, even a popular stop for the many tour buses that cruised through the area, with riders hoping to glimpse the familiar face of some current or past movie star. The mansion's seemingly countless windows reflected the sunlight. The fragrance of freshly mowed grass hovered about the estate like some natural lingering perfume.

A brand new, raven-black Cadillac limousine was parked in the mansion's carport, the highly polished surface of the automobile shielded from the sun's rays. From inside the mansion came the sound of music, a cut from the latest album by one of the latest and most popular longhaired rock groups participating in the so-called "British Invasion."

Inside the enormous house, a rather small and homely man with a skinny—near-frail—frame walked through the maze of luxurious furnishings that almost cluttered the vast living room. He sniffed the air that somehow retained the smell of the interior of a brand-new automobile. Aaron Van Aaron smiled, looking around at his collection of priceless paintings and other collectibles—the hanging tapestries, the sculptures, the state-of-the-art stereo record and audiotape system—basking in these reflections of his own wealth. Indeed, Van Aaron liked nothing more than being rich.

"All that money can buy!" Van Aaron stated, slamming his hands together in a loud and triumphant *clap*. Briefly Van Aaron stopped to admire himself in a gold-framed mirror. He smiled again, apparently seeing something other than the image reflected back at him. Perhaps his glasses were in need of a new prescription. For the multimillionaire seemed not to notice that he was gawking at a face much like the one Washington Irving had described for Ichabod Crane.

"Ah, yes! The life of a successful playboy and man-about-town," he spoke again. "It's nice to be both wealthy *and* good-looking." Then, as quickly as his attention had gone to the mirror, it shifted, attracted by movement detected via his peripheral vision from outside one of the living-room windows.

Turning to the crystal-clear glass and peering outside, Van Aaron smiled again, this time not because of his own biased sense of self-worth, but at the vision he was now beholding beyond the window. The smile now spreading across Van Aaron's hawkish face was a lecherous one—for the vision that had diverted his attention away from himself was out there, hopefully (this time, at last!) waiting for him.

Still smiling, this time in anticipation, Aaron Van Aaron rushed through the mansion's maze of opulently decorated rooms, exited via a back door, then hurried to an abrupt stop on the tiled surface that connected to the edge of his luxurious swimming pool. But it was not the pool—the biggest and finest that could be bought and pass the Beverly Hills codes — that had attracted his attention, but rather who was in it. Van Aaron's smile segued to a sheepish grin.

He coughed, nervously, before finally speaking. "Hello there, Miss Foster." His voice was nasally, somewhat high-pitched, almost rodent-like. There was also a dull and droning quality to it. And whenever he spoke to this vision of female pulchritude now gracing his pool it seemed to be even higher.

"Hiya, there, Mr. Aaron," the vision replied in a rather sensuous voice that was almost as high as Van Aaron's. That vision — a young woman barely twenty-two years old, and with looks comparable to those of either a movie queen or goddess from some long-extinct pantheon — swam gracefully to the edge of the pool, her incredibly long brown hair trailing behind her. Eyes big, red and open wide, she smiled at the multimillionaire, enticingly yet innocently. Then, moving with the grace of some sleek jungle cat, she slowly pulled herself out of the water, unveiling an impossibly perfect body covered only in the most strategic of places by a tiny white bikini. As he always did when Barbara Foster emerged from his pool, Aaron Van Aaron gulped.

She stood there for just a few moments — long enough for Van Aaron to take in her water-dripping beauty — the droplets on her magnificent body glistening in the sunlight. He never knew for certain if Barbara was trying to "turn him on," or if she was, like some innocent child of Nature, simply reveling in the sensations of water and sunlight against her *Playboy* "fold-out" good looks. Van Aaron did not really mind what her intentions were. He liked what he was seeing and stared until Barbara finally reached for a towel bearing the Van Aaron monogram and began to dry herself off.

"Are you going swimming today, Mr. Van Aaron?" Barbara asked in a singsong voice. "The temperature today is just perfect."

"Er . . . no thank you, Miss Foster," he replied. "You know I'm not the world's best swimmer. But I'm glad to see you're enjoying my pool again."

"I sure am!" Barbara said, offering him a pretty smile. She continued to dry herself with the towel, sensuously, rubbing dry the cleavage of her ample breasts, her long and perfectly muscled legs striking a model's type pose.

"You bet she is!" The voice was loud, deeply masculine and originating from the far end of the swimming pool. "Get another eyeful again today, you scrawny scarecrow?"

Still drying herself, the brunette goddess smiled, her cheeks flushing with self-consciousness, as she turned in the direction of the voice. With a gentle toss of her head, her long dark hair slapped wetly against her nicely rounded shoulders.

Van Aaron and Barbara watched as Dave Andrews swam across the pool with the speed and skill of an Olympic champion—a latter-day Buster Crabbe or Johnny Weissmuller, he liked to think of himself. Reaching the edge where the other two people waited, he quickly emerged from the pool. A moment later, Andrews, a handsome young man wearing blue swim trunks, was standing beside the young woman, his thick raven-black hair and sleek yet muscular body dripping water.

"Andrews!" stated Van Aaron with contempt sounding in his voice and showing on the smirk appearing on his skinny face. "Keep up with those insults of yours and, I promise you, I'm going to fire you!"

"Fire me?" laughed Andrews, reaching for another monogrammed towel. "That'll be the day. Never, pal—not as long as you want the best bodyguard hyphen driver money can buy. Not as long as there's someone like me to watch over that pitiful excuse for a body . . . and your millions. More likely, someday I'll quit."

Now it was Van Aaron who laughed. "You? Quit? Now that's funny. You won't quit, Andrews. You'll never quit. Not as long as I keep paying you the highway robbery you charge me for your services—a fortune compared to what you made breaking your bones for those dumb movies. And while I allow you the luxury of living in a plush mansion like this instead of in some skid row, quarter-a-bed flophouse where you belong."

"I think those prices may have gone up," Andrews chuckled.

"And let you use the limo in your free time. And let your girlfriend spend so much time hanging around here, too," Van Aaron continued, ignoring what Andrews had just said. "No, sir. You're not going to walk out on me—not now or ever.

You've got things too easy here . . . too sweet."

Upon hearing the word "girlfriend," Barbara started to laugh, louder and harder than either of the two men.

"Now what's the matter with *you*, Miss Foster?"

"It's just the way you two carry on all the time, Mr. Van Aaron," she answered with a gentle toss of her damp hair, "like a couple of kids."

"Come on, Barbie," admonished Andrews, "this is serious business."

"Serious business," she laughed again.

Once more Dave Andrews addressed his employer. "Listen," he barked, scowling, "if I'd never quit the stunt business, I'd probably, given the rising budgets and all, be making almost as much money in the movies and on TV today as you'd ever pay me. Besides, I miss the business—a hell of a lot. I had real friends back then, too."

Van Aaron cocked an eyebrow, skeptically. "The way I hear things, there's less call for your kind of work these days. Too much violence on the big screen and on the boob tube—no offense, Miss Foster—these days."

"That's a matter of opinion—the opinion of a handful of do-gooders," argued Andrews, flexing the muscles of his arms. "But if I'd stayed on at Democracy Pictures," the former stuntman went on, "like I should have and originally planned to do, I might have been all set up. Had a new contract in the works—with more money and a possible promotion to ramrod and then maybe second-unit direct, just like Yakima, in charge of all the action sequences. After that, who knows? I might even have got to direct a whole movie on my own."

"Might, might, might," snarled Van Aaron in his squeaky voice. "And I *might* have gone on to create some great work of art, if I hadn't spent all that time making the right investments. You just go on believing all that, you muscle-bound gorilla. And while you're at it, you can keep on enjoying your job with Aaron Van Aaron, Beverly Hills' most eligible playboy bachelor."

Reaching out, Andrews placed a hand around Barbara's trim waist and pulled her body against his. "So, *Mister* . . . Van . . . Aaron," he said with contempt, "did you come out here just to ogle Barbie, as usual, or do you have some actual work for me to do this afternoon?"

"I . . ." Van Aaron stammered, then cleared his throat.

"Maybe need your bodyguard to protect you from all those society ladies at Mrs. Snooty's Afternoon Club? If so, I'd better dry off and slip into my spiffy chauffeur's uniform and cap and rev up the big black Caddy."

"I . . ."

"Now that's really funny!" returned Andrews with a boisterous laugh. "Me . . . protecting you. When is that ever going to happen?"

"Someday it could," said Van Aaron.

"You flatter yourself, Mister . . . Van . . . Aaron. I mean, why would anyone want to attack you? I mean, be honest and think about that. I've had this job now for . . . what has it been? A couple years already? And not so much as a simple mugging."

"Better to be safe than sorry."

"That's what you say, Mr. Boss-man," said Andrews. He rubbed the towel through his hair, drying it to dampness. "The bottom line is that I'm sick of this job. Sick to death of it. And I'd quit in an instant, if. . . ."

"If I didn't pay you so damned much."

"If you didn't pay me so damned much." Andrews frowned. "And if that day ever comes, once that money of yours runs out, I'm cutting out of here and going back to my *real* job, doing stunts. That's where the *real* excitement is."

Barbara laughed again. "Can't you two ever argue about something different?"

"At least I still have other interests that keep me from flipping out over the sheer monotony of this lousy job," Andrews said. He tightened his arm around the young woman's waist. "All right, Van Aaron. What's it going to be this time? Where are we going today in the big limo?"

"A social event," Andrews' employer replied. "Tonight. In Brentwood."

"Why am I not surprised?" said Andrews.

"But this is no ordinary event. This one happens to be one of the *primo* social events of the season." Van Aaron's angular face almost glowed with enthusiasm.

"What kind of event? A dog show? No, probably something not so 'dangerous'. More likely a flower show."

"Very funny," Van Aaron retorted. His thin lips pursed into a scowl suggesting the appearance of a dried-up apple. "No, this is something beyond your own meager powers of appreciation. It's a party, yes—but the guest of honor is none other than Count Franz Lojos, a visiting nobleman from the Eastern European country of. . . ."

"I don't care where he's from," interjected Andrews with a disinterested grunt. "As long as the food is good."

Barbara, unlike Andrews, seemed legitimately impressed. "Ooh! A count! I've never met a real count before. I just hope he's not like Dracula. And we're invited?"

"*We're* . . . invited?" said Van Aaron in a mocking voice. He directed his attention from Andrews to the brown-haired beauty at his side. "I seem to remember only my name being on the invitation. I'm afraid both you and your overdeveloped boyfriend will have to wait this one out in the limo."

Stepping away from Barbara, Andrews walked up to his employer, striking an intimidating pose "Look, Mister . . . Van . . . Aaron, it's bad enough I have to drive you to these dumb affairs. But if Barbie wants to meet a count—even one of some insignificant God only knows what country—she goes along. And I go along with her. Otherwise I stay home and watch that new *Wild, Wild West* on the tube . . . see what I've missed by dropping out of the business . . . and you can drive yourself to your little shindig."

Aaron Van Aaron's scrawny body shook slightly in the presence of his employee, yet his face betrayed no fear. A defiant scowl on his face, he turned and started to walk back towards the mansion. He was, after all, the lord and master of this vast estate and all of its wealth.

Andrews and Barbara looked at one another. Disappointment showed on her gorgeous face, but the man she was gazing at only smiled. They had both experienced this routine many times before. They needed only to wait a few seconds longer . . . without looking back, Van Aaron said in a cold, matter-of-fact way, "Be dressed and have the limo ready to go by nine o'clock sharp."

Then he walked back inside the mansion, slamming the door behind him.

* * *

Just before nine o'clock, two attractive young people waited impatiently in the living room of the Van Aaron mansion, anticipating the usual grand entrance of the master of the house. They were facing the antique grandfather's clock that stood to the side of the spectacularly winding staircase that led to the upper floor.

At the precise moment that the clock chimed nine, the homely playboy appeared at the top of the stairs. Wearing the most expensive tuxedo Rodeo Drive could provide, Aaron Van Aaron — his attention apparently only on himself — strode down the stairs with the air of royalty.

"Mr. Van Aaron looks kinda cute, all dressed up like that," said Barbara Foster as her eyes followed the multimillionaire's descent. "What do you think?"

"Looks to me like some skinny penguin," grunted Dave Andrews, reaching into his pocket to withdraw the keys to the limousine.

Completing his descent, Aaron Van Aaron stepped from the last stair onto the soft cushioned rug that spread to every corner of the living room, his highly polished black shoes sinking into the plush fabric. That was when he finally took note of the two people who had been awaiting him. The playboy reacted with a start. Andrews was attired in his familiar black sports jacket; he wore no tie over his open-necked white shirt.

Barbara's appearance, while far more pleasing to Van Aaron's eyes, was dressed equally casually. Indeed she seemed to have been born to wear the new mod clothes that were rapidly dominating women's fashions. Her tight, black turtleneck sweater showed off the lovely curves of her breasts, and her black miniskirt, topped by a wide red belt, barely covered her matching black panties. Shiny black boots, reaching up to just below her knees, completed the ensemble.

Nice to look at though she was, Barbara's appearance — nor that of Andrews — exactly met the requirements of the invitation. "Look, you two," said Van Aaron with a gasp, "this is a formal affair. We're going to meet a damned *count*, for cripe's sake."

"Okay, Barbie and I will stay home, if you don't like the way we're dressed. Hope they have valet parking, because these big Caddies are a bear to parallel park. Come on, baby," Andrews said, putting the keys back into his pocket and taking his girlfriend's hand, "let's see what's on tonight in color."

Nothing more needed to be spoken on the matter. Van Aaron, obviously knowing better by now than to try arguing with his employee, especially with the clock continuing to tick away and the party imminent. Instead, as almost always, he kept silent. "Meet you two outside," Andrews stated with the sound of triumph in his voice. "I'll get the car."

* * *

This job is a real drag, Andrews thought, as he exited the mansion, then opened the door and slipped behind the steering wheel of the brand-new limousine. Unbearably dull. Have to be creative . . . find some way to make this job more exciting. Some way to get the old adrenaline flowing and heart pumping faster. Need some real kicks . . . some danger . . . even risking one's life. Those are the things that make life worthwhile! Yes, Dave Andrews was a man whose very existence depended upon action. That was why he originally went into business as a stuntman. But now, save for his daily workouts and his dips into the Van Aaron swimming pool, and, of course, his relationship with Barbara, Andrews' existence was basically action-free. Indeed, for the past few months, a thought was beginning to take birth somewhere in the back recesses of his mind . . . a wild and almost impossible idea that could bring some of that old electricity back into his life.

Sitting comfortably in the driver's seat of the big black car, Andrews felt the two weighty objects filling the opposing inner pockets of his sports jacket. As a legally licensed bodyguard with a very wealthy and influential Beverly Hills resident as his employer, the ex-stuntman always carried two shiny-black .38 snub-nosed revolvers on his person when working. As always each pistol carried six bullets. Moreover, Andrews' seeming-uncanny sense of balance almost allowed him to determine the number of cartridges these weapons contained by their weight alone.

Tonight, however, his sports jacket contained something in addition to the revolvers—three cloth items, neatly folded and compressed, that created a soft yet thickly padded lump within his inner left breast pocket. Items that could, if properly used, bring an end to the boredom currently pervading Andrews' life and into a world of excitement that not even the movies, with all their dangerous stunts, could offer.

A subtle smile turning his lips, Dave Andrews switched on the ignition, letting the mildly purring Cadillac motor idle for almost half a minute. Then he pressed his right foot down against the accelerator, revving up the engine as a signal to Barbara and his boss that they were ready to go off socializing.

Andrews waited, seeing his two passengers briskly walking towards the car. Barbara took her usual place in the front passenger seat, while Van Aaron occupied the seat of honor in the more spacious rear compartment. Then, smiling at the beauty sitting next to him, Andrews pulled into the driveway and cruised away from the mansion.

* * *

The Brentwood mansion where Count Franz Lojos was being entertained appeared to be not unlike Van Aaron's in relatively nearby Beverly Hills. "You see one of these boring places, you've seen them all," grumbled Andrews under his breath as he drove Van Aaron, the man whose body he was employed to guard, and Barbara, whose body he watched over for no payment at all, toward the stately building. The house was surrounded by a high metal fence. A long road led through the open gates and to the mansion's front door.

In reply, Aaron Van Aaron only grunted.

Every light in the mansion seemed to be burning this night, with the silhouettes of myriad guests flitting and dancing by the windows. Even outside and with the purring engine of the limousine, the sound of classical music could be heard emanating from the big house. Focusing his eyes ahead and down the road, Andrews could see the veritable army of people—men in tuxes and women in formal gowns—as they slowly stepped through the front entranceway.

Stopping the limousine in front of the mansion and turning the keys over to the valets, Andrews looked around, noting the array of obviously brand-new, high-priced, 1965 automobiles already lined up behind the Van Aaron car in humming procession. Then, feeling the cool night air, Andrews, Barbara and Van Aaron, the latter handing the man at the door his invitation, entered the party mansion.

Inside, the party was in progress with live music, social activity and a thick cloud of tobacco smoke. Almost upon their arrival, Andrews' and Barbara's garb went noticed by the other formally attired guests. Van Aaron even blushed as he noted the reactions some of them gave to Andrews' casual jacket and lack of a tie and to Barbara's form-hugging sweater and abbreviated skirt.

"I told you it was formal," whispered Van Aaron to his bodyguard as the threesome made their way across the main room of the mansion.

"Let them eat their hearts out," replied Andrews, one side of his face crinkling into an I-don't-care smile.

Barbara remained apparently oblivious to the glances and stares. "Where's the Count? Will he be wearing a crown so we can pick him out?"

"That's the Count over there," said Van Aaron. He nodded in the direction of an elderly, overweight bearded man wearing a military type uniform, weighted down by medals that shimmered and tinkled below the light of an overhead chandelier.

"Stuffy looking old coot," mumbled Andrews with a chuckle. "Kind of reminds me of someone out of Gilbert and Sullivan. I'm surprised he doesn't topple over with all that metal weighing him down. Bet a couple are from grammar-school spelling bees."

"*Shhhhh . . .*" was Van Aaron's only response.

"Why don't we go up and introduce ourselves to the old bird," Andrews continued.

"Can we?" asked Barbara, noticeably excited over the prospect of meeting someone with a title, even from such an obscure country.

"Given the circumstances and the way you two are dressed," Van Aaron cautioned, "I don't think that would be. . . ." But Andrews was already on his way, with the very willing Barbara hanging onto his arm, on a direct course towards Count Franz Lojos. Behind them, Aaron Van Aaron remained where he stood, rigid and speechless.

The nobleman turned at their approach, his attention immediately going to the young brunette, his gaze shifting down along her body to rest upon her pretty knees. There was a noticeable glassiness in his eyes and his tall form was slightly swaying, his condition explained by the almost-empty champagne glass in his hand. He smiled, almost lecherously at the woman.

Barbara smiled back naively and extended a hand. "I never met a real count before, Your Royal Majesty."

"And I've met few young ladies as attractive as you," he said, slightly slurring his words. Eyes widening, Count Franz Lojos accepted the young woman's dainty hand. "But I'm hardly a 'Royal Majesty,' yet from someone as lovely and delightful as you, I humbly accept the compliment, Miss . . . ?"

"Foster," she said with a cute giggle, "but you can call me Barbara."

"Barbara." With a polite bow, he kissed Barbara's hand. Immediately a pleasant smile spread across the Count's lined face. Bringing his hand to his mouth, he coughed, making it sound like an official pronouncement. "My dear," he said in the most perfectly spoken English, "I assure you that the pleasure of our meeting is all mine." That stated, the Count snapped as best he could to a position of attention and clicked together the heels of his shiny boots.

All the while, as Count Lojos and Barbara Foster proceeded to converse, Dave Andrews remained unaffected by all the pomp; in fact, he was mildly amused by it. Standing in the presence of one of noble blood meant nothing to the former stuntman, who would rather be hanging out with "Duke" Wayne or a group of rowdy cowboys. Indeed, Andrews' attention was rapidly shifting away to someone, presumably of less than noble blood, standing some fifty feet away in front of a hanging series of huge, ornate tapestries.

She was a bosomy young beauty with very large green eyes. Her blonde hair was fixed up in a seemingly impossible arrangement of curls and winds. Her obviously voluptuous figure was mostly covered beneath a form-fitting, strapless white evening gown, cut low in front to expose her generous cleavage, and with a hem that touched the floor. Against the thick tapestries, the gold of her mane and whiteness of her garb stood out strikingly.

The woman smiled at him, perhaps invitingly, not that the reason for her smile mattered. Andrews was not here tonight "on the make"; his love and loyalties were reserved for Barbara and her alone. Nevertheless, he was already bored by the open-ended chatting of his girlfriend and the nobleman, and craved something new to capture his attention.

The blonde was the first to speak. "Hello."

"My name's Dave," he said. "Dave Andrews. And what do they call you?"

"Hi, Dave," she replied in a low and sultry voice. "I'm Mary. Mary Smith."

Andrews grinned, having expected to hear something more exotic. "Just what I like, a good old-fashioned American name. Not that I don't mind all the Priscillas and Millicents, but you can't get any more good . . . old-fashioned . . . or American than that."

Mary Smith laughed, quietly and politely. She seemed to be by herself, which Andrews found a bit odd—a woman with Mary's looks being at such a swank social event unescorted. But this was the middle 1960s, he remembered, and, as Bob Dylan so aptly put it, "The times they are a-changing." "You don't seem to be having a good time," she said.

"It's that obvious?" Andrews looked around, noted the small orchestra made up of elderly, tuxedoed musicians. "Don't they have any Rolling Stones records in this freak show?" The music, to Andrews's tastes at least, was just rambling on; what it needed, he thought, was some sudden ear-piercing dash of electric guitar . . . a loud fuzz tone to cut through the monotony of—who was that he was hearing now, Beethoven or Brahms? He never could keep his classical music straight! "All sounds the same to me," he said.

Again, he looked around, noting the other partygoers—most of them just standing around in a single spot, some of them talking to one another. "And they all kind of look alike," he added, and then looked her up and down. "No offense."

"I wonder what they're all talking about?" she asked.

"Nothing of interest to me, I'm sure. Care for a drink?" Mary Smith nodded and smiled again.

Looking off towards Barbara and the Count, he saw a waiter—a man instantly notable for his strikingly red hair and who seemed to have a perpetual scowl chiseled onto his face— approach them carrying a tray with what appeared to be about a half dozen glasses filled with champagne. Count Lojos accepted a glass, but Barbara—who was not really a drinker of alcohol—graciously refused. Waving, Andrews tried to get the waiter's attention.

Instead, he got noticed by Barbara, whose gaze suddenly flashed from the nobleman with whom she was conversing to the blonde woman now taking up her boyfriend's time. For several protracted moments the two beauties stared at one another, while Dave Andrews—the cause of their mutual glaring—said nothing.

Andrews' attention, in that moment, was focusing elsewhere. Upon something held by the waiter serving the champagne . . . held in concealment beneath the tray holding the drinks. Something dark and shiny, its surface briefly flashing in the chandeliers' light. A flash of movement, the tray and drinks dropping away to crash against the floor, the red-haired "waiter" moved. Suddenly fire blasted from the thing in the waiter's hand—a .45 automatic semi-automatic—and three minor explosions echoed through the room, releasing the stench of gunpowder, capturing everyone's immediate attention.

A moment later, Count Franz Lojos was buckling forward, his once immaculate uniform now wet with gore, his collection of medals clattering against the floor. The music stopped, the various instruments of the small orchestra ending one after the other.

"Assassination!" an elderly woman screamed. "Another one!"

"King Lojos has been shot!" yelled a young man nearby.

"Where's the hell's our security?"

"Does this mean war?"

Dead! the ex-stuntman thought, noting the scarlet stain spreading rapidly across the nobleman's outfit. Immediately the Count's bodyguards and other security personnel began to act, hands reaching for concealed weapons. But before a single gun could be drawn, the waiter—that is, the red-haired man who had been masquerading as a waiter—pressed the barrel of his gun against the side of Barbara's head. "Careful," he warned, "unless you want to see her blood and brains spilled all over this nice floor mixed with the Count's!"

Barbara shut her eyes, apparently anticipating the worst. The security people relaxed their trigger fingers, lowered their hands. At the same time instant pandemonium broke out, as the guests, the musicians, the hired help, everyone agitatedly began moving about. Thus far only three shots had been fired. That meant there were, if the clip had been fully loaded, seven more bullets remaining in that weapon. The gunman could kill Barbara and still have enough ammunition to take down six more victims. By then the red-haired man was waving his gun threateningly about the room. "Now don't anybody move! Anybody! You hear me?" he ordered the assemblage.

Andrews' eyes darted in their sockets, noting that some of the people were already settling down, given the command and by the violence they had just witnessed.

"And get those hands up. Anybody plays hero and they get what the Count here just got!"

Andrews, of course, wanted to move, but given the present situation, could not. Barbara, her hands raised, stood motionless, just inches away from Count Lojos' bleeding body. Open again, her blue eyes looked toward her boyfriend, but he could offer her nothing more in return than an attempted expression of confidence. He knew that the slightest movement by either him or Barbara could result in one of the gun's remaining bullets ripping into her own spotless flesh.

Again his eyes shifting, Andrews saw Aaron Van Aaron, the

man he had been hired to protect, standing where he had left him, shaking like a scared infant. Never before had Dave Andrews felt this helpless. Inside the pockets of his jacket were two beautifully balanced revolvers loaded with a total of a dozen .38 bullets. And his skills with those guns—honed following many long hours on the target range—were without peer. Still, considering the danger to Barbara, Van Aaron, Miss Mary Smith and everyone else, those pistols were now no better than a child's cap guns.

There was absolutely nothing that Andrews could do—at least for the moment—but watch and wait and bide his time. The waiting was not for long.

Seconds later, three other men in waiter's outfits, each one stationed at a pivotal area of the room, joined the first, tossing aside their trays of drinks to reveal long-barreled .38 revolvers. Now there were four men with which to deal, each one brandishing potential death. Now, more than ever, Andrews was glad that he had not acted; for if he had, at least one of that foursome would have, by now, shot him down. Yet he could not just stand there doing nothing!

"You can't get away with this!" The slowly spoken voice had come from the far end of the room. A young man, drunk given the way he slurred his words, was already staggering towards one of the gunmen. No doubt, Andrews thought, the alcohol had bolstered his courage. He saw the young man's hands clench into fists.

Another eruption of gunfire!

The young man collapsed to the floor, his brains oozing out one side of his bleeding head. A middle-aged woman fainted, swooning loudly as she dropped.

"Anyone else think we can't get away with this?" said the gunman, the weapon in his hand still smoking. Several other women crumpled into unconsciousness, while their male escorts attempted, without success, to catch them.

Attention—that of the gunmen as well as the partygoers— went to the young man who had just been killed and also the fainting women, time enough for Andrews to do . . . something. Taking advantage of the commotion, Andrews moved quickly, slipping away from Mary Smith and between a small congestion of partygoers. So far, his luck seemed to be good; for no one yet had apparently noticed that the one male guest not properly attired was disappearing from the group and losing himself amid the wrinkles and folds of those towering tapestries.

A rush of excitement swept through Andrews' body, electrifying his spine, supercharging his blood, as he emerged from behind the other side of the tapestries, stepping into what seemed to be a hallway. Looking about furtively, he saw that he was alone. Everyone involved in the conspiracy must be back in the big room, where all the action was taking place. Great! he thought. With a modicum more of luck there just might be enough time remaining for him to do what he should have been doing long ago.

The moment he had long been considering—awaiting—had come! His right hand anxiously sought the contents of his left breast pocket—those three items that had produced that small bulge beneath his jacket.

First he removed a neatly folded object made of black cloth. Unfolding it, he pulled it down over his head until all of his face that remained exposed was his ears, the area from his nose to his chin, and—looking out from a pair of slanted holes—his dark brown eyes. He removed the pair of black gloves— protection of leaving behind incriminating fingerprints — slipping one over each hand. Then those gloved hands dipped into his jacket to produce the two coal-black snub-nosed revolvers. Finally, he quickly removed the black sports jacket, dropping it to the floor.

Black-hooded and gloved, he flexed his well-toned muscles. For several moments, images flashed through his memory— pictures of similarly masked characters he had seen as a boy in those old movie serials, characters with names like Zorro, Copperhead, the Masked Marvel and the Black Commando— heroes all, who risked their lives against seemingly impossible odds to bring down the world's evildoers.

The fact that he was now also hiding his identity seemed to impart new, almost preternatural strength to his limbs and an augmented sense of self-confidence to his very being. In a way Dave Andrews—former stuntman-turned-bodyguard-and-chauffeur—had ceased to be, replaced by a masked Twentieth Century knight whose very existence thrived upon action and adventure.

* * *

As no one at the party—not even Barbara and Van Aaron—had noticed Dave Andrew leave the room, likewise no one should him return. Everyone present would evidently be still too preoccupied with the horror that, just minutes ago, had occurred there and the threat of potentially more violence to come.

Silently the mystery man, his identity now concealed by black cloth, emerged from behind the tapestries, each gloved hand brandishing a loaded .38. The attention on the partygoers was still on the two bloody corpses and the four gunmen. Andrews knew that it would not be long before his returned presence was noticed. Delaying even a crucial moment or more could be fatal. There was no recourse for him but to act now.

"All right!" he shouted brazenly in his deepest and most commanding voice, trying his best *not* to sound like Dave Andrews. "All of you creeps—drop those guns!"

With his first words, the man wearing the mask was finally noticed.

Suddenly all eyes, including those of the four gunmen, were looking in his direction—at this bizarre, armed and hooded character. The hooded man smiled subtly; was he perceived as one of this gang of assassins, or yet some other and more deadly menace?

Boldly the masked man stepped back among the partygoers, walking past the startled Mary Smith, to face the four men with the drawn guns.

"Who in the hell . . . ?" began the phony waiter who had slain Count Franz Lojos. "Get that masked clown!"

Upon that command two of the other "waiters" jerked their gun-hands in the masked man's direction, simultaneously squeezing back triggers.

Yet fast though their actions were, their opponent moved quicker. Before they could discharge their weapons, twin spikes of flame erupted from the masked character's revolvers, delivering instant death to each of their skulls. The two men dropped, automatically firing their guns at the floor. Again the man in the black mask ordered: "Like I said, drop your weapons!"

Sweating, the red-haired "waiter," apparently the leader of this murderous band, cursed. His eyes looked furtively towards his accomplice. Then, slowly, he nodded. A moment later two guns banged against the floor.

For several seconds the hooded man said nothing, the eyes peering out from the slanted openings in his mask looking first to Barbara and then to Van Aaron. Both of them were watching his actions in amazement, but neither of them seemed, at least yet, to have recognized him. No doubt their eyes were more fixed upon the mask itself than the face it only partially exposed.

That was good, he thought. To be effective in this new guise—the persona that would afford him the thrills he so craved, without jeopardy to his "normal" life—it was best that his true identity remain unknown. So far the simple yet effective disguise was apparently working. And if it could fool Barbara and also his employer, people he knew so well, perhaps it could also keep his ID secret from anyone else.

All the while since his reappearance in the room, Andrews' sharp brain was working out a plan of action. And while his mind began to formulate that plan, he continued to watch the first "waiter." He noticed the slight turn of the man's head and the very subtle nod of his head, a signal to yet another accomplice—one not yet revealed—in the room.

But the masked man had waited too long. The signal had already been sent and received and, just seconds later, its recipient acted. Something small, hard and metallic slammed against his back—a sensation the mind of Dave Andrews remembered from scores of movies in which he had played bit roles as bad guys.

"Now it's your turn to drop your gun," spoke a familiar female voice as the little gun barrel pressed harder against him. So, Andrews thought, "Mary Smith" is also not what she seems. No wonder "Mary" was by herself, and her being "stag" had nothing to do with Dylan.

"Now where have you been hiding that little toy," he asked, disguising his voice and inching his body backwards to brush against her bosom, "as if I couldn't guess?" Glancing back, he took note of the silver-coated Berretta clutched determinedly in the blonde woman's dainty hand. "Looks like someone's been watching too many James Bond movies."

Again she jabbed him in the back. "Are you going to make me tell you twice?" Realizing he had been duped by the blonde's attractive face and figure, the masked man relaxed his grip on the revolvers and let them drop to the floor.

"Mary" walked around her captive. There was a sneer of triumph on her gorgeous face, as she looked the masked man up and down. Then she smiled, cruelly, and pressed the cold barrel of her small semi-automatic pistol against his exposed cheek. "Okay, now that fun time's over, let's see who thinks Halloween's come early this year," she said.

Moving sensuously, "Mary Smith" inched closer to the man in the mask, the Berretta still directed towards him. Her full lips parted temptingly and she pushed her full breasts against his chest. Then, slowly, she reached for the hood, touching the black material with anticipation. Obviously she was savoring this moment of revelation. Her smile broadened, her moment of triumph imminent. Gingerly her fingers began to slip beneath the cloth covering the upper part of the mystery man's face, drawing out the moment. "Mary Smith" should not have hesitated.

With reflexes trained to perfection following myriad screen battles, the masked man moved. A gloved hand, taking her by surprise, shot to the woman's wrist, shoving it away from the black hood. A fraction of a second later his other hand locked about the wrist of her gun hand, spinning her curvaceous body around so that her back was now against his chest.

"Mary" moaned as the masked man exerted pressure on her arm, forcing it into an unnatural position. In response her fingers loosened on the Berretta, dropping it. "Damn you!" she hissed, and then stomped a spiked heel onto his shoe. The masked man grunted, moved, just enough for "Mary," with a maximum exertion of strength, to slip away from his grip.

Capitalizing on that moment, the "waiter" moved again. In a flash his body darted toward the floor to retrieve the discarded gun resting just inches away from his feet. From that moment onwards everything happened incredibly fast!

The masked man also moved . . . leaping forward, slugging the man back to the floor, his fist stinging from the impact. In almost the same action he kicked the weapon, sending it sliding across the polished floor. But there was yet a fourth gunman garbed in waiter's clothes. Seconds later that remaining assassin was on the hooded man's back, pulling him forcibly away from the man who had shot the Count.

Almost simultaneously, however, the masked man spun around, a gloved fist striking his opponent with the seeming force of a jackhammer. Dropping, a hand rushing to his battered face, the fourth "waiter" groaned, "Man, he's a regular Jawbreaker!"

"I guess if you need to call me something," responded the masked man with a sly grin on the exposed part of his face, "Jawbreaker's as good as any." That said, the newly christened Jawbreaker slugged his opponent again. By now the partygoers were backing away.

Jawbreaker's peripheral vision detected several men—security, he thought—starting to draw their guns. He heard a familiar male voice. "Where's the phone?" yelled Aaron Van Aaron. "I'm calling the police!"

But the fight continued. The last "waiter" was already back and attacking his masked opponent. Jawbreaker felt the man's powerful fists slam with full force against his back. His body jerked, enduring the pain.

Before he could be struck again, the masked man caught his opponent around the neck. Recalling a trick he had learned during his stunting career, using leverage as well as speed, he flung the "waiter" over his head, sending him colliding into his other foe's body. Both men collapsed to the floor, groaning. As Jawbreaker fought, he heard through the confusion around him: "Shoot them!" someone cried out, apparently to one of the security people.

"All three of them? Maybe just the masked guy?"

"No, we can't risk firing in these close quarters."

"Where did that woman run off to?"

Three male bodies—one of them masked and gloved, two dressed like waiters—rolled across the floor and into a glass cabinet with smashing impact, releasing a flood of breaking dishes and glassware. Scrambling to his feet, Jawbreaker yanked at what was left of the cabinet, pulling it down atop the squirming body of the first "waiter." "Somebody stop them before they wreck the place!"

Taking advantage of the confusion, one of the gunmen—"waiter" number four—managed to get back to his feet. Reach a chair. Grab it and hurl it at Jawbreaker. The masked man was faster, though, ducking aside as the possibly priceless item of furniture was shattered against the floor.

"Stop them, somebody! That was an antique!"

But the fight went on, nobody able to stop it. Feet continued to kick. Fists pounded away. Bodies suffered relentless punishment. Finally a size-twelve shoe, launched by powerful leg muscles, collided with the masked man's face. Jawbreaker fell backwards, his body striking something on the floor. Something cold and metallic.

Another second passing, the gun was in the masked man's hand. Looking up, he saw the two "waiters" starting to make their way towards the front door. "Wait for me!" A streak of gold and white emerged from one side of the room, "Mary Smith," having retrieved her weapon and joining her fleeing cronies. "Stop right there!" roared the man in the hood.

Pausing, "waiter" number one turned and aimed his weapon at the masked man.

At the same time Jawbreaker raised and cocked his weapon. Apparently realizing that his foe was the superior shooter, the red-haired gunman grabbed his distaff accomplice and pulled her in front of him as a shield, just as the masked man fired.

The well-aimed bullet struck "Mary Smith" cleanly in the right breast. She groaned and started to drop, letting go of her pistol. Blood spilling from her wound, the red-haired man smiled.

A sickening feeling wrenched Jawbreaker's stomach. Killing a vicious gunman was one thing, but shooting a beautiful young woman—even inadvertently—was an experience he hoped never to have again. He paused, hating himself for what he had been forced to do, hesitating just long enough for the remaining "waiters" to escape through an open window.

"Get him!" It was Van Aaron's voice. "Get that masked lunatic before he shoots somebody else!" With incredible speed, Jawbreaker sprinted towards the crumpled body of the woman he had just shot. Crouching, he gazed down at her face, watching the tears well up in her eyes and her sensuous lips curl up into a look of hatred.

Obviously in pain, choking and spitting blood, "Mary Smith" said, "Not . . . your fault . . . *he* killed me. Matson . . . that bastard! Bastards, all of them . . . I'll tell you. Listen . . . Tomorrow night . . . ACME . . . Company . . . Fultons . . . master plan . . . careful . . . they can *destroy* . . ."

"Fulton?" he uttered. He knew that name, had experience with people bearing it. He wondered, could it be the same Fultons? No, that was a common name. That was impossible, insane even to consider. It simply could *not* be . . . before the blonde beauty could explain, her green eyes closed and her gorgeous body relaxed, limp and motionless.

The room was already erupting in a cacophony of voices, most of them threatening, swearing. In just another few moments the man calling himself Jawbreaker would be captured and unmasked, his usefulness over. And, from what "Mary Smith" had managed to tell him, Jawbreaker's work was just beginning.

Turning his head, he saw that the crowd—a few people holding guns—was already rushing towards him. From somewhere in the distance he could hear the sound of approaching police sirens. Clearly someone had reached a phone. Without further hesitation he bolted for the window, the same one through which the two assassins had escaped. In just seconds a flying leap, culminating in a somersault, catapulted him through the window and outside.

From somewhere off in the distance, getting progressively fainter, came the sound of an automobile speeding away. Looking up, Jawbreaker glimpsed the car—a black, late-model Pontiac Bonneville, no doubt the assassins' getaway vehicle, roaring off to freedom, already too far away to note the exact year or license plate number. In another few seconds it was gone, its raven finish merging with the night.

Concealing himself in the shadows, Jawbreaker waited, pulling off the mask and gloves to restore the identity of Dave Andrews. There he waited, outside and unseen . . . while the police squad cars arrived at the scene of violence and the people inside the building began to calm down. Eventually feeling the time was appropriate, he re-entered the house through a rear door. Then, moving with the stealth of a shadow, he returned to the place where he had left his jacket, donned it again, leaving behind the tapestries his incriminating mask, gloves and pistols.

"Barbie, baby!" he called out, spotting the pretty girl dressed in black almost immediately after returning to the assassination scene.

"Dave!" she returned, looking around and seeing him. She rushed up and threw her willowy arms around him. "Where did you go, sweetie?"

"No place, really, honey," he said.

"Andrews!" Aaron Van Aaron was walking up to the couple. "I should have known. Finally, my life's in danger, and you're nowhere around. Where did you go—to the bathroom?"

"I guess, in all the confusion, I just got lost in the crowd," said Andrews to both of them.

There were, of course, many questions to be answered—not to Aaron Van Aaron and Barbara Foster, but to the police. Once Andrews had told the police everything that he could without incriminating himself, and he was dismissed, he excused himself to use the bathroom—taking a quick side jaunt to retrieve the disguise and working tools of his new double identity.

As Andrews vacated the formerly festive place along with Barbara and his boss, he remembered what the woman calling herself "Mary Smith" had told him . . . first, apparently the name of the killer with the red hair, a man named Matson, seemingly the leader of that band of assassins.

More importantly, he remembered that she said something about the power to destroy. He knew that there were a number of companies named ACME in Los Angeles, not to mention the San Fernando Valley, Orange County and other related areas.

Something was to happen there tomorrow night at one of those companies, something involving that other name she had mentioned, "Fulton" . . . and some kind of "master plan," apparently involving destruction. Something, no doubt, of interest to his other and more dynamic identity.

Andrews also recalled the answers he heard that had been given to the investigating police. A visiting nobleman had been slain this night; no one could deny that fact. But the eyewitnesses' accounts concerning the Count's murder and its bloody aftermath, right down to the number of fake waiters, varied considerably.

About one thing, however, almost everyone questioned agreed: A masked character named "Jawbreaker" had taken the law into his own hands, and, as a result of his vigilante action, four additional human beings were now dead.

CHAPTER THREE: A LOT OF DISASTER

Dave Andrews did not relive the past events of his life, perhaps because he was not about to die. Indeed, the borrowed Impala exploded when its gas tank ignited upon the vehicle's violent contact with the canyon's basin. And a great cloud of smoke billowed into the night sky from that twisted mass of burning rubble. But Andrews—still wearing the mask and gloves of the adventurer called Jawbreaker—was not inside the doomed car when it blew up.

Rather, he was standing at the edge of the road above, his powerful body illuminated by the moonbeams, and staring down towards the burning wreckage. In the distance the faint rumble of a truck could still be heard, fading into the ambient sounds of night.

Breathing deeply, Jawbreaker rubbed the eyes that looked out from the slanted holes cut into his ebony hood, then pulled off the mask and stuffed it into his pocket. Then he did the same with the gloves.

Andrews sighed with profound relief, knowing that—had he not acted when he did—his flesh and bones would already be incinerated amid that raging conflagration. But he had acted, sparked by the reflexes and skills of a highly trained man of action. He had, just moments following the shattering of his windshield by his opponent's bullets, managed to spring up off the driver's seat of his car and leap out, as he had done in movies, rolling uncomfortably but safely alongside the road with the precision of a skilled stuntman.

A grim smile moved Andrews' lips, for he knew that a single second of delay or uncertainty would have resulted in his last moment alive on this Earth. He had saved his own life, but other than that, he knew, the night had been a bust.

It had taken too much time for Andrews to research the myriad companies in Los Angeles and its surrounding areas bearing the common name ACME of Roadrunner cartoons fame. To begin with, he had got a late start, having spent most of the day and evening at the beck and call of his employer. Then, by the time he deduced that the most logical of these companies for saboteurs and assassins to target for destruction was not ACME Used Cars, ACME Costume Rentals, ACME Book Shop or so many others, but the ACME Chemical Company less than a mile from the Hollywood Hills. By then, it was already mid-evening. Alas, the saboteurs struck too fast.

Andrews had more or less witnessed the explosion—at a distance and from the speeding limousine he had borrowed once more from Aaron Van Aaron—while on his way to the ACME factory. Seeing the fire and the smoke rising into the night sky, he grimly realized that actually preventing the destruction of the ACME Chemical Company had, in an instant, become a moot point. However, he—in the guise of Jawbreaker—might still be able to stop and bring to justice the perpetrators of that sabotage.

He did not, of course, want to use the limo in his capture of those felons. The big black Cadillac was registered to his employer and, if identified, could readily result in his career as a masked adventurer coming to a premature end, not to mention creating a quite embarrassing situation with Van Aaron. Someday, he thought, maybe he should use some of that fine money his boss was paying him and buy his own car; but, having such easy access to the luxurious Van Aaron vehicle, owning an automobile himself rarely occurred to Dave Andrews.

Fortunately Andrews had spotted the canvass-topped truck as it sped away from the burning crime scene, and it did not require an Ellery Queen to deduce that it had been involved in the sabotage.

The truck, in his estimation, seemed to be speeding towards the Hollywood Hills. Andrews knew well the winding, ascending and descending roads of those hills. Long had it been his job to know them, either as a stuntman performing the hazardous chases filmed by the second-unit movie crews, or as Van Aaron's chauffeur. He also knew the shortcuts and maze of connecting minor roads. It was no great feat for Andrews to drive the Cadillac up into those hills, park it on some inconspicuous side road, then — donning the guise of Jawbreaker — wait.

The wait proved to be less than fifteen minutes. Hidden within the darkness of the hillside, he had observed that same canvass-covered vehicle roar along his predicted road, ignoring the stop sign at the intersection . . . waited until another vehicle, an Impala convertible, slowed toward that intersection, stopped, and then began to proceed on its way . . . waited for the opportune moment to make the leap that, had it been in a motion picture, would have earned him extra money that night.

But tonight Andrews was paid nothing for his efforts; to make matters worse, he had failed both to prevent his foes from carrying out their act of destruction and to prevent their escape. There was nothing more he could do out here tonight.

Feelings of defeat weighed heavily upon Andrews' spirit as he made the long trek back to the road where he had parked Aaron Van Aaron's expensive automobile. During his walk he tried to imagine some link between the assassination of a European count and the destruction of an American chemical factory.

He thought about the gun battle he had engaged in before the Impala flew off into oblivion. One of the men — the one with whose red hair had been revealed by the moonlight, and whose bullets had shattered the windshield — was familiar. Andrews was certain that it was the same man who had posed as the waiter who, just a little more than twenty-four hours before, had slain Count Franz Lojos. The man, he remembered, "Mary Smith" — whatever her real name was, maybe the police knew by now — had seemingly identified as Matson. If nothing else, that identification positively established that the same gang of criminals perpetrated both heinous acts.

Andrews also dwelled upon that *other* name that "Mary Smith" had uttered just before she died. "The Fultons," she had said. If indeed there was some connection between the Fultons to whom she was referring and the Fultons he once casually knew – the two who sarcastically used to call him "Mr. Stuntman," some investigation on his part was required.

* * *

Within two hours, Andrews was parking the limousine in its usual spot—the driveway of the Van Aaron mansion. When Aaron Van Aaron asked Andrews where he had been that evening, the bodyguard and chauffeur replied with a curt, "Out."

The last thing Dave Andrews wanted to do that night was gab, especially with this boring playboy. He was weary and desired nothing better than a good night's rest. Ignoring his employer's incessant jabbering, he strode upstairs to his bedroom. It was already well past midnight and Andrews had exerted muscles tonight that had not been used to their full effect in many months. He was exhausted from his adventure and there was much to think about.

Andrews knew that he was now directly involved in some major chain of events having international implications— possibly some grand-scale conspiracy, one that without doubt involved both sabotage and murder.

The concept thrilled him . . . indeed, more than even the wildest movie stunts ever could. Like some addictive drug used by the hippies, the sense of danger . . . putting his very life on the line . . . fed his being. For the first time in many months Dave Andrews felt "alive" again—*truly* alive, with a sense of purpose, the feeling that his skills and strengths were about to accomplish something in this crazy world more significant than performing the comparatively safe stunts required for the movies.

Without undressing, he plopped down upon the comfortable bed that had been bought with Van Aaron money. The cushy mattress and bed coverings felt especially comfortable this night. He fell asleep rather quickly, his slumber deep and uninterrupted.

His dreams that night were mostly of blazing guns and automobiles screeching along dark and hilly roads. But he also dreamt that night of a lovely and curvaceous young woman with big eyes, an alluring smile, an unsurpassed figure and long brown hair.

* * *

Dave Andrews awoke early the next morning, fully refreshed, ready to face the world anew, already craving danger and excitement. After impatiently shaving, showering, dressing and combing his black hair, he strolled downstairs with the latest Beatles tune whistling through his teeth. Need to tape that one, he thought, that is, providing he got access to Van Aaron's new recorder when radio station KRLA plays it again. The atmosphere of the mansion was enhanced by the appealing smell of fresh bacon and eggs frying.

"Good morning, Stanford," he said as he stepped briskly into the kitchen.

Stanford, his employer's lanky English butler, was busy at the stove fixing breakfast, a lacy white apron around his trim waist.

Andrews gazed over at the two crackling frying pans that Stanford was fussing with, one containing a series of bacon strips, the other a half dozen eggs. He breathed in the tantalizing aroma as the butler flipped over the eggs.

"Just the way you like them, Mr. Andrews," said the man in the apron. "The eggs just a little on the hard side."

"Good," replied the ex-stuntman, the salivating glands of his mouth already in operation, "I hate it when the yolks have that slimy film."

From behind Andrews came a loud grunt.

Turning, Andrews saw his boss sitting at the kitchen table, a melancholic expression on his face and the morning edition of *The Sentinel* in his hands. The multimillionaire was staring intently, apparently barely noticing Andrews' presence, through the thick lenses of his even thicker-framed reading glasses. His long nose was directed towards the newspaper like the flesh-toned beak of some weird bird.

"My, my," quipped Andrews, "but aren't you in a cheery mood this beautiful morning."

"Obviously you haven't read today's paper," he replied without looking up. "That new 'ace reporter,' Rod Richmond, wrote the whole thing up."

"What?"

"Big explosion. The ACME Chemical Company. A security guard was killed. An Assassination one night, a big explosion the next. And all those other recent acts of sabotage we've been having lately. Reminds me the Fifth Columnist sabotage in World War II."

"Kind of reminds me of some of those old movie serials I used to see as a kid – at the movies and on TV," mumbled Andrews.

Ignoring his remark, Van Aaron continued. "Not to mention all those recent unsolved robberies—jewelry shops, banks, art galleries, you name it. And those killings—assassinations, mostly, of political figures, both foreign and American. And the murder of all those scientists! Remember that physicist two months back . . . and that visiting nuclear power expert from the Middle East? The whole town is going to hell in a hand basket, if you ask me."

"Actually, I didn't," said Andrews.

"And what gets you up so early?" remarked Van Aaron, still not looking up. "I didn't think you hit the pool before ten o'clock."

Andrews looked towards the clock hanging on the kitchen wall. Although he had climbed out of bed without effort this morning and was ready to face the world, he had neglected to note the hour. "Just what the hell time is it, anyway?"

"Let me see," said Van Aaron, raising his eyes in the direction of the clock, "the big hand is on. . . ."

"Never mind, 'Mr. Skelton'," interrupted Andrews. He saw that it was not yet eight thirty, at least a couple hours before his currently usual getting-up time, but still much later than his formerly usual rising time at the studios. Good, he thought. He had much to do today and being up already would afford him an early start.

He slid into a chair, joining Van Aaron at the table. "Whenever you're ready with that grub," Andrews said to Stanford, "I'll have my usual."

"Coming up, Mr. Andrews," said the butler, with his strong British accent, without looking back.

"*Mr.* Andrews," stated Van Aaron with a groan. "What a laugh."

Andrews, saying nothing in reply, just stared at his boss from across the table.

Following several seconds of silence, Van Aaron finally noticed the eyes glaring at him and lowered the newspaper.

"Well," he said, "what is it now?"

"You need me for anything this morning?" Andrews finally inquired. "Any poodle shows or art exhibits on today's agenda?"

"It looks like an uneventful day," replied the homely playboy. "Why?"

"Then since you apparently don't need me today, I'd like to have the day off. And since you don't drive, I'd like to borrow the Caddy again for a while."

"You borrowed it last night." Van Aaron set the newspaper down atop the table.

"I need it again today."

Aaron Van Aaron frowned. "When are you going to buy your own car?"

"When you pay me enough so I can pay cash for one."

"You still haven't told me where you went with it last night. What do you need it for today?"

"Here you are, Sir," interrupted the Englishman, as he began to serve the breakfast he had prepared. "Toast and coffee will be ready in just a minute."

Andrews' reply to his employer was in the nature of his expression. His eyes narrowed to slits and an almost threatening look altered his features. He prized his personal life and did not relish giving out explanations about what he did in his free time.

"Oh, all right, all right," Van Aaron finally acquiesced. "Take the day off. What's my word worth around here, anyway? I'm just the boss here, that's all."

"And the Caddy?" asked Andrews as he began to eat his bacon and eggs.

"Take it!" said Van Aaron, raising his voice. "Take everything—my car, my house, my blood, my toothbrush. . . ."

"That, Mr. Van Aaron, you can keep. Don't worry, I promise I won't dent your precious car."

* * *

Andrews enjoyed the tasty breakfast offered by Stanford, washing it down with a cup of the butler's freshly brewed coffee. Then, wiping his hands in his napkin and without excusing himself, he got up and strode off to the Van Aaron living room.

It was not yet nine o'clock in the morning when he picked up the receiver of the gold-colored telephone and dialed his most frequently called number. The phone rang for at least a half dozen times before a somewhat tired yet familiar feminine voice finally answered.

"Yes? Hello?"

"Barbie?" Dave Andrews spoke enthusiastically into the phone's mouthpiece. "Hope I didn't wake you out of your beauty sleep, baby, not that you need one. Guess who?"

"Dave," Barbara said, stating the obvious. "You know I know your voice, silly."

"None other," he replied. "What are you up to today, sweetie? Any special plans?"

"Nothing special, honey," she said. "I found a couple ads for modeling work in the paper, but I'm not really sure I want to do them. I think they involve nudity, and you know what a prude I am."

"Right," he said, an image of Barbara stuffed into one her almost illegally scanty bikinis suddenly flashing into his mind. "I don't want you taking your top off for anybody but me. And if anybody—any director or photographer, anybody—ever tries to get fresh with you, just remember some of those 'tricks' I taught you."

Barbara giggled. "Haven't had to use any of them yet. But I've been practicing, just in case." He imagined her making a fist and slamming it into the palm of her other hand.

Andrews smiled. "Then you're basically free today," he stated. "That's great."

"Why? Do you have something planned?"

"Get yourself ready to go in about an hour. I'll be by with the Caddy. And look your best—which should be easy—because you never know who you might meet. Who knows, maybe you'll be discovered."

"Go?" she asked with innocence in her soft voice. "Go where? Discovered by who?"

"Oh, yeah, baby, sorry. We're going to a movie studio today."

"A movie studio?" she replied, her voice louder now, higher-pitched and excited.

"That's right," he explained, "Democracy Pictures . . . where I did a lot of my stunting before selling my soul to Van Aaron. And with his limo, we'll go through those gates in real style."

"I can be ready in less than an hour," she said, giggling with excitement.

"Good," he returned. "I just have to brush my teeth. Otherwise I'm ready to roll. I think you're going to enjoy this, Barbie, baby."

* * *

In less than an hour, Andrews—his black jacket worn over a blue sports shirt—was on the twelve hundred block of Seward, a Hollywood residential street off Sunset Boulevard, double-parking the sleek limousine outside of Barbara's apartment building. Almost immediately upon blasting the car's horn Barbara appeared outside the building, smiling broadly, looking gorgeous as always in her tight-fitting black blouse and bright red miniskirt.

Leaning to his right, Andrews opened the passenger door. Automatically the two young people kissed as Barbara gracefully alighted on the black leather seat.

Then, with a revving of the big eight-cylinder engine, the Cadillac cruised off to Sunset, making a right turn on Highland Avenue and heading north towards the San Fernando Valley.

Democracy Pictures was located where it had been for years—on prime land in the Valley community of Studio City. Once the modest-sized studio was a bastion of mostly modestly budgeted, lowbrow screen entertainment—primarily serials and "B" cowboy movies, starring the likes of sagebrush singer Sundown Dawson, ground out on a weekly and even daily basis for the Saturday-matinee juvenile crowd. Yet Democracy also occasionally scored higher with reviewers with a higher budget feature, usually a World War II heroic drama or more prestigious "A" Western, some starring the "Duke."

Most of Democracy Pictures' "usual" youngster-targeted output had been filmed during the 1930s through the '40s and into the waning years of the 1950s. During those decades the studio had provided employment for many of the industry's greatest stuntmen, second-unit directors and special-effects wizards in the movie business, whether it came from Hollywood or elsewhere. Those talented people that worked for the studio on a more or less regular basis became known informally in the business as the "Democracy family." Moreover, some of the scenes shot during that rich period of movie history were so well executed and spectacular that they continued to turn up for many years as stock footage, either in other Democracy films or in movies made by other companies.

Indeed, when the requirement was for action, excitement and thrills, no studio—even the majors—could equal that offered on a regular basis by Democracy Pictures.

Dave Andrews had only worked for the studio a few years, but had been a big fan of its movies and chapter-plays since he was a child. By the time he worked his first day on the Studio City lot, Democracy had long "wrapped" its final episodic adventure, the twelve-chapter *Circus King vs. Crime, Inc.*, a rather lackluster last hurrah shot in 1955 and loaded with an abundance of footage originally shot for various earlier and far superior productions.

But even though he had been a member of the "Democracy family" for just a short time, appearing only in some of their lesser efforts, Andrews managed to build for himself a strong and commercial reputation. He became known, in fact, as more than just a stuntman of better than average abilities. He was hailed by his peers, some of them going back to the studio's glory days, as one of the best in the business—a veritable daredevil who was not afraid to take chances that other stuntmen would not, but always safely. By the time he had left the studio in reluctant acceptance of the offer for employment made by Aaron Van Aaron, Andrews had ramrodded several shows, answering only to the second unit director.

Driving slowly up to the studio gate, Andrews opened his wallet and proudly flashed the guard the lifetime pass that had been given him years ago by the one of the studio's veteran action directors. On the spot recognizing Andrews, the guard said cheerfully, "You don't have to show me that, Dave. You're always welcome on the lot." He smiled and tipped his hat to the pretty woman sitting in the passenger seat.

"Thanks, Woody," said Andrews with a warm smile. "Feel like I'm coming home. Is any of the old stunt team working today?"

"A couple," Woody the guard replied. "They're working on some low-budget Western today. None of the old stars in it. Otherwise, it's been pretty slow around here these days. Not much going on in the way of actual production."

"Thanks," said the driver of the limousine. "And I think I still remember my way around."

Woody grinned and waved the long black automobile through the gates.

Barbara, looking out the window as the car slowly rolled onto the studio lot, squirmed in her seat and giggled with delight.

As the Cadillac continued on its way, Andrews could see that the studio lot, despite the lull in production, remained virtually unchanged since its better days, having altered very little after the late 1940s. The old wooden rocket ship mock-up was still there, warping on the back lot and at the eroding mercy of the elements, since its last screen appearance during the early Fifties in the *Commando Cosmos* television serial. So was the dirigible hangar featured prominently in *The Adventures of the Black Scarab*, *The Scarlet Skull*, *King of the Seas*, *Phantom of the Carnival* and dozens of other Saturday-matinee chapterplays. The old barn set was still there, too, and the Western town, scenes of countless celluloid fist fights and gun battles. In the background, standing like some ancient monument, remained the fabricated cave set that had also seen its share of flamboyant screen action.

Unquestionably, being on the Democracy Pictures lot brought myriad memories back to Dave Andrews—mental images of fires, fistfights and floods, the "three Fs" as the stuntmen used to call them. And for a moment or two he felt like the child he once was, seated attentively in the darkness of his favorite movie theatre, devouring popcorn while his heroes battled the bad guys in production after production made on these very grounds.

Barbara, however, responded somewhat differently to their surroundings than did Andrews. Her eyes wide open, she was sufficiently impressed by the standing sets and props, and occasionally reacted with some sound of appreciation. But she seemed not to experience any real significance in any of them.

As Woody had said, there was not much activity anymore at the old studio. In truth the lot seemed almost deserted with just a few people visible, a far cry from those old glory days when Democracy Pictures was churning out its action product as if on an assembly line.

With hardly anyone present at the studio, finding an unreserved parking spot was easy. Andrews brought the limousine to a stop, then escorted his girlfriend out across the lot. Looking off towards the Western street, he thought that it reminded him more of an authentic ghost town than a movie set. In his mind he heard one of the old cowboy stars balefully singing about sky-riding ghost riders. Finally, someone called out in a southern drawl, "Davy? Davy Andrews, you old son of a gun!"

Andrews reacted with a start. Only one person in his adult life still called him "Davy."

Turning, Andrews and Barbara stopped walking as a tall, solidly built man in a cowboy outfit rushed towards them from across the lot. The man could have already been in his late fifties, but it was difficult to tell, given his healthy condition and youthful attitude. His smiling face was rather long and lined from many years spent working in the sun. As the man got closer Dave recognized the bulges in his elbows and knees—padding stuntmen wore when performing their impressive feats.

"Dale!" returned Andrews with an equally broad smile. "Dale Steele! And I'm still a lot younger son of a gun than you'll ever be again!"

Warmly, the two men hugged each other, and then shook hands. Andrews could feel that Steele, despite his advancing years, still could boast of a strong and steady grip.

"You still look great," said Andrews, jovially, looking the older man up and down, "for a guy who's been taking the falls for over thirty years."

"Gotta keep at it," replied Steele, laughing, "unless I want to start looking for an 'honest' job. And that may happen sooner than expected, what with the lull in production around here. No more singing cowboys. Hey, you don't look bad yourself, for a 'civilian,' that is. But I got to say, your friend here looks a hell of a lot better." Steele smiled at Barbara and she blushed, her cheeks suddenly almost matching the color of her skirt.

"Oh, this is my girlfriend Barbara," said Andrews. Barbara and the stuntman shook hands, obviously not so forcefully. "Pleased to meet you. I never met a real stuntman before."

"Uh, thanks!" said Andrews, forcing a frown.

"I mean, except for Dave," she said, blushing again.

"Dale's one of the best movie stuntman that's ever been in the business," boasted Andrews of his old friend.

"And—one of the oldest! So, old pardner, what has the Prodigal Stuntman been up to since leaving the 'family'?" asked Steele. "Haven't seen you down at the Association meetings for many a month."

"Gave it up, my friend," said Andrews with a slightly melancholy tone to his voice. "At least as a profession. But I still manage to keep in shape." Very briefly he described his job working for Aaron Van Aaron.

"Hmmm . . ." observed the other man. "You don't sound too happy about your new job, Davy."

"Who can complain? The pay's great."

"Didn't you once tell me that money isn't everything?"

"Let's change the subject," the ex-stuntman answered. "Tell

me about yourself? Still doubling Sundown?"

Dale Steele shook his head. "Mr. Dawson retired over ten years ago and is living off his record royalties. I heard he's thinking about buying a football team, the rich son of a gun. Me? Been working mostly freelance on TV shows. Not much theatrical shows shooting here anymore, and I keep hearing that Westerns are on their way out."

"That's too bad," said Andrews. "They're a tradition."

"I keep hearing rumors 29TH Century Fox, of all studios, is planning a TV show based on Batman. If that's true, it will need a some fancy action. And I think a lot of us old-timers from the serial days should find work there."

"Really?" Andrews responded with a chuckle.

"Yeah, real, far-out fantasy stuff. But what's so funny?"

"Nothing," he laughed, "nothing at all."

"So—when you stop laughing at what's not so funny, you can tell me what brings you back to your old turf. You here to reminisce or just to show-off your old place of business to your pretty girlfriend? Unless, of course, you'd like your old job again, in which case, welcome back, pardner."

As his old friend asked the question, Andrews could feel the smile dissolve away from his own face. He had not, in fact, returned to the studio for any of the reasons stated by Steele.

"Dale . . ." he began, "do you know what ever became of the Fulton brothers?"

"Howard and Theodore Fulton?" replied the stuntman with a smile of fond memory on his face. "Sure, they were still working here during your stay at Democracy, although they were getting up there in years—in my book the best trick-photography guys in the business when it came to miniatures and explosions. Ships, trains, barns, cars, you name it—they could build them in small scale and photograph them to look full size . . . and *real.*"

"And they were especially good at blowing those things up. Heck, I bet those two guys could blow up just about anything, small or even big, if they put their clever minds to it. To this day I've never seen anybody top their work, even the more famous guys working for the majors."

"I agree," stated Andrews.

"The Fultons could do anything, it seemed—just about whatever a writer could concoct for his script. Cars smashing into taxiing planes . . . whole oil fields burning up . . . planes crashing into dirigibles . . . you write it in and they'd shoot it. I remember those sci-fi things they did, too, years ago, the serials with those flying guys, like *King of the Marvel Men* and *The Adventures of Captain Rocket* . . . where they strung up those life-sized dummies and flew them across Malibu on wires. . . ."

Politely, Andrews interrupted. "But where are they now, Dale. Whatever happened to the Fultons? Are they still in the business, or . . . ?"

Steele rubbed his rather long jaw and gazed off towards the hills. "I don't know, Davy. They seemed to just . . . disappear."

"Disappear?"

The stuntman nodded. "The way I seem to remember it is that, just about a year after you left Democracy, something happened, although most of the facts got hushed up by the studio PR people. But there were rumors and a lot of guesswork going around when it happened. Seems to me that Howard— the real genius of the Fulton team—had some kind of 'accident.' A really bad one. The studio tried covering it up. There was, I think, an insurance problem, as well as lawsuits. . ."

"Never mind all that," asked Andrews, feeling himself grow impatient. "What kind of accident?"

"Well, like I said, Howard seemed to be the real brains of the team. Theodore was mainly Howard's assistant, lit the fuses, as we used to say. Anyway, late one night, Howard had set up this miniature chemical factory . . ."

Automatically Andrews reacted to those last three words, his body tensing, although he did not know why.

"And it was Theodore's job, as usual," Steele went on, "to set off the charge. Howard had rigged a squib— you remember, a little gadget that would ignite the explosives using a remote-controlled electrical charge—to set off the blast. Everything was ready to roll when—or so I'd been told—a prop man . . . the studio never revealed his name . . . wandered into the special-effects workshop, to drop off something or other, and naturally became fascinated by what the Fultons were doing. Howard happened to be bending over the miniature, making some kind of last-minute adjustment, when the prop man accidentally touched off the squib.

"I heard that Howard, clutching his face, bolted out of the workshop, his face on fire. Theodore, untouched by the explosion, ran out after him. The guard reported seeing their car exit the studio lot just minutes after the accident. And that's the end of the story."

"Then . . . ?" inquired Andrews.

"Then . . . nothing," replied Steele. "I'm told that, following the accident, Theodore came back a few times, I guess to gather up some of their stuff. But he kept his distance and didn't talk much to anybody. Actually, according to Woody at the gate, Theodore was here just yesterday . . . I guess to pick up some more of the Fultons' belongings. But I wasn't here yesterday, so I never saw him. But their workshop is still on the lot, never used again. That's because the Fulton brothers were never replaced. Not much call around here for their kind of effects these days."

Barbara shivered. "Ooh," she said, "that's a pretty gruesome story. Kind of like that old Vincent Price movie we saw on TV — about the wax museum."

"I suppose an explosion like that could really drive someone — especially a creative 'genius' like Howard Fulton — over the deep end," volunteered Andrews.

A puzzled expression spread across the lined features of Steele's face. "Are you driving at something, Davy?"

"I'm not sure," confessed the former stuntman in a somber voice.

"Well, then, you can tell me when you are. In the meantime, maybe you and your pretty friend might be interested in checking out what I'm working on these days. Actually, you two couldn't have come at a better time."

"How's that?"

"We're actually shooting something here today — the first Democracy production in quite a while." Steele took a pocket watch from his jeans pocket and checked the face. "I'm due back on the set in just a few minutes, anyway. Want to show the little lady something of the exciting kind of life you've been missing lately?"

54

Barbara's large eyes seemed to grow even bigger at Steele's suggestion. She looked at her boyfriend and smiled.

"Sure!" he said. "Why not?"

"Follow me," said Steele. "We're shooting on the same soundstage where you worked your last show."

"Really? That should bring back some nice memories."

As Dale Steele led them across the studio lot to a large wooden building, he said, "It's another oater, a real cheapie called *Requiem for a Bounty Killer*. I double the hero, a former leading man who's really got too old to be believable romancing the young ingénues anymore. I'm doing all his fights and most of his riding. There's lots of cameos in it too, old-timer cowboys who can use the work. Maybe even ol' Sundown will show his face in a shot or two."

* * *

"So this is where you used to work," marveled Barbara as Steele led her and Andrews through the building.

Andrews smiled. With the smell of hay and horses permeating the building, he really did feel like he was home again. The set was the usual Western barroom, with a familiar tall, craggy-faced old-timer standing behind it wiping out an empty glass. In one corner of the room, sitting at a table with a pack of cards in his hand, was an equally familiar elderly actor dressed in black and wearing a black ten-gallon hat. Looking around further, he saw that the director of this show was a youngish man whom he did not recognize. The director was off in a corner discussing something—probably the scene—with an actor bearing a superficial resemblance to—and wearing clothes identical to those worn by—his friend Dale Steele.

"I'm the ramrod on this show," Steele said with pride. "In the script it just says 'fight' . . . and from that point on, the show's all mine, with breakaway chairs and bottles and the whole bit. I'm doing today's fight with another old familiar face, Eddie Graham. We've already worked out all the choreography."

"Choreography?" asked Barbara. "Like in dancing?"

"Sort of," Andrews explained, putting his hand on her

shoulder. "It's all carefully worked out and rehearsed in advance, every move, so that the fight looks good and the stuntmen don't injure each other. The camera angles are set up so the stuntmen can miss each other by inches, with the punch sound effects put in later. For the close-ups, they bring in the real actors. And when you watch the whole thing all cut together, it looks like two guys are beating each other to death."

"Hmmm . . ." Barbara said, pensively. "It still sounds dangerous. I'm glad you've got a safer job now."

Andrews laughed and the work of the day commenced . . . the assistant director demanding "Quiet on the set!" with the subsequent orders following:

"Roll camera!"

"Speed. "

"Action!"

Yet as Dale Steele and his movie opponent began their carefully planned battle royal, stunt-fighting their way across the barroom set, they were suddenly interrupted by a cracking voice that interrupted the action:

"Attention! Let me have your attention, everybody — please!"

"What in blazes —?" the director shouted. "Cut! Cut! Am I mistaken or didn't someone just call for *quiet* on this set?"

As the director spoke, the action stopped, the cast and crew looking at one another, then at the cause of the interruption — a boy in his late teens, wearing a studio page's uniform, and with a horrified expression on his freckled face.

"You all have just five minutes to save our lives!" he yelled, gasping.

"What the hell are you babbling about, boy?" barked the director, glaring into the page's staring eyes.

Andrews looked first at Barbara, then to Steele, who was just releasing Eddie Graham from the fighting position they had been in just before the director brought the action to a stop.

Andrews felt Barbara's soft hand grasp his arm tightly.

"Top office just got a phone call," the page said, finally breathing normally again. "The caller said that, exactly on the hour, he's going to blow up one of the buildings on the lot!"

"Which building?" Andrews asked. He rushed up to the boy, stepping in front of the director.

"Didn't say," the page replied. "But the hour's in just a little more than five minutes now. We were told to inform everybody . . . so they could get outside where it's safer before the building—whichever one it is—blows."

"Nonsense!" said the director, as he turned his back to the messenger. "Studios get such threats all the time. "Probably a publicity stunt for some new thriller. Come on, people, let's continue. I don't want to have to pay you all for overtime."

"No, wait..." continued the boy. "This one's different, the man in the upstairs office said so."

"Oh? How so?"

"He said he thought he recognized the caller's voice. Somebody named . . . Fulton. Yes, Howard Fulton. Does that mean anything to anybody around here?"

For a moment or two no one spoke.

Then, huddling closer to Andrews, Barbara said, "I'm scared."

Andrews looked at his watch, noting the too-rapidly ticking second hand. Already he could feel the adrenalin rushing through his action-trained body.

"Howard Fulton," said Eddie Graham with both respect and fear apparent in his voice. "And you know what they used to say . . . ?"

"That he and his brother could blow up *anything!*" said Steele. "We all gotta vacate this place fast!"

"You mean that threat was for real?" asked the director.

"You want to stick around and find out?" asked Graham.

"Barbie," Andrews said, again glancing at his watch, "you go with Dale. He'll protect you."

"Me go . . . ?" she said, a look of horror on her face. "What about you?"

"Never mind me," he answered, shoving Barbara at Dale, who instantly clutched her arm. "I'll be okay. Just go!"

"Don't know what you're up to, Davy," said Steele, "but I'll make sure nothing happens to Miss Foster. Come on, everybody! Let's move!"

Again Andrews looked at his watch, as everyone, cast and crew alike, scrambled to vacate the building, with Dale Steele taking Barbara by the hand. There were four minutes left . . .

four quickly passing minutes before Howard Fulton — if, in fact, it was indeed the special-effects wizard's voice that the studio executive had heard over the phone — made good his threat.

Andrews dashed outside, noting that the lot was rapidly filling up with other studio personnel, all of them obviously having been alerted by other pages.

In that moment something was happening within Dave Andrews — in his veins, his very spirit. Certainly the adrenaline was pumping fast . . . faster . . . and the sense of danger, of possible death, thrilled him, as it had never done before. This was the kind of experience he craved and was living for. He would see it out through the end, whatever that might be.

Bereft of any real plan, Andrews was playing a hunch, probably a long shot but in these chaotic moments he had no options. There was a very slight chance that he could still save his old studio some damage, while at the same time reveling in life-threatening thrills and danger. Right now, however, his greatest foe was not Howard Fulton, but time.

His brain functioning like a computer, Andrews assessed the situation:

Presumably the telephone voice threatening destruction was that of Howard Fulton. Howard Fulton could very well have lost his sanity as well as his face in that explosion. Therefore, what piece of studio property would a madman find most appropriate to attack, even so many years following that event, especially if he held the studio responsible? What might give such a man a sense of personal satisfaction . . . his revenge?

According to the studio guard, Theodore Fulton had been on the lot the day before, presumably to retrieve some of the siblings' belongings. There was just one place at the studio that such items would be stored, Andrews knew.

He remembered the location of the special-effects workshop, the very place where Fulton's accident had occurred. With only three minutes remaining, the young man was already bolting across the pavement towards that very building. It was an old white-painted structure with the approximate dimensions of a modest-sized grocery store. One wall of the building still bore an old sign:

SPECIAL EFFECTS DEPARTMENT

The door of the building, of course, was locked. Probably no one had stepped foot inside the place since the Fulton brothers abandoned it. But the door's timbers quickly gave way to Andrews' battering body.

Inside, the place was probably much as the Fultons had left it, Andrews thought, littered with tiny tanks and ranch houses and other miniature replicas. Positioned among these artifacts of past movie projects were myriad sticks of what could only be dynamite. When this building was ignited, the explosion would be an incredible one, its devastation instantly spreading to other buildings on the studio lot.

But what would set off this array of potential destruction? Looking around furtively, Andrews saw no fuse . . . no timing device . . . or gadget to receive a detonation signal via remote control.

With time working against him and with his sight not revealing the answer, Andrews used another sense. He listened carefully, his keen ears quickly detecting a faint *ticking* sound. But the sound was faint, proving impossible to track to its source. At last the scenario seemed clear enough: Theodore Fulton, following Howard's accident, on one of his few return visits to the studio, had stocked this workshop with explosives and rigged up a hidden time bomb, set to go off today at the threatened hour. But where was the bomb concealed?

Two minutes and fifteen seconds remained.

Using logic more than his ability to hear, he looked quickly about the room. In one corner, resting atop a work bench, was a miniature factory. It was not the factory model itself, however, but the tiny sign painted on it that immediately drew Andrews' attention: ACME CHEMICALS!

A miniature chemical factory had destroyed Fulton's appearance and his career. Just the other night a real chemical ACME factory was destroyed. And now . . . poetic justice, Andrews thought, conceived in the brain of a lunatic.

Pressing his ear against the miniature, he listened intently. Yes, the ticking was definitely coming from inside. If he could open up the building and figure out how to deactivate the bomb. . . .

One minute and forty seconds left. . . .

Andrews grasped the roof of the scale-model building, exerting with all of his considerable strength. The roof did not budge. And there was no time to look around and — perhaps — find the proper tools to break the model open. Even if he could open the miniature, would he be able to shut the bomb down before it reached its explosive mark?

Less than a minute. . . .

There was no other course of action, Andrews knew. Rather than waste more time trying to open the miniature and then probably fail in attempting to deactivate the bomb, and instead of running off and let the time bomb ignite all the other explosives in the workshop, he lifted the heavy model in both hands, then ran with it outside. If he could run far enough away from the building, then drop the miniature and, with a bit more luck, get away from it before. . . .

He managed to get outside with the model. In the open space where the bomb, once it went off, might do the least damage.

No longer keeping track of the time, he continued to run, as fast as the heavy object allowed him. From somewhere behind him he heard Barbara shout his name . . . then Steele telling him to drop the thing he was carrying. He heard Barbara scream, heard the relentless ticking from inside the model factory.

That was when, the model obscuring his vision so that he could not see where he was running, Andrews fell, the miniature factory falling out of his arms and onto the ground.

He heard a deafening noise, felt the searing heat, as thick smoke rushed through his nostrils and clogged his lungs, felt his body flying through the air. He experienced pain as the effects of the blast struck him, bringing him darkness and oblivion. Dave Andrews' five minutes had come to an explosive end.

CHAPTER FOUR: HUMAN TARGETS

Smoke rose high above Democracy Pictures — not the smoke of a simple and well-controlled special effect, but of a device intended to cause real destruction.

Several hundred feet away, a small Western-clad crowd — the cast and crew of *Requiem for a Bounty Killer* — gaped incredulously at the scene of the explosion.

From where she stood beside stuntman Dale Steele, her arm still tightly hugging his, Barbara could see the man that she loved. Dave Andrews, his sports jacket ripped and marked by powder, lay face down in the dirt of the studio lot. His eyes were shut, his face covered in soot and bits of debris. He did not seem to be moving, but it was difficult to be certain at this distance.

"Dave!" Barbara yelled. Tearing herself away from Steele, Barbara bolted toward the apparently lifeless man.

"Careful!" Steele admonished her as she ran. "There could be another. . . ."

But Barbara paid the warning no heed. For the moment the young beauty's personal safety meant little. All that mattered was the man who had been hurled through the air by the force of the blast . . . the man now lying apparently lifeless on the ground . . . indeed, the hero who had risked his own existence at the expense of saving others and also that old piece of studio property.

Reaching Dave, she crouched down and gently touched his

face. "Dave, you can't be dead. I won't let you be dead!" Seconds later, Dale Steele and Eddie Graham were standing close to Barbara.

"Come on, pal," said Steele, apparently trying to keep up his spirits, "you've been through worse mishaps in some of our Western flicks. Open those eyes!"

After almost a minute of coaxing and cajoling, Andrews' eyes finally fluttered open. His body began to move, slowly at first, and his head turned. He looked up, reacting with a loving smile to the lovely vision standing over him.

"Barbie, baby. . . ." he started, as Barbara felt the tears forming in her eyes, "looks like I kind of . . . blew it."

"Oh, Dave . . ." Barbara returned, rubbing her boyfriend's powerful shoulder as his body continued to stir. "You're not. . . ."

Working up speed, plainly regaining his strength, Dave Andrews got back up onto his feet. "Me, dead—are you kidding? If I ever get killed by an exploding building, it's not going to be a toy like that one." He nodded towards the site of the explosion, which was now littered by pieces of burnt wood and chunks of plaster. Smoke still hovered about the scene—a pungent smoke that invaded Barbara's lungs and made her cough a few times.

She hugged Andrews, pulling his strong frame against her supple body, rubbing against him in the way that she knew he so enjoyed. But she could see that his attention was equally on someone else.

Grabbing both her arm and also Steele's, he led them both—with Graham in tow—away from the hearing distance of the other people who had gathered outside.

"Dale," he said in a sotto voice. "What are your thoughts on what just happened? You think Howard Fulton was responsible?"

"I think I'd be willing to bet my overtime on that possibility. That explosion had the look of a typical Fulton gag—only magnified a few thousand times over."

There was look of puzzlement on the other stuntman's face. "But if Howard did set that thing off, why did he bother to warn us about it—especially considering the fact that the old workshop was the target, and that no one was inside?"

Andrews shook his head. "Who can say, Eddie? Maybe the old guy still had a fondness for some of the old Democracy gang and didn't want them hurt."

"That doesn't see too likely," Graham responded. "Neither of the Fultons were close friends of any of us when they were based here, the way I remember it."

"Then maybe it was just Fulton's ego," Andrews speculated. "Maybe Howard — or Howard and his brother — simply wanted to have an audience for his greatest effect ever executed at Democracy Pictures."

"And maybe," Barbara volunteered with a nice smile, "he's just crazy — and that explains it all."

"Could be," said Andrews, although sounding as if he did not entirely accept his girlfriend's explanation, "but I still think there's something bigger . . . more complex going on here, something that also involves . . . Guys, help me out here. Do you happen to remember — that is, if anyone ever brought it up — where the Fultons bought their materials while they were here? Stuff like blasting powder, squibs, scaled-down car tires? You know, the things you need to buy when creating special effects."

"*Hmmm...*" Graham began, "seems to me like somebody once told me something about. . . ."

"I remember!" stated Steele with a big and triumphant grin. "They got their materials from a place that's been in business ever since the silent days. Let's see . . . Lyne, yes, that's the place . . . Matthew Lyne, Inc., over in Burbank."

"Right!" agreed Andrews, his eyes widening. "Now I remember hearing that a lot of special-effects guys get their stuff at Lyne's."

He grabbed Barbara's arm so tightly that she blinked.

"Nice seeing you again, Dale," he said. "You, too, Eddie. And thanks for the tour. It's been nostalgic — and informative."

"You're . . . leaving already?" asked Steele, a perplexed expression on his lined face. "You just got here. And after what just happened. . . ."

"I'm fine, really," replied Andrews. He removed his shredded jacket as he spoke, then patted his trousers, releasing several miniature clouds of dust. "But Barbie and I have a big day ahead of us."

"Come back and see us again," said Graham. "Soon."

"We will."

"Great!" added Barbara.

Barbara noticed that Dale Steele was about to say something else. But before he could utter another syllable, Andrews had taken her by the hand and was leading her back in the direction of the parked limousine.

* * *

"Are you sure you wouldn't prefer my driving you home?" Andrews asked the longhaired beauty sitting next to him. His eyes were not on her, however, but rather the scenery of Burbank as he drove Van Aaron's Cadillac down its sunny streets. "Wouldn't you rather lounge around under the sun for the rest of the day and keep working on that tan?"

"My tan's good enough," Barbara said, giving him a sly smile, "at least for now. Anyway, I heard somewhere that too much sun can dry you up like a mummy. Besides, all this Fulton stuff is starting to get kind of interesting . . . and there's still a whole afternoon ahead of us."

"But I warn you," he returned. "This could get really boring."

Barbara shook her head. "I rushed like crazy to get dressed up this morning—just for you, 'Davy' baby, and I'm *not* going home."

For emphasis Barbara crossed her long, mostly exposed legs, clearly making sure that her boyfriend noticed.

Andrews did. And he knew that there was no arguing with Barbara when she spoke to him like that, when she gazed at him with those big eyes, almost accusingly, and when she looked as good as she did now sitting beside him. Indeed, with just a look and a few words, Barbara could defeat him faster and more effectively than any criminal with a gun.

"Okay," he said with a long sigh, "but don't say I didn't warn you."

Ten minutes later, Andrews parked the limousine at his

destination—an inconspicuous brick building bearing the sign:
MATTHEW LYNE, INC.

And below that logo, in smaller lettering:

FOR YOUR EVERY SPECIAL-EFFECTS NEED.

"We're here," he said. After parking the car, Andrews and Barbara stepped inside the building, an electronic bell announcing their arrival.

The establishment was relatively small, the main room into which they had just stepped seeming to be the only room. Yet judging from the size of the building as it appeared from the outside, Andrews surmised that the place extended quite far towards the rear. A black curtain hung from the ceiling just behind the sales counter, covering the entire back wall. Remembering the old movie line about paying "no attention to the man behind the curtain," he continued to observe it, albeit surreptitiously.

He wondered: did something exist behind that cloth barrier that might warrant investigation? Something possibly having some connection—even a tenuous one—with the real-life scenario in which he was now involved?

"Doesn't seem to be anybody around," said Barbara as the two people walked towards the counter.

Andrews heard a rustle of cloth, then turned to see a bald man wearing a black, pirate-like patch over his right eye appear from behind the curtain. The ex-stuntman wondered if the man had lost that eye during the execution of some miniature explosion.

"I didn't mean to keep you waiting," said the man with the eye patch. "I had some work to do in back, but came as soon as I heard the bell. How may I help you today?"

Andrews was considering several possible replies when he heard something, a sound apparently originating from behind the curtain. Someone was back there, he was certain, doing something. Doing what? Andrews fought with his inner self not to get too curious. Becoming *too* suspicious could easily lead to paranoia.

Ignoring the sound and getting his attention off the curtains, he smiled at the man with the covered-up eye.

"I'd like to see the proprietor of this place," he said with an obviously forced smile and an affectedly friendly tone to his voice. "Mr. Matthew Lyne?"

"Call me Matt," said the man. "And what are you looking for? Are you in the special-effects business? I can supply you with everything you could ever need . . . from fog machines to artificial blood and everything in between."

"Actually," said Andrews, gripping his edge of the counter and leaning forward, staring Lyne in the eye, "I didn't come here to buy anything . . . except maybe some information."

"Information?" replied Lyne, looking puzzled. "I'm sorry, sir, but all we have here are materials for creating special effects . . . for the movies, TV, the stage, Halloween shows. Are you the police? If so, I must see some. . . ."

Andrews grinned and cut the man off. "Hardly. But the information I'm looking for . . . well, maybe you're the guy to provide it."

Taking out his wallet, Andrews opened it and withdrew a twenty-dollar bill. He let the currency go and flutter down to the table.

Gingerly, Lyne's hand started moving towards the twenty-spot.

"Nope," cautioned Andrews, thrusting his hand down onto the money, "first you tell me what I want to know."

"Which is?" asked Lyne. His face widened with a greedy smile.

"What can you tell me about Howard and Theodore Fulton?" demanded Andrews with verbal force. "I understand they used to buy their materials from you. Materials to make their miniature cars and whatnot . . . and to blow them up."

"Ah, yes," said Lyne. He looked up from the hand covering the bill, then back down at it. "How well I remembered those two when they were working for Democracy. They were the best in their day. Why, they could. . . ."

"I'm not talking about what they did years ago," grumbled Andrews, his patience beginning to wane, "but what they might be doing now. I want to know if the Fultons bought any items required for setting off explosions—and that includes big ones—and *recently*."

"Why no, sir," answered Lyne. "I mean, didn't both of the

Fulton brothers mysteriously vanish from scene just a couple years ago, after some kind of . . . accident over at Democracy?"

"Listen, Mr. Lyne, if you're trying to patronize me. . . ."

Andrews could feel the impatience . . . the rage starting to build up inside him. It was plain that the man behind the counter knew something and was toying with him. Lyne knew something; Andrews could tell when a person was trying to conceal some truth of which he had been asked. So, if Lyne was not going to talk to him, what next? Should he take a risk and try forcing the man to talk?

Before Andrews could do anything and before Lyne said anything more, the telephone behind the counter rang.

Excusing himself with a smile, Matthew Lyne stepped away from the counter and took the call. Almost immediately and in somewhat low tones, the proprietor began speaking what, to Andrews' ears, sounded like rather banal words concerning a shipment of modeling clay.

While Lyne continued to talk into the receiver, Andrews returned his attention to the curtain. He saw the ebony cloth move, although the proprietor during his phone conversation had not made contact with it, and there was no breeze in the store even to disturb it slightly. There was no doubt in the young man's mind that someone was behind that curtain. But what did that matter? There was no law stating that someone could not be working or even spying behind a hanging piece of cloth.

Paranoia, Andrews warned himself, he had to be careful of succumbing to its lure.

About the same time that Andrews stopped dwelling upon the curtain and what might lie beyond it, he noticed that Matthew Lyne's demeanor had somewhat altered. No longer was he talking about clay, but only listening. Gone was his forced smile, replaced by a very sober expression. Also, he was now taking notes—copious notes, it appeared—on a small pad of paper.

Finishing his phone conversation, Lyne tore the top sheet from the pad and stuck it into his shirt pocket. Then, his artificial smile not returning, he stepped back to the counter and looked Andrews squarely in the face.

"Then if you're not the police," said Lyne, almost threateningly, "who the hell are you? And why are you so curious about the Fultons?"

If the situation with the curtains were not proof enough, Matthew Lyne's sudden change in attitude surely added to the mix. Something was amiss at Matthew Lyne, Inc., and probably had very much to do with the overall mix. Now, however, was not the moment to pursue the matter further . . . not with Barbara present and not with him in his normal, everyday identity as ex-stuntman Dave Andrews.

"Look, Mr. Lyne . . . Matt," he said, at the same time retrieving his twenty-dollar bill and putting it back into his wallet, "I didn't really mean anything by that. I'm just interested in the Fultons' work, that's all. Call me a . . . an obsessive fan who's trying to learn everything I can about two movie heroes. Who knows, maybe I'll go into the effects business myself someday... or write a book about the Fultons."

"Well, then I suggest you buy your materials someplace else," Lyne said, his one good eye narrowing almost to a slit as it surveyed the man standing across the counter from him. "There are lots of other special-effects shops around. In fact Hollywood's full of them."

"Okay, then, I guess it's time that we be on our way," Andrews said. "But maybe you could kindly recommend one of those Hollywood shops. Maybe write it down for me so I won't forget?"

"All right, all right, just don't bother me anymore." Lyne picked up the notepad and hastily scribbled down a name and address. He tore off the top sheet, almost violently, and handed it to his apparently grateful "customer."

"Thanks, Mr. Lyne," he said, shoving the paper into his pocket and smiling at the man with the eye patch. "I won't be back. And that's a promise."

There was a look combining both curiosity and satisfaction on Dave Andrews' face as he turned and led Barbara out of the shop and out to the car. That expression would no doubt have been dramatically different, as he drove away with his girlfriend, had he been able to hear the conversation that commenced once Matthew Lyne vanished again behind that black curtain.

* * *

A man, sitting in an old wooden chair and clutching a highly polished .45 semi-automatic handgun, looked up at the proprietor of the special-effects supply shop. His hair was bright red and there was a concerned scowl on his rugged face.

"I don't like it, Matson," said Matthew Lyne to the seated man. "That guy asked too many questions that didn't ring true for someone claiming he might be going into special effects or writing a book."

"I know him," said the other man, "got a peek at him as he and the looker left. They were both there last night."

"Come to think of it, I think I know him, too."

"Who is he?" asked Matson.

"I don't know," replied Lyne. "But I seem to remember seeing him a few years ago on the Democracy lot when I visited the brothers. The 'looker,' as you say, I assume to be his girlfriend."

"They can both be checked out," said the other man. "But still, this isn't good. The coincidence of a former Democracy guy showing up now and asking questions about the brothers is just too pat. Maybe I should have plugged him while I had the chance. I got a feeling he's going to be trouble."

"How much do you think he knows?" asked Lyne.

"How the hell should I know? But we'd better be careful. And if that guy shows up again. . . ." He held up the pistol and patted its shiny black barrel.

"I think we should discuss this further," added Matthew Lyne, "with the brothers."

* * *

"Well, look who decided to come back," Aaron Van Aaron said as he walked out onto his backyard patio.

Dave Andrews and Barbara Foster were sitting together at a round patio overlooking the swimming pool, as Stanford the butler served them bacon, lettuce and tomato sandwiches and cold soft drinks.

"I thought you were taking the whole day off, Andrews. But I suppose one can't get everything he wishes for."

"Don't press your luck," said Andrews with a chuckle. He removed a plate from Stanford's tray and almost immediately started to eat his sandwich. "The day's not over yet. We just stopped by for a late lunch, but may decide to grace you with our presence until it gets dark."

The multimillionaire grunted. He looked away from his employee and over at Barbara, fetching as always, sitting with her legs crossed and her abbreviated skirt hem hiked almost up to her thin waist.

Trying not to stare too noticeably at the woman's legs, Van Aaron smiled, lecherously. "I guess there are some advantages in having you around, Andrews."

"Will there be anything else, Mr. Andrews?" the Englishman asked. Then, nodding to Barbara, he added, "Miss Foster?"

Eating her sandwich, Barbara shook he head.

"Right now we're fine, Stanford old man," replied Andrews. "Man, but no one makes a better BLT than you."

"Thank-you, sir," said the butler, who then bowed politely and walked back into the house.

"Sir, Mister Andrews, *bah!*" growled Van Aaron. "Who does that limey think he's working for, anyway?"

"Whom," Andrews corrected.

"I beg your pardon?" Van Aaron's eyebrows rose in amazement.

"The word is 'whom.' You said 'who.' But when you use the preposition 'for,' your word is the object of that preposition. That means you've got to use the objective case. 'Whom'."

"My, my," said the playboy, "look who's been reading the grammar books. What's really surprising to me is that an ape like you can read at all."

"Keep it up, Mr. Employer," said Andrews as he continued to chomp on his lunch, "and while I'm eating this BLT, you'll be eating that grammar book. It's been a long and busy day so far, and I'm not in the mood for your usual sarcastic lip."

"Busy?" said Van Aaron with a mocking tone. "Doing what? Like maybe flexing your overdeveloped biceps for little old lady tourists on Hollywood Boulevard?"

His mouth full of the sandwich's makings, Andrews gritted his teeth and glared at his boss.

At the same time Barbara smiled proudly at the skinny man. "Dave was a hero today," she said, beaming. "He saved his old movie studio from a terrible explosion . . . at the risk of his own life." Then, with great exuberance, she related what had happened at Democracy Pictures and how her beloved Dave was nearly killed in the performance of his heroic act.

Her report completed, Aaron Van Aaron grinned with skepticism.

"Ah, my dear," he said, "if only your imagination was as well developed as your other, rather obvious attributes."

"No," she protested, "it really happened, just like I told it."

"*Sure* it did," replied Van Aaron. "And I'm the Queen of Sheba."

"Maybe you're both telling the truth," laughed Andrews as, with one last bite, he finished off his lunch.

Ignoring Van Aaron, Andrews pushed aside his empty plate and took a sip of his cold drink. With a satisfied smile, he reached into his shirt pocket and withdrew the small slip of paper upon which Matthew Lyne had written down the information about some other special-effects supply house.

"Do you happen to have a pencil, Barbie?"

"I think so." Eyes opening wide, Barbara set her purse on the patio table, opened it, spent a few moments rummaging through its contents and finally removed a pencil. "Here, Dave." She handed the pencil to her boyfriend.

"Now what are you up to?" asked the multimillionaire. "Going to have a nice after-lunch game of tic tac toe?"

"Shut up," replied Andrews.

Of course the young man had no interest whatsoever in the words and numbers that Lyne had jotted down for him at his place of business. Rather, what seized Andrews' attention was what he hoped he would find there when he first asked Lyne to suggest some other supply house—those faint impressions of what Lyne had written on the pad's top sheet during his telephone conversation . . . the conversation that had changed his expression from forced smile to genuine concern. Lyne had torn off that top sheet and hidden it in his pocket, but traces of what he had written remained behind and were now in Andrews' possession.

It was an old trick that he had learned as a child, maybe in the Cub Scouts or from some movie, but it still worked. With Barbara's pencil in hand, Andrews ribbed the side of its point over the faint traces, until the hidden message—printed words and numbers, standing out white against the smears of graphite—finally began to appear.

"What the hell...?" asked Van Aaron.

"Oh, Dave," Barbara remarked with pride, "you're so smart . . . and clever, too."

Holding the sheet of paper so that only he could see its message, Andrews silently read the words revealed through the black smears. It gave an address located somewhere in the Highland Park area and a time, eleven o'clock. No more information was revealed on the sheet.

"What does it say?" asked Barbara.

"Yes, Andrews?" added Van Aaron. "Care to share that with the rest of the class?"

"Nothing that concerns either of you, I'm afraid," replied Andrews, as he crushed the message into a tiny ball and flicked it into the pool. "Why don't you get into your bikini and go for a nice long swim. I'm sure that should keep both you and also the boss man's eyes occupied for a while."

"I've no problem with that," stated Van Aaron. "And if, by chance, you forgot to bring your bikini, I'm a quite liberal man, so. . . ."

Glaring at Van Aaron, Barbara then looked over to Andrews again. "What about you, honey?"

"Me? No swimming for me today. I've got some planning to do."

* * *

Although very little information had been revealed on that slip of paper, Andrews had no choice but to assume the indicated time referred to eleven o'clock that very night. If his guess proved wrong, all that he would have lost would be a few hours of his time. Yet if his assumption proved correct. . . .

The former stuntman made certain that Barbara swam a lot that afternoon. In fact, she swam for most of the afternoon, rested for a while around sunset, then resumed the activity for a few more hours. Van Aaron, upon Andrews' subtle encouragement, heavily laced with his employee's left-handed compliments and also Barbara's naïve coaxing, had soon joined the brunette in the water.

By nine o'clock that night both Barbara and Van Aaron were sufficiently weary. This, as Andrews planned it, had a twofold effect: first, his girlfriend did not press him, as she usually did, to take her out on a date; and second, Van Aaron was satisfied staying at home watching his color TV.

That left Andrews to do what he had to do that night without interference.

It also freed up the limousine.

Just after ten o'clock, with Van Aaron munching away at a bowl of popcorn as he watched the local *Late Show* and Barbara already back in her apartment taking off her make-up, Dave Andrews—wearing a black shirt and trousers and his other sports jacket, this one charcoal gray—drove the limousine in the direction of Highland Park.

By approximately ten-forty, the big automobile was cruising along a hilly road in the Highland Park area, with Andrews' eyes seeking out the address revealed on the paper slip.

Within minutes of arriving in the area, Andrews found the sought-for destination—situated atop a hill in what appeared to be the proverbial "middle of nowhere," an old barn that had apparently been converted into a garage. The old building was dark, save for a sole light burning outside. The front door and the walls were decorated with torn and eroding posters advertising various fuels, lubricants and other items necessary to keep a car or truck running, the brand names of some of them being long defunct.

A dark car was parked outside the structure. Looking closer, Andrews realized that he had seen it before—the Bonneville that was getting away from the scene of that European nobleman's assassination.

Again not wishing to risk his boss' car being spotted and identified, Andrews doubled back, driving the limousine back down the hill, making a few turns until settling on a dark side street, where the big vehicle became lost among the other parked cars.

Andrews removed the black mask and gloves and the twin revolvers from the pockets of his sports jacket, then, in order to blend in better with the darkness, took off the gray garment and placed it on the passenger seat. Getting out of the Cadillac and locking it securely, hoping that it would still be where he left it upon his return — *if* he returned — he set off on foot, back up the slope of the hill towards his destination.

The moon, no longer full, still provided a modicum of light. Spotting some bushes growing along the hillside, the black-clad man slipped behind them. There, concealed by both the dark vegetation and also the shadows of night, he slipped on the black mask, then the gloves. Then, his identity suitably concealed, he peered out towards the barn-turned-garage.

It was Dave Andrews, who had disappeared into those bushes, but it was another man — an ebony-hooded avenger of the night known as Jawbreaker — who now emerged.

Moving rapidly up the hill under the protection of darkness, Jawbreaker spotted two men standing just to the side of the Bonneville. Both men wore dark suits and hats, their features revealed enough by the moonlight for identification. Both were familiar. One of the men was bald and wore a black patch covering one eye. The other man had red hair and his face had a familiar scowl. Matthew Lyne and the man "Mary Smith" had identified as Matson, Jawbreaker thought. Why was he not surprised?

Silent and unseen, the man with the hood edged his muscular frame, trained to spring into action at the slightest provocation, through the shadows and towards the old building, his back to the rotting timbers. Stepping behind a barrel that had been placed in front of one wall, he paused and spied upon the other two men; but nothing seemed to be happening.

He tugged at his left glove, exposing his wristwatch.

Still undiscovered, watching from behind the barrel, he saw Lyne check his own watch.

It was just one minute away from the hour of eleven, the

time that "something" had been scheduled to happen, according to Lyne's note. Jawbreaker continued to wait, as did the two men.

Then, almost precisely upon the awaited hour, another vehicle appeared, rolling up the rode that ran up along the hillside to the garage—a large, roaring truck covered in canvass. Jawbreaker believed he had seen that machine before too, charging through the Hollywood Hills; and the memories this vehicle brought back to him were hardly nostalgic.

The truck rumbled to a stop just outside the old building, and the driver, seemingly its only occupant, exited the cab.

"Right on time, Collins," said the red-haired man.

"Ain't I always, Matson?" replied the driver.

Jawbreaker continued his surveillance as Collins, quickly joined by the other men, walked to the back of his vehicle, then hoisted himself up under its canvass covering.

Collins' cronies watched, as he did whatever he was doing within that shroud-like canopy. When he appeared again, there was something in his hands—big, hairy objects that he began to toss, one after the other, down to the waiting hands of the other two men.

Furs, Jawbreaker thought. Stolen fur coats, no doubt mink. And lots of them, possibly enough to suggest more than one robbery, the whole collection constituting a fortune in purloined apparel. This old former barn must be the drop-off place for the furs, he deduced.

Again the hooded man's mind raced, his thoughts conflicting with one another, the facts seemingly not making any sense. What did stolen fur coats have to do with an assassinated count and a blown up chemical company? Did those crimes, in fact, as Van Aaron seemed to have naively and unintentionally suggested, connect in some way with all those other recent acts of theft, death and destruction that had been plaguing Southern California in recent months—acts that had been perpetrated before Jawbreaker got involved? Were all of these crimes the work of the same criminal gang?

More than that, how did all of those crimes tie in with the Fulton siblings and their attack on the movie studio that had formerly employed them? Maybe Barbara was right, he considered. Possibly all these crimes, different species though they were, could be simply explained away as the senseless machinations of madmen.

This was not, however, the time to solve this ever-expanding mystery. Sherlock Holmes-time would have to wait until later. This was, instead, the time for action—Jawbreaker-style.

The hooded man waited—almost ten minutes—until Collins dropped the last of the presumably stolen furs into the arms of Lyne and Matson, who then transported the items to the Bonneville. Once this operation was completed, he climbed back inside the cab and slammed the driver's side door.

The time to do something was now, before the truck drove off again, most likely to be followed by the Bonneville. If Jawbreaker were to stop these characters—not let them escape, as he had on two previous nights—he had to move . . . now!

His blood racing, his heart pounding, the masked man boldly stepped out from behind the barrel. In each gloved hand was a firmly gripped .38 snub-nosed revolver. In the eyes behind the slits in the mask was fire. Again the man behind the mask was doing what he had been born to do.

"Okay!" he shouted, his two guns covering his three opponents. "Don't make me have to use these things. Sometimes I'm such a good shot it scares even me, even in the dark."

"Jawbreaker?" Matthew Lyne was the first of the threesome to speak.

"You know, I'm actually getting to like that name," said the man in the hood, careful not to let Lyne recognize his voice.

"Take cover!" barked the man who, a couple nights before, had been disguised as a waiter. Seemingly from nowhere the familiar .45 pistol appeared in his hands, its long, rectangular barrel glinting an ominous blue-black in the moonlight.

Almost at the same time, Collins poked his head out the window of the truck's cab, then aimed a revolver at the masked man and fired.

But Jawbreaker moved. Spotting a barrel, as Collins' bullet whizzed by his exposed ear, almost slicing through it, his plan to capture these thugs interrupted, Jawbreaker leaped behind the barrel, taking cover behind its curved outer surface.

Jawbreaker fired back at the man in the truck. But, even though he prided himself on his shooting skills, aiming was difficult in the dim light. To make matters more difficult, his other two adversaries were already taking cover behind their parked automobile.

Once more, the truck's driver fired from the cab window, his bullets this time creating holes in the barrel behind which Jawbreaker was hiding, releasing two streams of bad-smelling water.

The masked man returned the gunfire, twin revolvers blazing, as Collins ducked back inside, his shots ricocheting off the cab's door.

"We've got to finish this creep off fast!" shouted Lyne, over the sounds of gunfire, "before these shots bring the police."

Jawbreaker continued to fire, his shots just barely missing their targets.

"Maybe there's a better way," yelled back Matson, laughing and ducking from the masked man's bullets. Craning his neck towards the truck, he waved to Collins, who peeked out the driver's window and waved back an "okay," obviously understanding the silent message. Then, again evading the .38 gunshots, the red-haired criminal dashed around the car to the driver's door. A bullet, blasting from one of Jawbreaker's pistols, shot through the door's window, shattering the glass.

In anger and defiance, Matson fired back through the broken window, his bullet ricocheting off the barrel, splintering wood.

His eyes beginning to adjust more to the darkness, Jawbreaker fired again, this time at Lyne—a moving target on his way to the Bonneville's passenger door. But it was still too dark to get a good aim. He saw the special effects shop proprietor rush inside the car and slam the door.

Neither Lyne nor the red-haired man behind the steering wheel fired again. Both men had stopped shooting and Jawbreaker wondered why. Something was in the works, the masked man sensed, the plan that had been silently conveyed by Matson to the man inside the truck. But what?

In just moments all was made clear. The hooded man heard the truck's mighty engine roar, as a blast of gray smoke belched out of an exhaust pipe. He saw the truck move forward, then abruptly turn, until its front end faced both the barrel and the man taking cover behind it. Saw the truck quickly pick up speed as it rolled towards the barrel, Collins looking through the windshield, his visage twisted into a sadistic smile.

He heard the Bonneville engine rev up loudly. With his peripheral vision he saw the dark automobile drive away to begin its descent down the hill. Yet the masked man's attention remained on the truck.

Jawbreaker's only salvation was to think and move fast. But there was little time to think and even less time to act.

The driverless metal monster was rushing towards Jawbreaker, blotting out everything else from his field of vision. There was no place to run . . . to jump . . . to roll. In just moments he would be squashed and torn and ripped apart by the tonnage of his onrushing juggernaut.

A look of horror showed on the face beneath the hood as he darted back behind the barrel.

The mighty truck engine growled and screamed, as, plowing forward, the huge vehicle crashed first through the barrel, sending water and wooden splinters flying in all directions, and then continued its deadly journey into and through the garage wall.

CHAPTER FIVE: SHAFTED!

Untouched by the mammoth vehicle concealing his body, the man in the black mask continued to press himself against the ground.

It was Jawbreaker's good fortune to possess the body of a stuntman, trained to move fast and with great agility upon the shortest notice. In this instance, as he saw the truck thundering towards him, he had dropped down to a prone position, letting the truck pass harmlessly over his body, its rotating wheels to either side, and then continue on its way through the building wall.

Still face-down on the earth, his backside covered with fragments of the shattered barrel that once served as a shield, Jawbreaker heard the truck continue on its way, no doubt in pursuit of the black Bonneville.

By the time the man in the hood regained his footing, both of the vehicles had vanished into the night. He whipped off his mask and gloves, then, shoving his revolvers under the waistband of his trousers, dusted himself off. Waiting for his heart to regain its normal pace, he turned towards the wreckage of the garage.

Once again Dave Andrews had escaped what should have been certain death, and for that he was grateful. He was alive and only mildly bruised, suffering several scratches and a few splinters, although the wall of the garage had been reduced to rubble. He wondered if the sounds of the shots had carried to the streets below and if anyone might have reported hearing those shots to the local police.

Andrews had to work fast. If the police caught him now, his secret career as Jawbreaker would come to an end and the remainder of his "regular life" might be spent in prison. He had, in effect, become an armed vigilante. People had been killed following his first donning of the now- infamous black hood, which technically made him a wanted man.

Still, the garage might provide some clues as to where the gang he had been fighting — and the Fultons, who apparently gave these criminals their orders — might strike next.

Stepping inside the ruined building, Andrews gave it a fast although fairly thorough search, finding nothing incriminating. No doubt this place had only been used by the gang as a drop-off spot . . . for those furs and possibly, in the past, other stolen goods. The inside of the garage, he reasoned, had probably not been used for anything other than waiting around for the truck to arrive.

Another place, however, might offer one or more significant clues.

From somewhere in the distance Andrews heard the sound of an approaching vehicle. Looking towards the road below he saw the revolving red light that heralded the oncoming patrol car. Yes, he thought, someone had heard all those bullets being fired and had phoned the police. In less than a minute or so that squad car would be here, its occupants investigating the scene of the gun battle.

Less than a minute, he thought — more than enough time for him to slip back into the shadows and make his way undetected down the hillside.

Reaching the bottom of the hill, he hid behind some foliage until the police car had passed, then preceded to the street where he had parked the Van Aaron limousine. The car was as he had left it, intact and unmolested. Slipping inside, he paused for a few moments before starting up the engine, regaining his breath, his composure and just thinking.

The night yet offered at least four more hours of darkness, time enough for Andrews — or Jawbreaker — to check out an additional place, one that could very well provide the clues he sought to continue his work. The mighty engine of the limousine purring, Andrews drove back onto the freeway. His destination: Burbank.

* * *

It was nearing one o'clock when the Van Aaron Cadillac slowed to a stop just a half a block away from Matthew Lyne, Inc. The building was dark now, not a single light to be seen anywhere, with no guards in sight.

In his guise as Jawbreaker again, Dave Andrews exited the parked limousine, armed and carrying a flashlight. Again he wore the dark-gray sports jacket, the inner pockets once more heavy with the weight of two revolvers. Hurrying through the shadows, he reached the back of the building, quickly finding a back door. It was locked — that was to be expected — and breaking it down might set off an alarm, he thought. Opting for a window, he forced the lock and pushed up the pane, surreptitiously gaining entrance to the special-effects supply house.

Switching on the beam of his flashlight, Jawbreaker found himself to be standing in the midst of an office that must have been, he surmised, located somewhere behind the slightly moving curtain he had spotted earlier that day.

Near one wall was an old wooden desk, atop which were various pieces of paper. A quick perusal of the sheets revealed nothing more incriminating that receipts for special-effects materials sold to various customers, mostly the sometimes-recognizable names of people working in motion pictures and on television.

The desks of the drawer were all open and devoid of any contents. Someone — Matthew Lyne, obviously — had seemingly made a rather hasty exit from the place, taking along whatever those drawers had once contained. No doubt, taking into account Dave Andrews asking those curious questions about the Fultons, following Jawbreaker's appearance at the Highland Park garage, Lyne had realized that he was now under suspicion and decided, as quickly and efficiently as possible, to vacate his own base of operations, taking with him any records that might further incriminate him.

But perhaps Matthew Lyne had, in his haste and fear of

being caught, missed something—left behind some important scrap of information that could be of use to Jawbreaker.

His flashlight beam darting about the room, the masked man spotted something in the corner of the place just a few feet away from the desk. The wastebasket was stuffed with papers; evidently either Lyne had not deemed its contents important, or he had simply neglected to dispose of them when he removed the other items.

Remembering an old adage, Jawbreaker silently mused that Matthew Lyne's trash could well prove to be Jawbreaker's treasure. Anxiously he turned the wastebasket over and let its paper contents spill out onto the floor. Upon shuffling through the collection, he found most of the papers to be more of the same species that he had found on the desk—all, that is, save one that instantly caught his attention.

A black-gloved hand brought the slip closer to his eyes. The paper had been burnt, as if to destroy some potential evidence. Yet enough information remained on the brown-charred paper for identification. Evidently the burnt slip constituted the remains of a receipt. Good luck apparently on his side again, Jawbreaker noted that at least part of the company name had not been obliterated by the burning, what appeared to be the words "...JACKSON, FRIEND..."

"Jackson . . . friend..." he stated aloud.

Looking around again, flashing his beam, he found something else that Lyne apparently had not deemed important enough to take with him. A stack of telephone directories, both "yellow" and "white" pages, rested atop a bookshelf, some from the general Los Angeles area, others from the San Fernando Valley, Orange County and other areas. As he did not know what kind of business the words "Jackson" and "Friend" might represent, and because he was not even certain that "Jackson" was the first word in the company's name, he immediately began looking up the name in the "white pages."

Several phone books later, in the directory including North Hollywood, Sherman Oaks and Van Nuys, his gloved finger pointed towards an entry:

CHARLTON L. JACKSON, FRIENDLY NEIGHBORHOOD TRUCK DEALERSHIP.

Furthermore, above the name of the company was a surviving purchase order number.

That could be the very item for which Jawbreaker had been searching! A truck—probably the same one—had been used in both of Jawbreaker's recent encounters with this gang. Trucks had to be bought or rented from *someplace*.

Charlton L. Jackson's dealership, according to the phone directory listing, was located in nearby Sherman Oaks.

The night, he thought, had been a quite active one, perfectly fueling his need for action. It was not yet over. He debated: should he continue on his quest now, while his heart was still racing and his enthusiasm was at its peak. Or, more sensibly, should he return to the Van Aaron estate, get some needed rest, possibly a late-night snack, maybe even drop in on Barbara, who probably would welcome his presence regardless of the hour.

Stuffing the receipt fragment into his pocket, Jawbreaker switched off his flashlight and bolted outside. He did not remove his mask and gloves as he sped off again into the night, heading west in the direction of Sherman Oaks.

* * *

Just past two o'clock, Jawbreaker exited the parked limousine once more and, making sure that no one was on the street to notice him, strode boldly toward a large structure identified by a big sign:

CHARLTON L. JACKSON, FRIENDLY NEIGHBORHOOD TRUCK DEALERSHIP.

Jackson's dealership was, in actuality, a reconverted, multilevel indoor parking lot. Its exterior lights were left on during the night, revealing the row upon row of trucks of all makes and models. Even at ground level, Jawbreaker could see that some of the trucks were of the canvass-topped kind that he had encountered before.

Surprisingly Jawbreaker found a side door to the structure to be unlocked.

Upon entering he heard a popular country and Western song . . . a radio playing from somewhere inside the building.

83

Apparently, given the unlocked door and the music, someone was still on the premises despite the late hour.

Moving silently, Jawbreaker followed the music to its source, an office located on the first floor at the end of a long corridor. The door to that office was ajar and light shown from inside. As he got closer to the office he could hear that the person within that connecting room was humming along with the music.

To be safe, Jawbreaker drew his revolvers from his jacket.

Using his elbow to push the door open wider, he noted the man inside, a middle-aged, overweight character seated behind his office desk. The man had a full mustache and beard, both of them black and streaked with gray. He was decked out in a gaudy cowboy outfit complete with white Stetson hat, reminding the masked man of some remnant from one of Democracy's gaudy old musical Westerns.

"Working late tonight?" asked the man in the black hood with sarcasm in his voice. "Or were you just waiting up for me?"

Dramatically looking up, the bearded man reacted with a start to his nocturnal visitor. "Uh, if you're here to rob me, masked man," he said in a deep and almost jovial-sounding voice, affected by a Southern accent, "I gotta warn you. I don't keep much cash in the safe after closing time."

"I'm not a thief," said Jawbreaker.

"No? Then why the hell are you wearin' that damn mask?"

"That . . . Mr. Jackson, I believe . . . ? That is *my* business."

"Okay," replied the man behind the desk, nodding, "then if you're not here to rob me, why the hell are you here? If it's for 'trick or treat,' I don't have no candy, neither."

"I came here for information that I think maybe you can give me."

"Tell you what, masked man," said Jackson, flashing him what must have been his best "friendly neighborhood" smile, "you lower those shootin' irons of yours, and I might be more inclined to tell you what you want to know."

Eyes shifting behind the black mask, Jawbreaker surveyed the premises. No guns or knives in sight, at least; and if Jackson made a move for any concealed weapon, he could always whip out one of his own pistols. He had been, after all, one of the movies' quicker and more accurate fast-draw artists.

Although still somewhat reluctant, he stuck the two revolvers back inside his jacket.

Jackson smiled broadly. "Now, sir, how can I be of service?"

Removing from his pocket the burned slip of paper he had salvaged from Matthew Lyne's office, Jawbreaker handed it to the Western-attired truck dealer.

"Well now, sir," said Jackson, examining the fragment, "this looks like one of my own receipts. But judging from the look of it, somebody didn't think too highly of my always fair deal."

"Don't play coy with me, Jackson," said Jawbreaker in his most threatening voice. "Just do what I tell you to do."

"Meaning what?"

"There's what's left of a number on that piece of paper," he said. "Somebody bought a truck from you, probably not that long ago. I want to know who that person was—even though I think I can guess. More importantly, I want an address for that person. You should be able to check using that number."

"*Hmmm...*" replied Jackson. He brought a hand to his chin and struck a pensive pose. "You're asking quite a bit, mister . . . asking me to break the bond of confidentiality I share with my. . . ."

Grabbing Jackson's studded cowboy shirt, Jawbreaker warned, "And I'll break more than that unless you don't cooperate."

Jackson grinned, sheepishly. "*Er* . . . follow me."

He got up from behind the desk, at the same time raising his arms and opening his hands, as if to assure the masked intruder that he still carried no weapons.

"Where are we going?" asked the hooded man.

"All my records of past sales are kept upstairs. If we kept 'em down here, the place would be one hell of a mess."

"All right, then," replied Jawbreaker. "But if you try anything. . . ."

"No need to worry about that," interrupted Jackson. "Hey, the notion of stayin' alive has really grown on me."

With Charlton L. Jackson, the friendly neighborhood truck dealer, leading the way, Jawbreaker followed, his hands always within reaching distance of those twin revolvers.

* * *

Two men—one of them wearing a black hat, the other sporting a white cowboy hat—stepped inside the ancient-appearing elevator that would transport them to the upper levels of the truck dealership.

"Remember," admonished the masked man, "no fancy moves."

"How can I forget?" said Jackson, chuckling jovially. "With those two nasty looking snub-noses stuck in your belt?"

The Western-attired man cranked a wheel on the elevator control panel. With a sudden jerking movement accompanied by a loud clang, the rickety old elevator car began to rise. Over the door a mechanical arrow began to move from one number to the next.

"Just where are you taking me?"

"Big storage room on the top floor. I keep all the company records . . . all the receipts, contracts, whatever your heart desires, up there in a big ol' vault. Never throw anything away, you see. Never know when something might come in handy . . . or when some outlaw like you comes by asking to see one of them."

"I'm not an outlaw," said the masked man. "That is, not exactly."

The arrow above reached the ultimate number . . . seven.

"No? Then, like I said before, why you wearin' that . . . oops, we're here." Jackson drew open the elevator door, revealing the top floor.

The masked man grunted. He still did not really trust Charlton L. Jackson, despite the man's obvious attempts to be liked. How could he trust anyone who had dealings with the murderous gang bossed by Howard and Theodore Fulton? With Jackson still leading, he stepped out of the elevator, always ready to grab his pistols at the slightest indication of trouble.

Looking around, Jawbreaker found the top floor, devoid of trucks, to consist of a series of rooms—more offices and storage facilities, according to the little signs on their doors. The room into which Jackson led him was a rather large place filled with filing cabinets, desks and other kinds of office furniture and equipment.

An average-sized vault—over six feet high and approximately four feet wide—dominated one corner of the storeroom; and seemingly an old vault, possibly dating back to the earlier part of the Twentieth Century. The masked man confirmed his suspicions as to the vault's age by noting the brand name stamped near the bottom: READING VAULT COMPANY, INC., 1908.

Painted onto the black surface of the vault, above the shut door in large, bold silver lettering, was the familiar company logo: CHARLTON L. JACKSON, FRIENDLY NEIGHBORHOOD TRUCK DEALER. In the center of the door was an imposing combination-lock dial.

"In there?" asked the hooded man, motioning towards the vault.

Jackson nodded. "And if you'll just give me a minute, I'll get the blamed thing open. Good thing I know the combination by heart."

"No more chatter," said Jawbreaker. "Just *do* it."

"Yes, sir. . . ."

Very slowly, the truck dealer began to turn the dial, first several times to the right, then back to the left, then to the right and left again. All the while the masked man watched his actions, observing cautiously every movement of Jackson's chubby fingers.

He did not, however, pay attention to Jackson's left foot, as gingerly. . . subtly . . . almost imperceptibly, and at the same time his hand worked the combination . . . the sole of his shoe slipped over a barely discernible button rigged to the floor, pressing down on it. Nor could Jawbreaker have been aware of the electrical signal the depression of that button now sending to somewhere else in the building.

"Hurry it up!" ordered Jawbreaker.

The thought came to him that Jackson might have been deliberately moving so slowly because he knew something that he was not telling; that the truck dealer was stalling for time. That suspicion was affirmed as he saw a strange twinkle appear in Jackson's eyes, followed by a weird smile on his face.

"What's so funny, Jackson?" he blurted out without thinking.

"Just this!" The voice was a mocking one, originating from somewhere behind the masked man.

"Why, you didn't really think I'd be workin' this late in a big, dark warehouse all by my lonesome?" laughed Jackson, "not when there's masked vigilantes running around town? I mean, you really didn't think that, did you, Mr. Jaw . . . *Breaker?*"

Jackson's implication was obvious. Jawbreaker had not been careful enough, and if Jackson was involved with the Fultons he had probably already been briefed regarding the vigilante's existence. Indeed he should have been more cautious. But he was not, and now he had to deal with the results of his carelessness.

Frowning, feeling stupid, turning abruptly, Jawbreaker saw a man in a security guard uniform rushing into the storeroom. In the man's hand was a long-barreled .38 revolver. A moment later the man was leaping at him. No time to grab his own revolvers, Jawbreaker zipped aside, the guard's momentum sending him crashing hard against the floor.

In another moment a second man, this one wearing a blue jumpsuit identifying him as a mechanic, appeared from the outer corridor. Seconds later, the mechanic joined the guard, rushing towards their masked prey with reaching, grease-marked hands, one of them brandishing a wrench.

But fast though the second man was, Jawbreaker was faster. Grasping the hand holding the wrench, stopping it, the masked man slugged the mechanic hard with his free hand. The man in the jumpsuit collided with one of the room's many filing cabinets, knocking the metal thing over. At the same time his hand relaxed and the wrench went sliding across the floor.

"Get that masked owl hoot!" yelled Jackson, arousing Jawbreaker's attention.

Turning again, Jawbreaker grabbed the man with the cowboy attire, almost simultaneously slamming him in his bearded jaw.

Falling back against a desk, apparently unhurt, the big man

quickly regained his senses. Looking from side to side, Jackson spotted a large metal paperweight, shaped like an elephant, and hurled it at his masked adversary. In time, Jawbreaker ducked, avoiding impact with the heavy object.

A flying leap, the result of man-hours spent at the gym, sent the masked man's body crashing against Jackson's. Another punch with those rock-hard fists knocked Jackson over the desk and to the floor, his white hat falling off and slipping along the floor.

There were still, however, two other adversaries — thugs, although wearing the garb of employees, more accustomed to physical conflict than was Charlton L. Jackson — with which to deal.

Again the man in the guard's uniform was almost immediately charging him. Jawbreaker swung once more, the impact of his gloved fist against the felon's jaw sending him tumbling back. Before the man could regain his senses, Jawbreaker continued to act, tipping a metal storage shelf onto his body, briefly trapping him. By then the mechanic was already back in the conflict, driving his fists hard into Jawbreaker's stomach, then onto his back and neck.

Stunned, in pain, Jawbreaker did his best to retaliate considering the circumstances. But his body, so in need of rest, was already beginning to buckle under the night's strain. Through the corners of his eyes he could see that Jackson was already reviving and the security man was pushing aside the heavy shelf. And as the masked man began slamming both fists into the third man's skull, one blow following the next, he was already being attacked by the two other men.

If only the hooded man could pause long enough to reach his guns. But the battle was too relentless, never affording him the time.

Suffering the onslaught of fists and feet, Jawbreaker staggered, his body racked by pain, his vision beginning to blur. He felt the guard's arm capture his throat as if in the jaws of a vice. Gasping for air, Jawbreaker struggled, lashed out, tried to strike anyone . . . anything . . . but Jackson and the other man seized his arms. Seeing . . . even breathing was becoming more difficult, almost impossible, by the moment. . . .

"What should we do to this character?" asked the security person, never relaxing his grip on the masked man. "Shoot him?" He gazed over to his lost revolver.

"Save your ammo," replied Jackson, breathing heavily. He retrieved his hat and placed it back neatly atop his head. He bent over and handed the uniformed man back his gun. Simultaneously the mechanic retrieved his wrench.

"Too much fuzz in this neighborhood," Jackson continued. "But we gotta do something. I'm told this Jawbreaker character's been causing a lot of trouble the last couple days, which means he must be on to something. But I got a better idea."

Jawbreaker continued to struggle as, his neck still in the suffocating grip of his opponent's arms, he was virtually danced out of the storeroom and back into the adjacent corridor. Dazed, his consciousness gradually slipping away, he could guess where his captors were taking him. Their brief journey ended at the closed elevator door.

Smiling gleefully, Charlton L. Jackson pushed a button on the wall. Almost at once the elevator door opened. Quickly stepping inside, the truck dealer made an adjustment of the elevator's controls, then moved back outside.

The group watched as the elevator began its jerky descent towards the building's lowest level.

"Nice thing about these old-fangled elevators," stated Jackson, a proud smile turning the left side of his mouth, "you can keep the doors open even while the dang thing is goin' down, if you know how to rig 'em just right." By now the elevator shaft resembled a deep mine shaft, a yawning...waiting space of darkness.

"Let's make sure our masked friend doesn't feel too comfortable on his last journey. But make sure he stays conscious. I don't want to miss out on this little shindig."

Smiling back at Jackson and giving a nod, the mechanic slugged him again, this time with the wrench—first in the face and then in the abdomen.

The masked man groaned. He tasted the warm blood streaking from his exposed lips. The eyes behind the slanted holes narrowed to slits. And a sound—either a muttered curse or simply a groan of pain—issued from his partially opened mouth.

Jackson laughed. "I think that ought to hold the hombre. Okay, you know what to do."

That stated, the man in the uniform shoved Jawbreaker forward, sending him plunging down through space like some black-masked movie-prop dummy.

CHAPTER SIX: IN SAFE KEEPING

In mere seconds, Jawbreaker's drop through the dark elevator shaft would come to a smashing climax.

However, in this moment of peril, the mind of the man behind the black mask did recall past events. His thoughts, however, focused upon only one aspect of his life — the gorgeous young woman with the long brown hair. Hauntingly, Barbara Foster's image flashed before him in one psychedelic montage, instantly bringing back to his mind countless moments of mutual bliss . . . their swims together in the Van Aaron pool, their jaunts in the limousine through the lively streets of Hollywood, their more intimate moments where the rest of the world barely mattered.

Either as a last-moment effort to embrace the woman he loved, or as the fast reflex action of a seasoned movie stuntman, Jawbreaker reached out. Almost instantly his black-gloved fingers wrapped around something cold and metallic.

Jawbreaker's body jerked, his descent mercifully halted, his feet dangling in space.

Reacting quickly, he found that he had seized one of the thick elevator cables. His strong hands gripped the cable more tightly. Looking down he could see the top of the stopped elevator, approximately a dozen feet below him, a short distance for a stuntman to jump.

Almost immediately upon landing atop the elevator, Jawbreaker drew his revolvers and aimed them toward the three men—Charlton L. Jackson, the security guard and the mechanic—looking down at him from the top of the shaft.

"Is he dead?" asked the man in the working togs. "I heard something hit bottom."

"Don't know," replied the security guard. "It's so dark down there, hard to see."

"One way to find out, I reckon," suggested Jackson.

Jawbreaker watched from the dark depths of the shaft as Jackson, his overweight body moving with remarkable speed, disappeared from view. Moments later the masked adventurer heard the sound of machinery and felt the surface upon which he was standing push up against the bottoms of his feet. The elevator was rising again, slowly bringing him back to the floor from which Jawbreaker had been shoved to an apparent doom.

Before the elevator could transport him upwards beyond one floor, he fired—one bullet from each gun, each one ricocheting off the edge of the shaft's summit.

"Whoa, there!" exclaimed the big man wearing the Western clothes. As he spoke he briefly appeared again at the top of the shaft. Then he again disappeared from view. "That dude's got more lives than a mountain lion."

The security guard and the mechanic also moved back, vanishing from the masked man's field of vision.

Jawbreaker felt the surface below him jerk to a stop.

Looking up, he noted that the elevator car had just barely started making its ascent when Jackson obviously shut it off. He was closer to his enemies now, he realized, and a better target. But his guns still held five bullets each. Possibly, if they showed themselves again, he could pick off each one of them before their own weapons found their target.

"What now, Mr. Jackson," he heard one of the unseen men ask, apparently the mechanic. "If we finish him off, I think the cops will buy our story that he was here to rob the place. I mean, with that mask and those guns. . . ."

"And, with him in the dark down there, he might shoot us first." It was the recognizable voice of Jackson speaking. "Better check first with the big bosses. Maybe they got some other notion of what to do with that polecat. Meantime, I got a hum-dinger of an idea."

A pause of nearly a minute . . . then Jackson again appeared at the top of the shaft. This time he was holding something in one hand.

"Now don't shoot, you hear, Mr. Jawbreaker or whatever you call yourself—until you've heard me out," he said. "You see I'm unarmed." He raised his hands in full view of the man below, showing that one hand held only a flashlight and the other was empty.

"Okay, I'm listening," stated Jawbreaker fearlessly, his voice resounding through the narrow chamber. "But I warn you. . . ."

"I know, I know, one false move and you'll let me have it. I have a proposition for you, masked man."

"I don't usually agree to propositions."

"Oh, I think you'll agree to this one, my hooded friend. My deal is this: you drop those two shootin' irons of yours and get those hands up, or I shut this here door, go back to the elevator controls up here and send that car with you on top of it on a one-way trip upstairs. You won't look so 'heroic' once your body is squashed between the elevator roof and top of that shaft.

Jawbreaker tried remaining calm. "You don't fool me, Jackson. Not even you could be that sadistic."

"Oh?" said the man standing high overhead. "We'll see about that."

He nodded to one of his men, still out of view. Again there came the sound of machinery and the elevator started to ascend.

Jawbreaker looked up, see the ceiling above, with all of its gears, looming ever closer.

"And now I'll close the door," said Jackson, laughing. "I'm kind of squeamish when it comes to blood—and crushed bodies."

Again Jawbreaker thought fast. No doubt if he gave in to Jackson's demands, the man—or more likely his superior—would have some other unpleasant fate in store for him. Either way he would be dead, he believed. Yet if he did what he was asked now, laying down his weapons, he would have time on his side—time to plan perhaps some way of getting out of this situation alive.

94

As the door above began to close again, Jawbreaker shouted: "Wait!"

The door to the shaft opened again, Jackson smiling down at him. He motioned to someone out of view and the elevator stopped.

"Bright boy," said the man in the Stetson. "Now if you'll kindly put down those guns? And be real careful about it. . . ."

Again the security guard and the mechanic appeared at the edge of the drop-off to the shaft, this time both of them holding revolvers, their barrels trained at the masked man's head.

Slowly, cautiously keeping his hands in full view, Jawbreaker set his guns down atop the roof of the elevator car.

"Like I said . . . bright boy. Now if you'll keep bein' a bright boy and behave like I tell you, we'll get you out of there."

"You win," said Jawbreaker with defeat sounding in his voice.

Raising his hands in subjugation, he waited docilely, while Charlton L. Jackson brought the elevator car back to the level of him and his two henchmen. Without further resistance, the man with the mask stepped out of the car and back onto the floor from which he had been pushed.

The mechanic began to reach for Jawbreaker's mask.

"I can't wait to see who's under that hood," he said, only to have his wrist suddenly seized in the grip of the bearded man.

"No!" ordered Charlton L. Jackson. "I think we should save that little ol' pleasure for the bosses."

"And when's that gonna be?" asked the guard.

"Right," added the mechanic. "We can't hold this guy forever."

"Allow me to disagree," stated the man in the Western garb in a matter-of-fact tone. "I got me a 'safe' place to store our masked friend while we're waiting." Jackson began to laugh, his heavy body shaking. "A really 'safe' place. Follow me."

With Jackson leading the way, the four men—the masked one forced along at gunpoint—returned to the room which, just minutes ago, had been the scene of their fight. Nodding to the large cube-shaped object that dominated one corner of the room, Jackson said, chuckling, "But first, let me finish what I'd started before you two fine hombres interrupted. He wanted me to open this . . . so that's what I'm gonna do."

Both the guard and the mechanic nodded, sadistic smiles on their faces.

Laughing now, Jackson strode over to the vault and gave the dial an additional turn to the right. Then, with a hard yank on the vault's big metal handle, he opened the reinforced door.

"You know what to do," said the guard with a nudge of his pistol to Jawbreaker's back.

"Not too hard to guess," Jawbreaker remarked as he let himself be escorted to the open vault.

"Should be enough air inside there to hold you until the bosses arrive," Jackson gloated, then nodded towards his men.

Time, Jawbreaker thought again. Perhaps if he had just a little more time. . . .

Taking a deep breath of what might be the last fresh air he would ever intake, Jawbreaker stepped inside the vault. Looking out from the dark chamber, he stared hatefully at the three men who had apprehended him, a trio almost certainly in the employ of his greater enemies, Howard and Theodore Fulton.

A subtle grin appeared on his face, for even though this seemed to be the end of Jawbreaker, the sharp mind of Dave Andrews was already at work. Planning.

Then, a triumphant smile on his bearded face, Charlton L. Jackson reached for the heavy vault door and slammed it shut, bringing a flood of blackness to Jawbreaker's eyes.

* * *

Smiling contentedly, Charlton L. Jackson spun the combination dial, and then turned away from his company vault. "That should hold him," he addressed his two henchmen with a look of satisfaction on his chubby face. "And if his air runs out before the bosses show up, well . . . either way, we won't be bothered by Jawbreaker anymore." Jackson walked out of the room and back to the elevator.

The security guard and the mechanic, smiles on their faces, followed their burly employer. As they walked, the uniformed man shoved his service pistol back into its holster and snapped the leather flap over the gun's handle.

The group rode back down to the main floor, and then stepped into Jackson's office. The bearded man stopped behind his desk and reached for the receiver of his telephone. Anxiously he dialed a familiar number. For almost half a minute he waited in quiet expectation. Then his eyes opened wide and his smile broadened.

"Uh, hello, Boss?" the man with the beard spoke into the telephone mouthpiece. "Yeah, Boss, Jackson. Yes, yes, I know it's late, but this is important. Listen, Boss, I got something here I think you'll be interested in dealing with yourself . . . locked snugly away in my vault."

He paused, listening to the voice coming through the receiver.

"No, nothing like that," continued Jackson. "But I'll give you a hint. He's wearing a black mask and gloves."

Another rather lengthy pause, as Jackson's face beamed proudly.

"You got it, Boss. I thought I'd leave that up to you. How soon can you be down here? I don't know how long the air in there will last . . . unless, of course, you don't care if he's alive or dead.

Jackson nodded to his two cronies, who exchanged smiles.

"Yes, we'll be waiting for you," the bearded man said, and hung up the phone.

"The bosses are coming here?" asked the security guard.

"Just one of them," answered Jackson, looking up at the big clock hanging on the wall. "Should be here within a half hour. That masked ranny should still be alive by then—assuming, of course, he don't breathe *too* much."

All three men began to laugh.

* * *

Less than thirty minutes later, two men arrived at the establishment of Charlton L. Jackson, Friendly Neighborhood Truck Dealership. One of them was bald and sported a black eye patch and carried a small suitcase. The other man was a rather ordinary yet distinguished-looking middle-aged man, wearing a black continental suit.

Rapidly and succinctly, Charlton L. Jackson briefed the two newcomers on what had occurred before their arrival, his recounting stopping short of revealing where the captive had been confined.

"Well," said the black-suited man in a stern voice, "where is he?"

"Upstairs, Mr. Fulton," replied Jackson, pointing upwards with his finger, "on the top floor."

There was a noticeable look of disappointment on Jackson's face.

"Is there something wrong, Jackson?" asked the man in the continental suit. "You don't look happy for someone who's just captured our greatest enemy."

"Oh, nothing, Boss," he said. "I guess I was just hopin' to show off my 'catch' to both you and your brother."

"You know that Howard doesn't get out much unless he absolutely must. Besides that, he's busy, you know, working on that great 'master plan' of his."

"Oh," said Jackson. "Guess I figured that capturing Jawbreaker might be a big enough deal to bring your brother out. Never mind. But what's *that*?" His gaze went to the suitcase that Matthew Lyne was carrying.

"That?" answered Theodore Fulton, smiling. "Oh, just something that will rid us of that masked menace — with flair and style."

"I hope so, Mr. Fulton," said Lyne, clutching tightly the handle of the suitcase. "That guy's even luckier than the heroes in those old movie serials you used to do effects for."

Theodore Fulton grunted, then looked towards the man in the Western clothing. "It's late and I'm tired, so let's get this over with. Jackson, it's your show."

"This way, Boss," said the truck dealer, obediently leading the other four men out of his office and back to the waiting elevator.

* * *

Five men stepped out of the elevator and onto the seventh

floor. As Charlton L. Jackson led the group in the direction of the storage room, Theodore Fulton spoke:

"I think my brother would have preferred a more fitting end for our self-styled mystery man," he said, "you know, something slow . . . elaborate, like one of those crazy death devices the props department used to rig up for those old cliffhangers."

"You mean like tying him to a log headed for a giant buzz saw?" asked Jackson with a laugh. "Or tying him to a railroad track . . . or better yet, maybe strapping him to a platform while a swingin' pendulum blade slowly came down to cut him in half? Ah, yeah, Boss, those were sure the days, all right. I remember in one of those old cliffhanger things, the hero, another dude in a mask, but a cowboy, was tied to a. . . ."

"Be nostalgic later, Jackson," barked Fulton. "This Jawbreaker character has been a thorn in my brother's and my sides since he first showed his hooded head. Best thing is to skip the more melodramatic ends we might devise for him and just kill him. That's why I had Matt bring along what's in that suitcase."

"And I'll admit," said Lyne, "that I'm looking forward to using it." He patted the suitcase as he continued walking.

"And I know that my brother Howard will also get a lot of satisfaction knowing that our 'thorn' has been removed, once and for all."

"In here," said Jackson. Waving his hand, he bade the four men to step into the storage room where he had confined the masked man.

Fulton and Lyne looked around, noting that, save for themselves and Jackson's group, the room was bereft of any humanity. "Well, I don't see anybody in here, masked or otherwise."

Beaming, Jackson pointed toward the corner of the room where the company vault, with its ostentatious lettering of identification, silently waited like some metallic mausoleum.

"He's in there?" asked Matthew Lyne, as a small area of his cheek began to twitch nervously. His hand gripped the handle of the suitcase tighter, so much that his knuckles began to pale. In response, Jackson nodded. Theodore Fulton glared at the friendly neighborhood truck dealer. "You'd better not be mistaken about this," he warned.

"I locked the door on him myself," boasted the man in the Stetson. The security guard again snapped open the flap of his holster, an action that did not go unnoticed by Fulton.

"No need for that," the former special-effects artist stated.

"No need . . . ?" returned the guard. "But when Mr. Jackson opens that door. . . ."

Smiling knowingly, Fulton looked at the man with the suitcase, raising his eyebrows as he gave the order, "All right, then. Matthew, it's 'show and tell' time."

Nodding and smiling back at his boss, Matthew Lyne opened the suitcase, exposing to full view the four highly polished Thompson submachine guns.

"Man, where did you find those?" laughed the mechanic, his eyes opening wider. "In some antique shop? I think I'd trust my wrench a hell of a lot more than those museum pieces."

Fulton frowned. "Actually, I found these weapons gathering dust in a virtually forgotten corner of the Democracy Pictures prop department. Old, yes they are — but with a little tinkering, those Thompsons now work again as if they're brand new — and fire live ammunition most efficiently . . . and accurately."

"Real classics," added Lyne.

"Well," said Fulton, "I didn't bring these down here just for you three to gawk at. There's one for each of you — unless our mechanic friend here would still prefer his wrench."

Once more the security guard snapped shut his holster.

Charlton L. Jackson was the first to grab one of the historic weapons. He cradled the submachine gun as if it were a baby, then noted its weight and balance. A smile spread across his chubby face. "It ain't exactly a Winchester '73," he said, slipping his finger behind the trigger, "but I think it'll do the job just dandy."

Next the guard and then the mechanic removed their weapons from the suitcase. "Makes you feel kind of powerful just holdin' one of these babies," said the uniformed henchman. "Kind of like Humphrey Bogart. . . ."

"Or Eddie G," added the mechanic.

"But won't these shootin' irons make an awful lot of noise?"

asked Jackson. "Someone's bound to hear. . . ."

"This is a trucking dealership!" interrupted Fulton. "I'm sure people have heard backfires before."

"If you say so, Boss. . . ."

"All right, then," said Fulton, "now that you've all had your little thrill at playing old movie gangsters, I suggest you train those Thompsons where they'll do the most good."

Virtually in unison, like some half-trained military firing squad, three of the four men with the submachine guns aimed their weapons at the vault door.

Resting his own weapon against the ebony door, Jackson stepped closer to the combination lock, the fingers of his right poised just inches away from the silvery dial. He paused, looking back at Fulton for some signal to proceed — one that came in the form of a subtle nod of the head.

Slowly and deliberately, careful not to go beyond the correct marking, Jackson began to turn the silvery dial, first to the right, then the left and continuing.

As he performed this action, three fingers rested securely against three triggers . . . and three pairs of arms steadied the antique weapons upon the vault door.

"Be ready to fire as soon as that door opens," Theodore Fulton commanded. "That Jawbreaker seems to be a clever and resourceful character. And we have no idea what other weapons he may have hidden on his person."

Again Jackson looked to Fulton, the expression on his face informing the ex-special-effects man that the combination of numbers had reached completion. When Fulton responded with another slow nod of his head, Jackson gingerly reached for the vault door's shiny handle, gripping it tightly in his right hand. He gave the handle a hard yank, pulling it down and to the left, at the same time producing the metallic sound of the vault being unlocked.

At the same time, he reached out with his left hand to retrieve his Thompson.

With all the strength and speed his right hand and arm could exert on the heavy vault door, Jackson pulled it wide open.

"Now!" roared Theodore Fulton.

A moment later, four submachine guns simultaneously

sprayed their hot death into the darkness of the vault.

CHAPTER SEVEN: THE SCARLET SKULL

"Hold your fire!" The booming voice of Theodore Fulton attempted without success to cut through the continuing blasts of gunfire.

But there was no need for the ex-special effects artist to be heard over all the noise. Suddenly, as smoke from the barrage of bullets wafted from the darkness of the open Jackson company vault and began to settle, it was painfully evident to the four men firing the Thompson submachine guns into that metal container that they were simply wasting ammunition.

"Are you fools blind?" yelled the man in the black suit.

At the same time, Charlton L. Jackson, Matthew Lyne, the security guard and the mechanic finally stopped shooting and, dumbfounded expressions on their faces, lowered their weapons.

Thompsons still smoking, the four gunmen gawked with wide eyes towards the yawning interior of the vault.

There was no blood within that dark interior—no bullet-riddled body of a man wearing a black hood and black gloves. No human being at all, only papers, some of which had been blasted to shreds by the four men's relentless firing.

"The damned thing's empty!" gasped the security guard, stating the obvious.

"Where'd he go?" added the mechanic. "He couldn't of just disappeared!"

Jackson, as though not believing what his own eyes were

witnessing, rushed inside the vault and looked around, feeling its walls and ceiling for assurance. He scratched his bearded face and tilted his Stetson hat at a crooked angle. Yet the truth was obvious and indisputable. The man that had been locked inside the vault—the mystery character known as Jawbreaker— was nowhere to be found!

"I just can't believe it," Jackson said. He was still looking around the vault's interior. "I locked him in here myself—and there's nobody else in the world that knows the combination to this vault."

"Mr. Jackson's telling the truth," echoed the security guard.

"We both seen him lock that door," added the mechanic. "No one coulda unlocked that vault and let the masked man out."

"I still can't believe. . . ." continued Jackson.

Fulton cut off his words: "I'll tell you what happened. Somehow, Jackson you fumbled . . . screwed up! Somehow, through your incompetence, the greatest enemy to my brother's and my plan has been freed—freed to continue this one-man war he's been waging against us!"

"No, Mr. Fulton, I swear I didn't. . . ." he pleaded, his large body starting to shake.

"Then would you mind telling me where the masked man is?"

"No need for that," came a deep voice from behind the five men, "when I can tell you myself!"

"Jawbreaker!" snarled Charlton L. Jackson. "I'd never forget that voice."

As a unit, the five men began to turn.

"Uh, uh," the man behind them spoke again. "First put down that hardware. But I warn you, no fancy moves. I have all of you covered."

"Don't believe the dude," said Jackson. "We made him lose his guns."

"Guns that are 'lost' can also be retrieved," Jawbreaker returned, "while you guys were all down in the office, spending so much time gabbing. Now—do you want to believe me that I'm armed, or do you prefer listening to this second-rate 'Sundown Dawson' here and take a chance that I'm not?"

"Let's do as he says," advised the man in the continental suit. "If he is lying . . . well, I think you can figure out what comes next." Without further question, the four gunmen set their weapons on the floor.

"Now . . ." said the man standing behind them, "turn around . . . slowly. And raise those hands and keep holding them high."

Obediently, the five men turned, their arms lifting

Jawbreaker stood, confident and triumphant, in the doorway of the storage room. Although bruised and cut, the hooded man was quite alive. And, as he had boasted to his five captives, each gloved hand clutched a .38 snub-nosed revolver. A smile appeared on the visible part of Jawbreaker's face. Even as he held Jackson and the other men at bay, he thought of his actions following his egress from the vault—how, moving swiftly, he had opened the door to the elevator, then worked the controls that brought the roof of the car to the level of the seventh floor. From that point on it was a simple matter to just pick up his discarded firearms.

"Okay, Mr. Masked Man," said Jackson, clearly still amazed. Slowly, deliberately, he stepped back out of the vault and stood beside the black-suited man. "Tell me—how'd you get out?"

"Easy to explain," stated the man in the hood, his eyes shifting in Jackson's direction. "That Reading vault of yours is an old one—and made so it's almost impossible to break *into* . . . but not *out* of. It's relatively easy—once you know how . . . and if you have a dime to spare." The masked man laughed, as he happily remembered. . . .

* * *

Actually, it was Jawbreaker's resourcefulness that had gotten him out of Charlton L. Jackson's vault. Darkness had come with the shutting of the vault door. But realization had also come, the knowledge that his life depended upon remembering something Dave Andrews had read years ago. . . .

Details typed into the scene descriptions of a script for a mystery movie in which Dave Andrews was performing stunts. A movie whose detective hero had been similarly trapped inside the vault of a bank. Apparently the writer of that script, a stickler for accuracy, had put in those otherwise unneeded details to make his story more plausible to the director and actors. If those details were indeed accurate . . . if Jawbreaker remembered them correctly and moved swiftly enough . . . they could set him free.

He had felt his way through the darkness looking for something like a switch. Most vaults, the script had told him, included interior lights. Finding something that felt like a small metal chain, he pulled it, bringing instant illumination to the vault's interior.

So far the script had been correct.

The place was littered with paper. Doubtless the very information for which he had come to this truck dealership lay among the pads and sheets surrounding him. Now, however, he was looking for something else, yet another instructional detail recorded in the script.

That item proved easy to find—the rectangular metal plate affixed to the inner side of the vault door. Four screws, one in each corner, held the plate to the door. He removed his gloves, letting them drop to the floor of the vault. Searching through his pockets for something that might function as an ersatz screwdriver, he produced a dime.

He slipped the dime into the first screw and, straining, exerted all his strength. After a few seconds the screw began to turn to the left, eventually coming loose. Repeating this action three additional times, he removed the plate, exposing various sets of tumblers inside the door -- tumblers, he thought, that reflected the correct combination for unlocking the door. It was now, according to that overly written script, a relatively fast and simple matter to line up the tumblers. That accomplished, Jawbreaker slid to one side the bolt that kept the door locked.

Hastily he replaced the metal plate, setting the four screws back into their slots, his fingers giving each a few turns to the right. He slipped the gloves back over his hands, then pulled again on the light chain, bringing darkness back to the vault's interior. Then he pushed against the door. Miraculously, it seemed, the door opened.

Quickly stepping outside, Jawbreaker then shut the door again and spun the combination dial. He tugged at the handle on the door, assuring himself that the vault was again securely locked.

Now Jawbreaker smiled. His escape from the vault had taken only minutes to accomplish—time enough for him to run back to the elevator shaft and retrieve his prized revolvers.

* * *

"I suggest you might consider investing in a newer model," Jawbreaker continued speaking just moments later, "that is, if you get out of this little mess alive."

"You blundering idiot!" The man in the continental suit glared at Jackson. "Because of your incompetence . . . and your stinginess . . . this . . . this . . !"

Jawbreaker's eyes narrowed behind the holes cut into his ebony mask. His gaze was no longer on Jackson, but fixed upon the man wearing the continental. In that instant his eyes seemed to glow as he finally recognized the man who was speaking.

Before that man could continue berating the truck dealer, Jawbreaker interrupted.

"So . . . ." said the masked man, "if it isn't the once-famous special effects wizard, Theodore Fulton . . . the lower half of the old Fulton Brothers double-bill."

"You know who I am," stated Fulton. "I take it an old-movie buff hides behind that mask. Well, Mr. Jawbreaker—am I supposed to be flattered?"

"No, you're supposed to do what I say—starting with kicking those weapons over in this direction where you can't use them . . . slowly and carefully."

The five men, again, did as Jawbreaker ordered them. Their hands still raised, they used their feet to send their abandoned weapons sliding across the floor in the masked man's direction. One of the Thompson submachine guns—the one kicked by Matthew Lyne—slid to a halt about midway between him and his five enemies.

"So, Mr. Lyne," chuckled Jawbreaker, "how're things in the stolen furs business these days?"

Matthew Lyne spat on the floor. "You tell me."

"And you, Fulton," he taunted, addressing the man whose

face he had recalled since his employment at Democracy Pictures, "how's your brother Howard? Must have really smarted when that miniature blew up in his face. I hear that he's in retirement now, working on some big 'master plan.' Care to brag about it, 'little brother'?"

"You seem to be on top of everything, Jawbreaker, or whomever it is under that stupid mask," answered Fulton, apparently not intimidated by the man holding the revolvers. "So, like Matt just said, you tell me."

"I guess you didn't hear me, Fulton," said Jawbreaker. "And I'm not too fond of repeating myself." He trained one of his pistols directly at Fulton's chest. "Now where the hell is your brother and what is he planning to do. I know that the two of you are behind all these recent crimes — the assassination of that count, the explosions at the chemical factory and the movie studio, even the theft of those furs.

"I also know that all those crimes somehow tie into some kind of 'master plan' that you two have concocted — and one that seems to involve destruction. Now *talk*, Fulton . . . talk or I'll . . . "

Jawbreaker's gloved fingers tugged at the triggers of his perfectly matched pair of weapons. Yet he knew that he was not capable of gunning down a man "in cold blood" — even a criminal who probably deserved dying, as Theodore Fulton seemingly did. Indeed, the masked man was banking on the fact that Fulton probably did not know that he would not murder him. If his ruse worked long enough to scare Fulton into talking. . . .

He never had the opportunity to find out.

In a blur of movement Fulton turned, grabbing Jackson and spinning him around, so that the still-startled truck dealer crashed fast and hard against Jawbreaker's body. The unexpected impact of that collision knocked the masked man against the wall. From that moment on, everything happened as if in various flashes of movement.

Already recovering, feeling stupid and even embarrassed for being caught off guard, Jawbreaker saw Fulton make a dash out of the storage room in the direction of the elevator. "Kill him!" he heard Fulton shriek as he vanished from sight.

He saw Lyne, the security guard, the mechanic, and finally the recovering Jackson scramble to get back their Thompsons. There was no time for Jawbreaker to pursue Fulton. With his four remaining adversaries now armed like soldiers on a battlefield and out for his blood, there was no chance of him — with his relatively puny snub-nosed weapons — fighting them off. In just moments, he knew, he would be cut to pieces by four hails of submachine-gun fire.

Still, there might be one chance to win such a mismatched encounter. One of the Thompsons was still on the floor where Matthew Lyne had kicked it — between Jawbreaker and the other men.

The four men were moving fast, already aiming their weapons at him. But Jawbreaker, his body trained for action, moved considerably faster. He dropped his twin revolvers. In another streak of motion he managed to reach that fourth submachine gun and snap it up. This time the situation was not murder, but self-defense. Without hesitation he pulled the trigger.

"Die, rats!" Jawbreaker shouted, although the stream of gunfire, belching out at his four adversaries, drowned out his words. He moved the Thompson from left to right, then left again. Four men screamed, as the spray of bullets from Jawbreaker's purloined weapon ripped through their bodies. Three Thompsons dropped from bloodied hands and four groaning bodies crumpled forward. Then, silence.

For several moments Jawbreaker stared incredulously at the four corpses now lying at his feet in a river of their mixed blood. Then he looked with distaste upon the weapon in his hands — the implement that, in just moments, had taken the lives of the four men who had sought to steal his own. A violent act, he admitted, but a necessary one — an act that ensured that his life would continue onwards to combat and, hopefully, thwart the Fulton Brothers and their destructive secret plan.

Jawbreaker's work here was done and, although Theodore Fulton had escaped to plot anew, at least this night had accomplished something — four of the Fulton Brothers' henchmen would no longer pose a threat to the masked man or to anyone else. Now all that mattered was leaving this place, best now, before all the racket made by all the gunfire alerted the attention of anyone.

Dropping the submachine gun to the blood-smeared floor, he grabbed up his familiar pistols and shoved them into his jacket pocket. Then, quickly finding and descending the back stairs, he yanked off the mask and gloves, becoming once again bodyguard and chauffeur Dave Andrews.

* * *

Dave Andrews spent most of the next day in the solitude of his room at the Van Aaron mansion, tending to his battle wounds, generally pondering what had gone before and simply recuperating. The excuse he gave Aaron Van Aaron for his apparent "antisocial" seclusion was that he had a bad headache and could not face the world again until it went away, thanks two a couple of aspirins, which would probably occur by late afternoon.

When Van Aaron queried where his employee had been all night with his expensive limousine, Andrews terminated that line of questioning abruptly by—once again—threatening to quit his job. And when Van Aaron proceeded to threaten firing him, Andrews—at least this time—let his boss win the argument.

Fortunately, Andrews' employer had nothing pressing on his agenda for the day, which afforded the young man the time he needed by himself. Any and all errands that required transportation, Andrews suggested, could be handled by the butler Stanford.

Of course Andrews was quite hungry, following all the exertion of the previous night. Rather than join his boss for breakfast, lunch or dinner, however, he requested that the butler serve all of his meals in the quiet privacy of his room. Moreover, Andrews left instructions with both his boss and the butler to refuse any phone calls intended for him, especially, for a change, any from Barbara Foster.

Thus, Andrews spent the day alone in the comparative peace and quiet of his room, much of that time enjoying a long and much needed sleep. The hours passed slowly, as the sun again began its repeat journey back towards the horizon.

* * *

Miles away from the Van Aaron mansion, nestled away on a remote and isolated hilltop in an otherwise rather open area of the Hollywood Hills, stood the main warehouse of the Langley Storage Company. The old building stood out against the dwindling light of sunset, a kind of "eyesore" compared with some of the expensive homes in the surrounding area.

In years past Democracy Pictures utilized the warehouse for storing the studio's original motion picture negatives and nitrate prints. But the building had not been utilized for that purpose in several decades. Since then, following the clearing out and vacating of the premises more than a dozen years ago, the place was abandoned, with several big "CONDEMNED!" signs prominently adorning its walls.

There had been at least several noble attempts, over the last decade, to have the warehouse torn down. Once that was accomplished, perhaps it might be replaced by a house or houses that would be decidedly more pleasing to the eyes of Hollywood Hills residents. Those plans, however, never reached fruition. Thus, so many years following its gutting and evacuation, the Langley Storage Company warehouse remained where it had always been since the halcyon days of Democracy Pictures.

No one entered the warehouse anymore—legally, anyway. The place, condemned as it was and with its myriad rooms, clearly was a potential deathtrap. Anyone would have to be a fool—or something worse—to open its warping wooden doors and, risking the place's collapse, step inside.

Tonight flickering lights shone inside the warehouse. The lights—a series of candles in a small back room on the first of the building's three floors—could not be seen from outside. All of the windows had been painted black long ago, preventing anyone from seeing inside the place—or the other way around.

The candlelight cast only dim illumination about the room, producing shadows about the creaking wooden walls—eerie shadows, two of them having human shapes, thrown about the drab walls of this place that was believed to be unoccupied.

The light also fell across a large poster thumb-tacked to one wall, a more than twenty-year-old "one sheet" for *The Scarlet Skull*, a Democracy Pictures movie serial in fifteen chapters. Glaring down from the poster, depicted in luridly effective artwork, was a grinning crimson skull with burning yellow eyes, framed by a deeply red, monk-like hood.

In that dim illumination sat two men, the agents of those shadows. An old wooden table, atop which the candles steadily burned, separated both men. One of the duo, clad in a black continental suit, was standing. The second man, his back to the first, was seated in a swivel chair. Like the character shown on the poster's artwork, he was wearing a red outfit resembling the garb worn by monks.

There was a look of revulsion on the face of Theodore Fulton as he looked down towards the back of the other man's covered head.

"Really, brother," said Fulton with the sound of exasperation in his words, "must you always insist on wearing that get-up? I mean, I've seen you in it so long now, it's hardly what you'd call 'effective.'"

Dramatically, the man in the swivel chair at him, bringing his face — or what substituted for one — into the dim candlelight. For the countenance that Howard Fulton presented to his brother, partially obscured by the shadow thrown by the cowl, was a reasonable duplicate of the image on the poster, but in vivid three dimensions. The visage seemingly consisted of a red skull, its bony features barely covered by skin or muscle, veins or arteries, or any other soft tissue.

Indeed, it was like the face of the Grim Reaper . . . the Red Death . . . a crimson Phantom of the Opera...or more accurately, the once-famous Scarlet Skull — the titled masked mystery villain in that old chapterplay — that perpetually grinned back at Theodore Fulton with bared yellowed teeth. The only recognizable features of Howard Fulton were the two brown orbs that looked out from the sunken eye sockets of the red death's head.

"What's wrong, brother Theodore?" replied Howard Fulton, finally, his voice icy and without emotion. "You never minded looking at the face of the Scarlet Skull every day when we were doing the effects on that show back in '44."

"I was getting paid for looking at it then," explained the younger Fulton brother. "And that job was just for a few weeks. Besides, I don't see the point in your wearing that costume when the two of us are alone. Who are you trying to impress?"

"Call me a frustrated 'method actor,' if you like," replied the skull-faced man, "something we didn't have at the studio in those days when we shot *The Scarlet Skull*. But wearing this outfit keeps my mind focused. It symbolizes death . . . death also of my human spirit . . . and is a constant reminder to me that . . . now . . . I *am* death . . . Death Personified."

"I understand all that." Theodore Fulton gasped, shrugging his shoulders. "But I'm your *brother*, for God's sakes, Howard. Surely you could take off that mask, put on a nice business suit like me, and let me see you as you really are."

"My face was burned terribly in that explosion."

"But the plastic surgeon..."

Howard Fulton shook his skull-like head. "The work that doctor—that is, that *late* doctor—did upon my face must remain a secret forever. My true face must be kept secret even from you. My soul as well as my features was destroyed in that blast, Theodore. Thus, the being you knew once as Howard Fulton must remain forever beneath the guise of the Scarlet Skull."

"All right," the other man said. "If there's one thing I've known since we were kids, there's no arguing with you once you've made up that crafty mind of yours. I just wish you'd internalize more your identification with death . . . and find some other disguise that's easier on the eyes."

"Ah!" said Howard. "Enough small talk about masks and death symbolism. We've wasted too much time already talking about things trivial. Tell me—what's the latest on this...this Jawbreaker character?"

Pulling a chair from across the room, Theodore Fulton sat down in front of the table. A frown swept over his face and he bit down on his lower lip.

"Jawbreaker!" he grumbled loudly. "He seems to lead a charmed life. So far every attempt our men have made to kill him has ended in failure. It's as if the gods have smiled on that masked creep or something, the way he's escaped us at every turn."

Howard slammed a fist onto the table.

"Idiots!" he exclaimed. "Dolts, all of them. And you, too, brother!"

"Then why don't you go off on some of these field missions instead of sending me all the time?" Theodore complained, grunting. "It's just like the old days when we were doing effects—I light the fuses, while you. . . ."

"That's because I'm the brains of our team, while you've always been better at actually getting things done . . . until now, that is. I'm the mastermind and you are my spearhead villain, as the scriptwriters referred to those characters. My Capone to your Nitti. Besides that, dressed as I am now, well, you might say I'd rather stand out in a crowd."

"But Howard . . . !" protested the other man.

"There's no getting around it, Theodore. You should have stayed at Jackson's place when you had the chance—and killed Jawbreaker yourself—rather than running off like a coward."

"I couldn't, Howard!" he explained with emotion. "Really, I couldn't. If I hadn't left when I did, he would have killed me. Didn't you catch the news today? Jackson, Matt and the other two were found dead this morning, almost cut in half by submachine gun fire."

"Submachine guns, I might add, that *you*—brother—supplied."

"Guns intended to kill Jawbreaker," Theodore reminded the other Fulton.

"But they didn't, did they?"

"They would have . . . if that blundering nut in the cowboy suit had kept him locked away."

"Four more men—dead. Of course, they're replaceable . . . but I'll admit I might miss Matt, considering the long history he and his company have had with us." For a moment or two, the eyes looking out from the crimson skull got misty. "At least we've still got Matson. He gets things done. And we must get rid of Jawbreaker before he jeopardizes my ultimate plan."

"Your 'ultimate plan'!" complained Theodore. "And just when are you going to tell me what that is? All these crimes we've been perpetrating . . . all this destruction . . . What are they all leading to?"

"You'll know when it's time for you to know, little brother. Right now your main concern is the man in the black mask."

Theodore shook his head. "You know, Howard? I'm beginning to wonder if this Jawbreaker guy is even human, the way he moves around and constantly escapes death. I'm starting to wonder if he even *can* be killed."

"That's nonsense," said the man in the Scarlet Skull garb. He glared threateningly into Theodore's eyes. "Every man can die, dear brother—even *you*."

"Yes, I . . ." he said with a nervous flutter in his voice. "But I've never known anyone so lucky before."

"Or—so well trained."

"What are you suggesting?"

"I'm not sure just yet," answered Howard Fulton. "But for the present, maybe killing this Jawbreaker isn't our biggest problem."

"No? Than what the hell is?"

"Knowing *who* he is," stated the older Fulton with certainty, "I mean behind that black mask. If we knew his true identity . . . his motives for risking his life to put a stop to our enterprises . . . maybe we'd have a better idea of how to destroy him."

Theodore paused, a pensive look on his face.

"Something occur to you?" asked Howard.

"I'm not sure," said Theodore. "But I was wondering . . . maybe we could get to Jawbreaker . . . through his friends."

"His friends?" Howard's body moved forward. He rested his elbows on the table and stared hard into his brother eyes. "How the hell are we supposed to know who his *friends* are . . . if we don't even know who *he* is?"

"This may be just a hunch," said Theodore, leaning closer to the skull face, "but . . . Jawbreaker doesn't seem to be the only person who's taken a recent interest in our operations. At the party for that foolish count . . . at the studio . . . and then at Matt's place . . . all three times this guy and, also for the first two, this pretty girl were present."

"Oh?" Although the expression did not change on his skull face, the tone of his voice revealed new interest.

"I don't yet know the girl's name. But I've already done some checking on the guy," said Theodore Fulton. "It seems that the man in question was Dave Andrews. Does that name sound familiar?"

Howard's hand grasped the bony chin of the Death's head. "Andrews . . . Dave Andrews . . . seems I do recall someone. . . . Yes! Wasn't he a contract actor who came onto the Democracy lot just before the . . . accident?"

"A stuntman," corrected Theodore.

"Yes," said Howard, "now I remember. "A very good stuntman, if I recall, maybe even one of the best.""

"Obviously there's some connection between Jawbreaker and Dave Andrews," Theodore deduced.

"Yes, I believe Andrews may just be the key to the masked man. Either the two are friends, or possibly Andrews may even *be* Jawbreaker. Unquestionably his stunt training would serve him in good stead during the kinds of action our mystery man has recently been engaged in. Do you know what Andrews is doing these days? Is he still a stuntman?"

Theodore arose from his chair and shook his head.

"Seems he gave it all up years ago, not long after we left Democracy. Now he's working as a bodyguard or chauffeur — more likely both — for some very rich man named Aaron Van Aaron."

"Hmmm . . ." thought Howard. "Van Aaron must have offered Andrews a better deal than Democracy did, which wouldn't surprise me. Given that, I don't think I can go to the next step and say that Andrews *is* Jawbreaker. I mean, why would someone with such a well-paying job — as he must have — risk his life for . . . for nothing? I sincerely doubt that, like some character out of those old pulp magazines or comic books, he would magnanimously put his life on the line just to thwart evil or see justice done. No, that doesn't make sense. This Jawbreaker person must be someone else."

"Nevertheless," said Theodore, "there does seem to be a connection of some kind between Andrews and the guy in the black mask. Maybe if we kidnapped Andrews we could force him to tell us what we need to know about Jawbreaker. But I must warn you, Andrews seems to be a pretty tough character.

There's no guarantee that, once we've got him, that he'll eventually crack and give us the information we want—even under torture."

"There may be a better . . . easier . . . more foolproof way . . ." Howard's skull visage seemed to smile more hideously in the poor lighting. His brown eyes widened as he moved closer towards the array of candles. "You mentioned a young woman," he said. "Obviously she and Andrews have a . . . relationship. Otherwise they wouldn't have been together when they crossed our paths."

"According to my reports, she's quite beautiful . . . a real 'looker.' I know what you're getting at," said Theodore.

"I doubt this . . . this 'looker' is as tough or durable as her ex-stuntman boyfriend. Once we have her, getting Andrews to tell us what we want should be a comparatively simple chore. I don't think he'd be too reticent to talk to us about Jawbreaker if his girlfriend's beauty . . . even her life . . . were at stake. It's settled, then."

"Your plan, Howard?"

"First we find out her name and where she lives," said the skull-faced man, "which should be an easy job for someone with your talents. Maybe start with the Van Aaron estate. She's bound to turn up there with Andrews sooner or later, probably the former. Then we get Matson, and . . . "

"And then . . . ?"

"Then, tomorrow, we'll do . . . this," said Howard Fulton, leaning so close to the candles that his body obscured most of it, bringing almost total darkness to the room.

CHAPTER EIGHT: STALKED

Andrews wanted to sleep late again the next morning. The bed—a king-sized one set against the wall of the spacious bedroom his employer had awarded him at the Van Aaron mansion—felt especially comfortable today. His wounds and bruises, not yet entirely healed, and his still-weary bones enjoyed the comforts the bed had to offer.

Yes, he could and would—*should*—have slept much later, but he knew that employer Aaron Van Aaron was not about to let him slack off for two consecutive days. Van Aaron was paying Andrews—paying him quite handsomely, in fact—to perform his almost token duties as his bodyguard and chauffeur. Even if he were not actually guarding Van Aaron's body or driving the multimillionaire someplace, Andrews had, at least, to be *present* on the job. He had to be *there*, ready to drive and escort his boss wherever and whenever he wanted to go. That was part of the verbal arrangement Van Aaron and the ex-stuntman shared with one another.

Also, it seemed, the Fates were against his sleeping in today. The morning sun was brutally shining through the bedroom window, flooding his eyes with light. His stomach growled, Andrews not having eaten anything since the previous afternoon. More than that, someone was pounding on his closed bedroom door, making it impossible for him to slide back into the realm of pleasant dreams. Eyes open to slits, Andrews gazed over to the clock on his nightstand. It was almost nine o'clock, an hour past his usual time of getting out of bed.

He ran his fingers through his black hair. His head moved across the pillow and, his eyes blinking, he focused his vision on the door. "Yeah?" he grumbled. "Whoever's out there, you better be telling me the building's on fire to get me up at this God-awful hour."

The reply was spoken in a polite and proper British accent. "Mr. Andrews, Sir . . . it is I, Stanford."

"Go away," grumbled Andrews. "I'll be up in a half hour."

"But Sir," Stanford went on from behind the door, "it's the telephone — for you."

"If it's the White House, tell LBJ I'll call back after I've had my coffee."

"Uh, it's not the President, Mr. Andrews . . . but Miss Foster. She would like to speak to you, Sir."

"Tell her I'll call her back once I'm completely awake," Andrews groaned. "In a couple days."

"Sir. . . ." replied the butler, "Miss Foster also phoned yesterday . . . several times . . . when you were sleeping."

The man in the bed moaned. "Oh . . . Tell her I'll call her back. But I need to get some caffeine in my system first."

"Very well, Sir," said Stanford. "I shall inform Miss Foster that you will call her back shortly when you have fully awakened — perhaps in a couple days."

Andrews sat up in the bed and shook his head, as he heard Stanford's footsteps diminish as the butler walked away from the door. He was never certain if the butler actually did have his own unique sense of humor or if he really did take most of what he heard literally.

But, being honest with himself, Andrews missed Barbara. It had been well over a day since he had last seen the brunette beauty . . . seen her, gazed into those expressive eyes, embraced her perfect body and made love to her. Even though Barbara could be somewhat of a nuisance at times, especially when he needed to be alone in order to carry out his chores as Jawbreaker, she meant more to Andrews than anything else in his crazy life. Even his almost narcotic-like need for adventure and action ran second place to his desire and need for Barbara

Foster.

There was no question about it; Dave Andrews would get no more sleep this morning. The sun and Stanford and Barbara's phone call had already accomplished their destructive work. It was time to make himself presentable and face his duties of the day.

Moving slowly, Andrews went through his usual morning routine . . . shaving, showering, dressing and combing his hair. Looking into the mirror of the bathroom that adjoined the bedroom, he could see that his face still showed the telltale reminders of his recent physical battles. They were healing fast, he thought; and he looked a hell of a lot better than he did the day before. His routine completed, he exited the bedroom and stepped into the kitchen, his nostrils reacting to the smell of bacon and eggs.

Stanford was at the stove, a white apron tied around his waist.

Aaron Van Aaron, still wearing his expensive pajamas and — although he did not smoke — his shiny blue, Hefner-like smoking jacket, was seated at the kitchen table. As he usually did at this time of day, he was engrossed in reading the morning edition of *The Sentinel*, his face almost completely hidden behind the newspaper.

"I took the liberty of making one of your favorites," said Stanford, a little smile on his otherwise serious face. "With the eggs over easy, Sir . . . so the yolks aren't . . . 'slimy'"

Andrews grinned and sniffed at the aromatic air. "Caffeine ready?"

"If you'll be seated, Sir, I'll pour you a cup," said the butler, "as soon as I can step away from this frying pan."

"Never mind, Stanford," returned Andrews. He walked over to the coffee pot and began to pour himself some of the steaming brew. "Just keep working at hardening those yolks."

"Well, look who just got up," said Van Aaron, his homely face looking up from behind the newspaper as Andrews, coffee cup in hand, sat in his usual place at the table. "What did it take to get you up, 'Sleeping Beauty' — a kiss from some beautiful fairy princess? Of course, judging from the way you look this morning, you could have used an hour or more of beauty sleep."

Lifting the coffee cup and saucer as a unit to his lips, Andrews sipped, then replied to his boss with a grunt.

"So, Mr. Andrews," Van Aaron continued, his eyes noting the various dried cuts and bruise marks on his employees visage, "what happened to you? Walk in to a door or something?"

"Or . . . something," he replied. He set the combination cup and saucer down on the tabletop.

"I'd like more of an explanation than that," said Van Aaron, his voice sounding to Andrews as if he were trying hard to be threatening."

"What I do on my own time is my personal business," said Andrews.

With force, Van Aaron set down the newspaper. "Not when it involves the use of my car!"

"You said I could use the damned car when you didn't need it," Andrews reminded him. "You didn't need it the other night. I did. Case closed."

"Damn it, Andrews!" exclaimed the multimillionaire. "When you stay out all night, then come in looking like you'd just stepped out of the ring after a round with Cassius... er, Muhammad Ali. . . ."

"If you don't like what I do on my off time," Andrews interrupted, "then maybe I should just quit and find another job. I hear bodyguards and chauffeurs are in big demand these days."

"Quit?" Van Aaron laughed, as he had so many times before. "Not if I fire you first!"

"Your bacon and eggs," interjected Stanford, "exactly the way you prefer them."

The butler set a plate down in front of the man who was not his employer. In addition to the bacon and eggs were two freshly popped slices of whole-wheat toast, already buttered.

Ignoring Van Aaron, Andrews took in the aroma of the morning meal, smiled, and picked up his fork and knife. After spreading some jam over both pieces of toast, he began to eat.

"You're *not* going to tell me what happened?" asked the multimillionaire.

"No," Andrews stated in reply, chewing his food while cutting off another chunk of his bacon and eggs. No more was said concerning that topic.

Aaron Van Aaron picked up his newspaper again, his hawk-like face vanishing behind it. "Hmmm. . . . " he began, clearly trying to divert the morning's conversation into a different direction, "it appears that masked outlaw — Jawbreaker — has made the news again."

"Is that so?" said Andrews, trying his best to sound disinterested. He took a bite from one of his pieces of toast. "So what did he do this time? Rob a mom and pop candy store?"

"Very funny. No, it looks like he's killed again . . . and this time he's really done it in grand style."

"Really? How so?"

"Richmond wrote the whole story up," he said, his attention still on his copy of *The Sentinel*. "The whole thing smacks of the old days of Prohibition, a real Gangland type killing right out of *The Untouchables*."

Andrews' attention was gradually perking up as his employer continued to paraphrase what he was reading in the newspaper. "According to Richmond's report, a bystander had heard what sounded to him like gunfire coming from the Jackson truck dealership building. This bystander is quoted as saying that it sounded to him like Vietnam, with machineguns blasting and everything. Says here he saw someone exit that building, then disappear into the shadows — a man wearing a black mask."

"Anybody can wear a mask," said Andrews. "Even you or I could."

"*Could*," said Van Aaron, "but not necessarily *would*. Anyway, this innocent bystander then phoned the police. When they arrived on the scene they found Charlton L. Jackson, the owner of the dealership, plus three other men — one of them a Matthew Lyne, owner of a time-honored company supplying special effects materials for the entertainment industry — lying dead in a pool of their own blood, apparently the victims of machinegun fire."

"Another assassination?"

"Not . . . exactly. Each of the victims was found with his

hands clutching or near a Thompson submachine gun."

"Then it sounds more to me like that . . . that Jawbreaker guy might have been acting in self-defense."

"Could be," said Van Aaron, "but be that as it may, this Jawbreaker is now wanted for just about every crime in the book, outside of spitting on the sidewalk. The city is going to post a ten thousand dollar reward for his capture. Maybe you, during some of that off time you cherish so much, should try and bring that nut to justice. I'm sure you could use the extra money."

"No thanks." Andrews started biting at his second slice of toast. "Working for you is dangerous enough."

"I wonder. . . ." said Van Aaron, setting the newspaper aside and staring off towards the kitchen window, "who'd be crazy enough to put on a mask like that and get himself into so much trouble?"

"Maybe he's really the Lone Ranger," said Andrews with a chuckle.

"Or possibly the Green Hornet?" suggested Stanford, drolly. His eyebrows raised and his eyes seemed to twinkle in the morning sunlight. Both Andrews and Van Aaron looked towards the butler and frowned.

"Er . . . would either of you care for more coffee?" he asked, stepping back towards the stove.

* * *

A half hour later, Dave Andrews walked into the living room of the Van Aaron mansion, picked up the telephone receiver and dialed Barbara Foster's number. He let the phone ring for more than a minute before he hung up the receiver again.

"What's wrong?" asked Van Aaron, striding into the room from the kitchen, the newspaper in one hand. "Your girlfriend finally see the light and stood you up?"

Andrews frowned. "Listen, Van Aaron, just because you. . . ."

Before he could finish, the doorbell rang.

Within seconds, Stanford was at the front door, apron gone,

the usual dignified and professional expression on his countenance. He opened the door and his expression instantly metamorphosed to a smile.

"Ah, Miss Foster," the butler said as he beheld the young beauty standing just outside. "You've come to see Mr. Andrews, no doubt."

"No doubt," Barbara replied with a pleasant smile. "Hi, Stanford."

"Barbie!" said Andrews in a loud voice. He stepped away from the phone and walked briskly towards the front door where the woman he loved was standing. His heart pounded a trifle faster; seeing her was just the medicine he needed following the pain and physical damage he had suffered two nights before.

Indeed, Barbara seemed to look better this morning than she ever had before, which, Andrews had to admit, was virtually impossible. She was wearing a tight blue halter-top and briefest white shorts that left little of her spectacular figure to the imagination. Her hair had that special sheen to it that Andrews found so attractive. About her was the scent of the young man's favorite perfume.

"Hi, there, stranger," she told him in her melodious voice, kissing him on the cheek.

"Stranger?"

"I've been trying to get you on the phone since . . . Oh, how do you expect me to remember? It's been *so* long. . . . "

"I'm sorry, Barbie baby," he said, placing his hands on her bared hips and pulling her closer to him.

"Uh, Andrews . . ." protested Van Aaron from across the room. "Do you mind?" Turning away, the multimillionaire sauntered off into an adjoining room. Altogether ignoring his employer, Andrews said to the woman he was holding, "I apologize, really I do, baby. I've just been busy . . . *very* busy, and tired."

Barbara placed a hand under his chin and slowly raised his head higher. Her smile instantly faded, replaced by a look registering sorrow and concern. Her gaze moved from one facial wound to another. "You look like you've been busy. What happened, sweetie? Looks like you've been in a fight."

Certainly Andrews did not want to lie to Barbara. Throughout their over-a-year relationship he always strove to be totally honest with the young woman. But what was he supposed to tell her now? That he'd been nearly killed several times over in the past two days and nights while in the guise of a man wanted by the authorities, a vigilante—outlaw, even— with a hefty price on his hooded head?

"Yes, a fight," he said, careful not to give out too much information that might expose his other identity. "But you know me, I used to make my living off fighting on the screen."

"Those were fake fights," she reminded him, "using choreography, just like in a dance routine."

Grasping her trim waist, he pulled her body against his once more and squeezed her tightly. "But I obviously came out of it whole and intact," he said. "So don't worry about it. Okay, baby? What's done is done, as they say. So let's forget it ever happened."

"All right," Barbara said. She pressed her face against his and kissed his ear gently. "But you've got to promise me you'll be more careful from now on, okay?"

"Okay," he said. "Scout's honor."

"In the meantime, maybe I can help those battle wounds get all better a little faster."

"Sounds like a fine idea to me," he said, glancing over at Van Aaron. "But let's do it outside, where the air's a lot fresher." Taking Barbara by the hand, Andrews led her outside to the backyard. They sat down in a pair of lounge chairs several feet away from the swimming pool. Somehow, the ex-stuntman surmised, his wounds did not look so ghastly in the bright light of the sun.

Barbara took a handkerchief from her purse, dipped it into the pool water, and then, careful not to hurt him, lightly dabbed the wet cloth against Andrews' cuts and bruises. "How's that?" she asked as she continued her work.

"I can feel those wounds going away already," he said. "Just what the doctor ordered—tender loving care."

"Did the doctor also order this?" she asked, as she took the handkerchief away and began to kiss the marks on his face.

"No," said Andrews, "but maybe I did. . . ." He kissed her

back, on the mouth and with passion. When they parted again, Andrews asked, "So, my dear, what would you like to do today? So far, Van Aaron hasn't asked me to drive him anyplace. Want to go for a swim? I'd rather wait until my breakfast entirely settles, but after that. . . ."

"Sorry, honey," she said, "but not today. I've got a modeling gig this morning, in less than an hour. Luckily it's sort of close by . . . in Bel Air."

"Oh?" asked Andrews, curious and always protective, suspiciously cocking one eyebrow.

"No, nothing like that," she laughed, getting up from the lounging chair. "It's for a swimsuit ad—for a mail-order catalogue. The top stays on the whole time."

"Where is it?"

"That little studio in North Hollywood, the one off Laurel Canyon."

"Oh, yeah." Standing, he said, "What time do you get done?"

"I'm not sure," she said. "It's supposed to be a five-hour session. But you know how these things sometime take longer."

"Then call me when you're done," he said. "If you're not too tired and I don't have to work, we'll do the town tonight, maybe go down to the Strip and check out that new Purple Shadow nightclub."

"Sounds cool," she said, again kissing him on the cheek. "*Ciao.*"

Andrews turned and accompanied Barbara back into the house, passing Van Aaron along the way. As they continued onwards toward the front door, Stanford was already present opening it.

Behind him, Andrews heard his hawk-nosed boss grumble to himself.

"Just what does that moron have that I don't?"

* * *

The black Pontiac Bonneville had been parked on the street below the Van Aaron mansion for several hours. In the front seat of the sleek automobile, two black-suited men impatiently waited.

Theodore Fulton, the man in the passenger seat, looked through the windshield towards the driveway of the estate, where two cars were parked. A long black Cadillac limousine occupied the space within the carport; behind that expensive vehicle, its right wheels on the nicely cut lawn, was a 1964 Ford Mustang.

"How long are we going to wait for that bimbo to come out, Mr. Fulton?" asked the red-haired man who sat squirming behind the Bonneville's steering wheel.

"As long as it takes," returned Theodore Fulton gruffly. He tried to sound as though he were in complete control of the situation. "Be patient, Matson. She can't stay in there forever."

"No?" said Matson, grinning lecherously. "If I was that Andrews guy and had a chick like that for a girlfriend, I'd keep her locked up in there forever."

Although he said nothing in reply, Theodore Fulton had to agree with Matson. The haunting image of Barbara Foster, so fetching in the revealing outfit she was wearing when she entered the mansion, still lingered in the man's thoughts. At times like this he had to question whether he had done the right thing in following his brother into this life of crime and destruction. How much more rewarding his life might have been if, upon leaving Democracy Pictures, he had simply settled down to enjoy a normal life in the company of such a beautiful woman.

"But unfortunately," Matson continued, "I don't have that long."

Certainly Fulton was as bored as Matson seemed to be. Following Howard Fulton's instructions, he had taken the gamble that, sooner or later, Dave Andrews' girlfriend would show her lovely face and figure on the Van Aaron property. They could be waiting in their stakeout for the duration of the day and into the night, if not longer. Luckily, however, the brunette had arrived on the estate that very morning.

Theodore Fulton could not, however, even guess as to how long she would remain inside the stately house.

"My brother said that we should wait until she leaves," said Theodore Fulton, "and that's just what we're going to do."

"Yeah? Well, something better happen soon. I haven't had breakfast yet and I'm starving."

"I'm hungry, too," Fulton replied. "But we have our orders and that's that."

"*Our* orders," moaned the other man, sarcastically, tauntingly. "Don't *you* ever give orders in this set-up? I mean, I thought you and your brothers were partners. How come it's always he—?"

"I give the orders to you, Matson, and. . . ," interrupted Fulton. Matson's words stung him, stabbed bitterly into his soul, for they were true. Ever since he and Howard were children, then following through their professional life in the special effects business, he had been the "little brother" . . . the brother who took the orders . . . the one who lit the fuses.

Now, here he was again, out working "in the field," without the slightest inclination as to what the "master plan" of his more prestigious brother even was. Saying no more concerning the topic, Fulton suddenly reacted with a start and pointed towards the front door of the Van Aaron manor house. "Looks like our wait is finally over."

Matson's head snapped in the direction indicated by Fulton's fingers. The front door of the big house was opening. Moments later, two young people stepped outside—a ruggedly built man and a movie-star gorgeous woman.

Instantly the henchman with the red hair reacted. "It's them, all right—I remember from the night we took care of that stupid count . . . Man, that's what I call a real babe. Could give Bardot a run for her francs. That bastard Andrews! Some guys got all the luck."

"Shhh, quiet," said Fulton in a sotto voice, suppressing an urge to agree with Matson. "I want to hear what they're talking about."

Yet at that distance, even with his automobile's windows rolled down, it was impossible to hear what Barbara and Andrews were saying. It was not, however, too far to note the lingering kiss they both shared before Andrews escorted the beauty back to the Mustang.

"Do we make the snatch now?" asked Matson.

"No," said Fulton, "not with Andrews out there. He's too

volatile and we don't want to deal with him now. We'll wait . . .
follow her. Then, when she's at a safe distance from Andrews
and the mansion, we'll strike." Thus, the two men continued
their wait, until the brunette finally stepped away from
Andrews and slipped into her Mustang. The engine of her car
purred as she backed it out of the driveway and then into the
street. Offering a final wave, Dave Andrews returned inside the
house.

"That's our cue," said Fulton, giving the man seated next to
him a slight jab from his elbow. "Don't follow too close . . . and
don't give her even a hint that she's being followed. But don't
lose her."

"I've never lost anybody yet," bragged Matson, throwing the
Bonneville into gear and cruising off in pursuit of Barbara
Foster. The pursuit continued for at least a half hour. Seemingly
unnoticed, the black Bonneville continued to pursue Barbara's
white Mustang, the two cars eventually continuing north on
Laurel Canyon Boulevard—leaving behind the general area
occupied by Democracy Pictures—heading in the direction of
Victory Boulevard. Several blocks short of Victory, the Mustang
turned right.

"Where do you think she's headed?" asked Matson.
"Home?"

"We'll know soon enough," said Fulton, his vision never off
the white Mustang. "I think we may be reaching the end of the
line."

Turning the wheel of the Bonneville to the right, Matson
continued to follow their quarry. Still at a safe distance the two
occupants of the black car watched the other car slow down as
it approached a large office building . . . then turn again,
descending the ramp leading to an indoor parking lot.

"Keep close to her," ordered Fulton. "We have to do this fast
and efficiently, while there's nobody around. But let her park
first, so everything looks normal even after we've nabbed her."
Obediently Matson braked the black car to a stop.

Fulton and his accomplice waited and observed as Barbara
Foster pulled her own vehicle into one of the unused parking
spaces. From out of his pocket Fulton drew a small bottle filled
with liquid, along with a clean handkerchief. He looked at the

label, which identified the bottle's contents as chloroform, and a satisfied smile appeared on his face. "All right," said Fulton, again nudging the man in the driver's seat. "We're doing it!"

* * *

Inside the Mustang, Barbara Foster shut off the ignition, and then paused to check her make-up and hair in the rearview mirror. She had been primarily hired for this modeling assignment because of her exquisite figure, but her face would be photographed also. Secure in the way she appeared, she opened the car door and swung her long legs to the side to make her exit.

With her peripheral vision she noted the arrival of a black car, as it pulled to a stop in a nearby vacant parking stall. But she paid the vehicle no heed.

Opening her purse, she withdrew a business card and, for reassurance, checked the name and suite number of the modeling agency. The time of her appointment was written on the card in ballpoint pen. Dave had, during the early weeks of their dating, taught her to be punctual. And since that time, as he often told her, punctuality had become one of her finer non-physical traits. She smiled proudly; her arrival here was more than ten minutes before the designated hour, plenty of time to take the stairs up to the studio and get a little additional exercise.

Ready to meet the people with the cameras, Barbara exited the car. Paying no attention to the two men who were getting out of the black car, she started making her way across the indoor parking lot towards the door leading her to the upper floors.

As she walked, Barbara could hear the footsteps of the only other two people in the parking area. They seemed to be walking slowly or at a natural pace. Then, gradually, the men were walking faster, their footsteps becoming louder against the pavement. A creepy chill rushed through her body as she realized that the men might be stalking her. At last reacting to the men's footsteps, Barbara stopped and turned her head.

"Uh, Miss . . . ?" asked one of the men. He was wearing a

nicely tailored continental suit.

"Yes?" Barbara regarded both of the men. The other man, the one with the red hair, looked familiar, although she was not yet certain why. "Do I know you? Are you from the studio? I guess I am a bit early."

"Yeah, that's right," said Matson, forcing a smile. "We're from . . . the studio."

Something was not correct here, Barbara thought. She had posed for the cameras at the upstairs photography studio on several occasions, but she could not recall ever seeing either of these men on the premises. Nevertheless, she had definitely encountered the red-haired man before . . . somewhere.

Pensively her pretty face wrinkled, as she studied the man's features. "Wait a minute," she said in grim surprise. "I know you from someplace. But not the studio."

"I don't think so, lady," replied Matson. His smile suddenly vanished and his eyes narrowed.

"Let me think . . . *yes!*" Barbara gasped. "That night . . . at the party, where that count was . . . Oh, my God!"

"Do it fast, Matson!" commanded the other man.

In an instant Matson was grabbing the young woman, squeezing her arms with such strength that she groaned from the pain. But Dave Andrews had taught Barbara more than just being on time. He had shown her how to move fast and thrust hard . . . how to utilize leverage . . . take advantage of an adversary's size and strength and, as fighters do in the Orient, turn them against the opponent. He had taught Barbara how to turn that luscious body of hers into a kind of living weapon. Now was the moment to put into practical use the skills she had learned from her ex-stuntman boyfriend.

A quick upward thrust of Barbara's arms broke Matson's hold on her. "Come on!" she said, her voice echoing through the underground chamber. "I'm ready for you!"

Already prepared for more aggression, she took a step back from the two men. Again Matson rushed at her, his powerful arms grabbing her from behind, one hand holding her waist and the other pressing tightly against her throat. Valiantly she squirmed, moaned, kicked, tried to lash out against her attacker. "Holy . . . !" exclaimed the man as he continued to restrain her. "She's a human wildcat!"

Barbara had to remember fast—what was it that Dave had taught her to break this specific hold? Was it a sudden jab of her elbow to her attacker's gut, or . . . ? But thinking was difficult, considering the pain resulting from that choking pressure.

Yet no time remained for Barbara, none to think let alone actually to fight back. For the other man, the one in the continental suit, who, although not personally joining in to restrain her physically, was by no means idle. While the man he had called Matson continued to exert force upon her, the second man was brandishing something small and made of glass . . . that, plus a white piece of cloth.

She saw the other man pour some of the bottle's contents into the handkerchief . . . saw, in a flash of whiteness, the cloth thrust firmly against her face . . . smelled the fluid drenching the cloth . . . tried to resist its suffocating fumes, fought her best not to breathe them in. . . .

Her leg kicked out, striking nothing, her muscles going limp. She tried to turn . . .to fight . . . not to give in to the fumes. But they were already taking effect upon her body, making her drowsy, dimming the light and closing her eyes. The last thing Barbara saw, before the darkness enveloped her entirely, was the grinning face of the man in the continental suit.

CHAPTER NINE: CAPTIVE BEAUTY

It was almost evening when Dave Andrews, seated in one of his employer's comfortable living-room chairs, again dialed Barbara's telephone number. It was Andrews' fourth attempt that day to call his girlfriend. As with the other three attempts, he left a message on her answering machine — one of those compact new models that he had bought her, almost as expensive as the one that Aaron Van Aaron had.

"It's me again, baby," he said into the phone's mouthpiece. "The photo session must be taking longer than I thought. Hope you're getting paid overtime. Call me when you get back. If I'm not here, leave a message. Love ya." Hanging up the phone, Andrews knew there was no reason yet to start worrying about Barbara. Sometimes those photography sessions could go quite late. Still, when Barbara usually worked late, she called to let him know, especially when they planned to go out on an actual date.

"Well," said Van Aaron sarcastically as Andrews stepped away from the phone, "if you've finished trying to reach your girlfriend for a while, I've got a few driving chores for you to do — assuming, of course, that you're still working for me."

Frowning at his boss, Andrews reached into his pants pocket and withdrew the keys to the black Cadillac limousine. For the next several hours, Dave Andrews played his monotonous role of dutiful chauffeur and bodyguard, driving Aaron Van Aaron to the usual places — on this day, those places being a brief tea party held at the home of a Brentwood society woman, followed by a brief stop at an art opening and reception held at one of the more exclusive La Cienega Boulevard galleries. All the while he was working, however, Andrews' thoughts remained on Barbara.

By just past eight o'clock that evening, Andrews and his employer were back inside the mansion living room and in the company of Stanford the butler. Eyes shifting towards the telephone answering machine, Andrews noted that its little red button—the one that told if anyone had called and left a message—was not blinking. He looked inquiringly at Stanford.

"I'm sorry, Mister Andrews," the butler replied with a long face, "but Miss Barbara did not ring."

"Thanks," said Andrews flashing Stanford a forced smile. Then he looked at Van Aaron.

"Go ahead, use it," said the multimillionaire. "But you might consider using some of that excellent money I pay you to get your own private line."

For the fifth time that day Andrews phoned Barbara, again getting nothing more than the pleasant sound of her voice as recorded on her answering machine's outgoing message. This time, however, he did not leave a message of his own. He looked at his wristwatch. Odd, he thought, for her not to call him, especially so close to the time of their intended date.

Determined not to let Barbara's unexplained absence worry him, relatively certain that she would call him in plenty of time, he proceeded to get ready for the night's fun and entertainment. Barbara was, after all, a punctual young woman. She had rarely been late for a date, and then never more than about fifteen minutes. And she had never—not since they originally met—"stood him up."

Showering, dressing, grooming himself and looking his best, Andrews went back to the telephone. It was getting near nine o'clock, the time that he usually picked her up before hitting the town's "in" spots. One more time he dialed Barbara's number . . . again hearing nothing over the phone receiver other than several rings, followed by that familiar taped message.

By now Andrews was getting worried. This time he would not ask his boss for permission to use the Cadillac.

* * *

Less than a half hour later, the Van Aaron limousine was rolling into one of the parking spaces in front of Barbara's Hollywood apartment building. A minute later, Andrews was rushing up the stairs to the second floor. Quickly reaching the door to Barbara's apartment, he rang the bell . . . several times. No one answered; nor, as he finally noticed, did any lights seem to be on inside her apartment. Again he rang the doorbell; then, in frustration, he began to knock, loudly. "Barbara!" he shouted, loud enough to be heard by anyone inside the apartment.

But no one replied and the door did not open. "Can I help you?" The voice was not Barbara's. It was the rather shrill voice of an elderly woman's and was coming from the patio down below.

Rushing to the second-story landing, Andrews looked down to see, gawking up towards him, a rather slovenly, heavyset woman with unkempt gray hair, and wearing an apron. He recognized the woman as the building's manager, known by the tenants simply as "Mrs. O." Barbara had often complained to him about this eagle-eyed woman, who apparently had a reputation for being a busybody who saw everything and minded her tenants' business far more than her own.

"Oh, hi, there," said Andrews, trying his best to sound friendly and not worried. "Yes, you can help me. I'm looking for Barbara Andrews. Have you seen her today at all?"

"You mean that model with the long legs and big garbanzos?" The old woman shook her head. "Not since she went out this morning. She hasn't been back all day. I'd of seen her if she had. Car's not back in her carport, either. Must be out on a date."

"Uh, thank you for the help," he said with a frown.

"My pleasure," said "Mrs. O" with a toothy smile. "Always like to help out."

There was one other possibility, Andrews thought, as he hastily descended the stairs and made his way back to the parked Cadillac. The photo session was indeed taking longer than planned. It would be a simple matter to call the studio where Barbara had been booked for her shoot. Unfortunately, he did not know the studio's phone number. And Barbara had never bothered to tell him the name of the studio or its photographer; nor had he bothered to recall the name on the door.

Still, Andrews knew the address of the studio. He had been there once before to watch her work. If Barbara had not yet left, he might reach that location before she left. Within twenty minutes Andrews was driving the long black car down Laurel Canyon in North Hollywood, consistently keeping within just ten miles over the thirty-five miles per hour speed limit.

Myriad thoughts invaded Andrews' mind, as he got closer to the remembered destination:

Might Barbara be seeing another man? No, that made no sense at all. She was quite clearly in love with him, as he was with her, and loyal, so he feared no rivals. That something might have happened to Barbara was entirely another matter. Since assuming the mask of Jawbreaker, his life had taken on new dangers replete with enemies. Was it possible that someone had uncovered his deepest secret and had taken the young woman in revenge? Andrews shuddered.

Yet Barbara was an adult who could handle herself in a "situation"; of the latter he had seen to himself. Most likely he would find her at the photographer's studio, he thought, trying valiantly to remain calm. The studio, however, located on the third floor of an office building, was locked when Andrews finally reached it, and dark save for a dim nightlight radiance seen through the door window. Looking inside, he could identify no clues attesting to the fact that Barbara had even shown up for her session.

Something seemed to speak to Andrews from the back of his mind, words spoken in the craggy voice of Barbara's apartment building manager. She had mentioned that Barbara's car had not returned to its carport. Mention of that carport prompted Andrews to bolt down the stairs that led down into office building's parking area. Fortunately the door leading from the stairs and to the area was not locked.

Stepping into the semi-darkened area, Andrews furtively looked around. As most of the cars had obviously vacated the building for the night, his search was not a long one—for there he saw it, standing out in the darkness—Barbara's white Mustang, silent and abandoned.

* * *

Light.

Barbara Foster rubbed her eyes as she slowly returned to consciousness and took in a deep breath. The air was musty, having the smell of an old basement that had not been opened for many years. And the illumination was dim, almost semi-darkness. Her surroundings were finally coming into focus.

Barbara was sitting in an old wooden chair behind an equally old wooden table, atop which burned a single candle. She seemed to be inside some large warehouse or former factory, she surmised. But who brought her here—and why— she could not imagine.

Her eyes noted the large poster affixed to the wall—*The Scarlet Skull*, she remembered, one of those old Democracy Pictures productions that Dave had often told her about—with its lurid depiction of the titled, crimson skull-faced menace. A shadow, tall and human in form, crept ominously across the poster, as if possessing a life of its own.

"Good evening, Miss Foster." The voice, eerie and unfamiliar, issued from behind. "I'm glad to see that the ether has finally worn off." Barbara turned around in response to the voice, then gasped, a thrill of horror rippling through her body.

For the red-garbed creature slowly ambulating towards her through the shadows, its crimson face revealed in the candle's light, seemed neither alive nor human. Rather, it had the near-skeletal visage of someone or something that had died long ago . . . the Scarlet Skull given life, as though the masked-villain character had literally emerged from the poster.

Instinctively, Barbara moved to get up from her seat. But the "Scarlet Skull" moved faster, a distinctively non-bony hand thrusting against her chest, forcing her back into the chair. "Don't waste your energy and my time by trying to run away," he told her. "I assure you that you wouldn't get far. My little sanctuary is very well guarded."

Looking around quickly, Barbara observed another man—the one in the continental suit, the man who had shoved the ether-drenched cloth against her face—step out of the shadows. She stared up at the Death's-headed figure looming above her.

"Who . . . *what* are you?"

"I prefer 'who,' Miss Foster. And honestly, I'm surprised that you haven't guessed by now."

"Don't tell me," she said, her pretty face frowning, "the Scarlet Skull."

"How observant, Miss Foster. I've chosen the persona of that old chapterplay villain for several reasons—one of which is because my brother and I happened to have worked on *The Scarlet Skull*, creating all of its special effects. Another reason is that the look of that character seemed appropriate for me, given what happened to my face during that explosion at the studio."

Barbara paled. "You're . . . Fulton," she said incredulously. "Howard Fulton!"

"My, my," said the man with the red Grim Reaper face, "you actually seemed surprised. I'm wondering if you really didn't know it was I in this guise."

"I . . . I didn't," she replied, her body trembling. "How could I have known?"

"I guess I thought you knew more about me and my operation than you actually do," Fulton said. "No matter. Because your use to me has little or nothing to do with what knowledge you actually have in that pretty head of yours."

"What . . . why have I been brought here?" she asked, becoming more scared by the moment. "What're you going to do to me?"

Fulton moved closer to her, uncomfortably close, the red surface of his countenance now only inches away from Barbara's face. As he got nearer, the woman detected a familiar smell emanating from his hideous visage. It was an odor that she knew from her experience as a model and occasional actress, the sweet aroma of theatrical make-up.

"You'll know everything in due time, my dear," he said.

"You could have saved yourself a lot of time by dropping all these phony theatrics," she chided him. "Just tell me what do you want of me."

Turning his head, Howard Fulton nodded to the man in the shadows, signaling the other person to step up beside him.

"Shall we tell her now?" Howard asked the man in the continental suit.

"Why are you asking me, Howard?" he answered. "Like always, it's your show."

"I hope I didn't detect a hint of dissatisfaction in your voice, brother. Remember, as always, we're in this together."

The man that Barbara now knew to Theodore Fulton scowled — subtly, yet enough to be noticed even in the meager lighting. Clearly, she recognized, something was going on here besides brotherly love. She recalled something that Dave's stuntman friend had told him that day at the studio, something about Howard being the brains and Theodore lighting the fuses, not that the memory served Barbara in her present situation.

"Just tell me," Barbara repeated with courage and indignation sounding in her voice, "What do you want?"

"That's a very simple question to answer, Miss Foster," said Howard Fulton, matter-of-factly. "We want . . . Jawbreaker."

Barbara's face revealed her perplexity. "Jawbreaker?" she said. Her eyes opened wider. "You mean the candy?"

Theodore took a step further. "Don't try to be funny, Miss Foster. My brother and I don't have much of a sense of humor."

"I'm talking about the masked man who has recently decided to take the law into his own hands . . . the man who appeared for the first time that night of Count Franz Lojos' assassination."

Jawbreaker?

Barbara's mind raced. Yes, she had been present on the night of that murder. She was there when the black-hooded mystery man appeared, as if out of nowhere, and made his own unique contribution to the violence of that event. But what connection did *she* have with that hooded vigilante?

"I'm sorry," Barbara finally said, almost disappointed, "but I don't know the guy. Sure, I was there when the Count was killed, but I never talked to this Jawbreaker . . . had anything to do with him. Heck, the two of us weren't even introduced."

The skull-headed man laughed, momentarily glancing at his brother. "No, my dear," responded Howard, "perhaps you don't know this Jawbreaker character. But you are associated with someone that I believe does, in fact, know him."

"Really?" Barbara shot back, genuinely ignorant as to the meaning behind Fulton's implication. "And just who, Mr. Scarlet Skull, might that be?"

"Andrews," volunteered Theodore Fulton. "David Andrews."

"Dave?" she replied, a look of surprise on her face. "But Dave doesn't know Jawbreaker. And if he did, he'd have told me. Dave tells me everything—even things I don't particularly want to know."

"I'm sorry to disappoint you, my dear," said the man in red, "but Andrews' connection with Jawbreaker is something he's obviously decided to keep to himself. Somehow Andrews has to be directly connected with that hooded vigilante. And once we have Andrews under our power, it goes without saying that we'll soon have Jawbreaker."

Barbara relaxed in her chair and looked away from the man with the skull's face. She was smiling for the first time since her kidnapping —not at her two captors, but at the thought that her beloved Dave would betray a friend.

"Obviously you don't know Dave as well as I do," she said with a chuckle. "If there is some connection between Dave and this Jawbreaker guy, if they're friends, Dave just isn't the kind of person who'd sell a friend out."

Howard Fulton took a few steps, walking to the other side of the table. His cold eyes, gazing down from sunken sockets, focused upon his beautiful captive. "Which is where *you* come in, my dear," he said.

Barbara already suspected the truth. "Me?" she said, a chill cascading through her.

"Andrews would probably not betray a friend . . . unless the welfare of another friend, an even more special friend, a friend with whom he enjoyed a more . . . *intimate* . . . relationship...was at stake.

Barbara's chill became a cold shudder. She knew that what this fiend was telling her was true. Dave would do anything—give up his own life, if necessary—to ensure her happiness. No, she thought; she loved Dave too much to put him at such risk.

Without saying another word, Barbara shot up from her chair, her mind again racing with aggressive maneuvers and defensive techniques that Dave had taught her.

"Careful!" Theodore shouted in warning. "She's a wild one and knows how to handle herself."

Barbara's hands clenched into fists and her body snapped into a threatening martial arts pose. But it was still difficult seeing in the dark and she had still not entirely thrown off the effects of the ether. Within moments both Fultons were upon her, grabbing her arms, holding her back in restraint, forcing her back down into the chair.

With the back of his hand, Theodore Fulton prepared to slap the young beauty. Then he stopped, as if unable to go through with the action.

"You always did fall prey to a pretty face and shapely figure," said the man in the guise of the Scarlet Skull, completing his brother's action by slapping Barbara with stunning effect.

Barbara, her tongue licking the little trail of blood now dripping from one lip, glared up at the red face, saying nothing.

"You didn't have to do that," said Theodore solemnly to his brother "We can handle her."

Then Theodore looked down at Barbara, still bleeding from Howard's blow. "And your boyfriend will do whatever we tell him to do," he said, "once he knows that we have *you*."

"The trap is ready and you are the bait, Miss Foster," said Howard Fulton, speaking slowly, deliberately. His grinning skull of a face seemed to broaden as he smiled. He brought a finger to Barbara's cheek and touched it, his flesh cold against her skin. "And I must say, you make most lovely bait indeed."

* * *

At the Van Aaron mansion, Dave Andrews again tried phoning Barbara, again getting no answer. In desperation he looked up and phoned "Mrs. O," the manager of Barbara's apartment building, hoping the perpetually snooping old woman might have got a glimpse of Barbara either coming or going, again with a negative result.

141

By now Andrews accepted the reality that such efforts were futile; nevertheless, he had to try. Perhaps she had worked late and—inadvertently, inexplicably—left her Mustang in that parking area after the place was locked up for the night. Or her car would not start. Maybe even now she was on a bus or in a taxicab on her way back to her Seward Street apartment. No, if that were the case, why had she not telephoned him by now? Too many "maybes"!

Barbara's most logical course of action, had Andrews' speculations been true, would have been to call him, so that he could pick her up at the photographer's studio and then simply drive her home.

At least once per hour he deliberated over contacting the authorities and reporting Barbara as a missing person. But, he believed, she had not been gone long enough to qualify as one of society's missing. By the time that she did, something terrible might happen to her, he thought. Never before in his life did Andrews feel this helpless.

In between his unanswered phone calls to Barbara, Andrews tried occupying his thoughts with more mundane activities— watching Van Aaron's big color TV, listening to the new Beatles LP on the multimillionaire's giant stereo, even engaging in his traditional arguments with Aaron Van Aaron himself. Nothing, however, worked, and his thoughts almost immediately focused back upon the woman he loved.

An hour after such attempts at occupying his time, and having made three more obviously useless attempt at reaching Barbara by phone, Andrews strolled into the living room and slumped, defeated, into an easy chair and glanced toward the TV set. Aaron Van Aaron was sitting on the couch, his attention riveted on *Gilligan's Island*.

As Andrews' attention gradually began to focus upon the latest inane escapade of the Skipper and his crew of castaways, a familiar and long anticipated ring. Reacting, quickly getting up from the chair, Andrews saw Stanford the butler walking with dignity towards the phone.

"I'll get it, Stanford!" Andrews said, his voice rising in pitch, "on one of the extension phone." He rushed silently out of the living room and into the kitchen, where another phone was ringing.

The kitchen telephone rang several times—and seemingly louder than ever—before Andrews answered it. Indeed, by now, he was almost afraid to pick up the receiver, his mind being immediately flooded with thoughts of what might have befallen his girlfriend, none of them good. When he finally did bring the receiver to his ear, his hand was on the verge of shaking. He waited a second or more before speaking.

"Yes. . . ." he said, speaking quietly so as not to be overheard by either Van Aaron or the butler.

"Dave Andrews, please."

The voice that came from the earpiece was not Barbara's; rather, it was a male voice, deep and sinister in its tone. Moreover, there was a familiar sound to the voice. Andrews remembered hearing it before, perhaps years ago.

"Speaking," Andrews said into the mouthpiece.

"We want Jawbreaker, Andrews." The reply was spoken slowly yet clearly and to the point, sounding to Andrews as if being read from a script. "You will provide us with him."

"What?" replied Andrews. "Who the hell is this? And what are you talking about?"

The first thought entering Andrews' mind in that moment was that someone had, at least, discovered his dual identity. Perhaps someone who was either after the sizable reward that had been posted for the apprehension of the masked adventurer. Or someone who, through blackmail, might try to expose Andrews and possibly collect an amount even surpassing the ten thousand dollars offered by the city.

"We know that you and Jawbreaker have some connection—that you're involved in the same case." Hearing those words, Andrews sighed in relief. Apparently the caller was not, as he had erroneously feared, found out that he and Jawbreaker were the same man. Yet. His secret, at least for now, was still safe.

"Who is this?" he asked. "The cops?" The telephone caller laughed. "What's wrong, Mr. Stuntman, don't you recognize me?"

The words "Mr. Stuntman" immediately prompted one of Andrews's memories—a recollection harkening back to his days working on the Democracy Pictures studio lot. A mental image formed and a wry grin appeared on his face. "Fulton," Andrews posited, "Theodore Fulton."

"I guess I should be flattered," said the man on the phone, "considering how long it's been."

"So how are things, Teddy, old boy?" asked Andrews with a quietly taunting laugh. "Still lighting your brother's fuses?"

"Keep that up and you'll only make things worse for you, Andrews. Howard and I want Jawbreaker, and we believe you can deliver him to us."

"Oh? And if I could bring Jawbreaker to you, then what?"

"We'll leave that up to your imagination."

"I see," said Andrews. His mind produced a half dozen possible murder methods, all derived from the old Democracy Pictures serials, that the Fultons might recreate to eliminate their black-hooded foe. "And just what makes you so sure I can even contact Jawbreaker?"

"Don't take me for a fool," said Fulton. "We know that you're associated with him in some way. Just bring him to us and don't ask any more questions."

"Just one," stated Andrews. "Assuming I can bring Jawbreaker to you, what makes you so damned confident that I will?"

"Just this," said the telephone voice.

There was a pause of at least ten seconds, during which time Andrews listened intently, waiting to hear more.

"Dave! They've got me, Dave!" The voice was that of Barbara, sounding as courageous as she must have been afraid. Andrews' heart seemed to sink. He had expected the worst, but what had apparently happened to Barbara clearly exceeded even his expectations. Somehow she had fallen into the custody of the very people he was fighting to defeat.

"Barbie!" he replied, squeezing the receiver tighter. "Where . . . ? What have they . . . ?"

"We've done nothing," Theodore's voice broke in again, "at least not yet. And we promise not to rough the young lady up more than we have to—she's quite a fighter, as you probably well know—as long as you cooperate with us. Of course, looking as fetching as she does in blue and white, we might also find some 'other' ways to get physical with her, before . . ."

After a few seconds of silence, Andrews said with grim resolution, "Sounds like I don't have much choice."

"Actually, Andrews," said Fulton, laughing, "if you care for this girl, you have no choice whatsoever."

"The terms?" asked Andrews. "Assuming again that I can bring Jawbreaker to you, how and where will this be done?"

The telephone voice chuckled. "My brother and I think it would be most fitting if you perform the execution. Being that you seem to be Jawbreaker's friend, we feel it would be someone ironic if yours is the hand that does him in."

Ironic? Indeed, Andrews thought, it would be more ironic — suicidal, even — than either of the Fultons currently suspected. "I need more details," he said.

"We want to witness Jawbreaker's execution," said Fulton. "Enjoy it . . . savor every moment of it. We'll leave it to you to decide how he is to die. But we insist that his demise is imaginative . . . like something the Scarlet Skull might have thought up to get rid of the hero in his own movie serial."

"Just remember, Fulton," said Andrews almost threateningly, "in the old serials, the hero always escaped death, no matter how imaginative, while the bad guys always lose."

"And you keep in mind, Andrews, that this isn't the movies anymore. When you kill Jawbreaker, he'd better be really dead . . . and *stay* dead."

"How long do I have?"

"Until tomorrow. We're leaving everything up to you, Mr. Stuntman. And I warn you — say nothing of this, nothing of Miss Foster's abduction, to anyone . . . not to Mr. Van Aaron . . . especially the police. Otherwise her life will be forfeit, regardless of what you do with Jawbreaker."

"And if I do this, then what of Barbara?"

"Once Jawbreaker is dead, Miss Foster will be let go."

"How do I know you'll keep your word?"

"You don't," Fulton said coldly. "But you can imagine what might happen to her if you don't do what we want."

Andrews' reply was somber. "I'll see what I can come up with . . . something imaginative."

"I'll phone you again tomorrow at approximately this same

time," said Fulton. "By then I'm sure you'll have had everything worked out. Remember, Andrews, Jawbreaker must die by your hand before our eyes. Remember, too, that we have Miss Foster."

"And you remember this, Fulton," warned Andrews. "Just so much as touch Barbara, even muss her hair, and I swear I'll. . . ."

There was a *click* from the receiver's earpiece, followed by a portentous dial tone.

Andrews slammed down the receiver.

For several moments, the ex-stuntman stared off into space. He bit his lower lip and a look suggesting defeat before it occurred swept across his face. The Fultons had dictated to him what seemed like an impossible situation—murdering before their witnessing eyes his very own alter ego, with the life of his beloved in the balance. Like Theodore Fulton informed him, Andrews had no options. He was their puppet and the two special effects wizards were manipulating the strings.

More than that, Andrews had begun his career as a masked crimefighter basically to alleviate his boredom and satisfy his need for action and adventure. Now that second life had suddenly veered off into a new and previously unexpected direction. The safety and very existence of a person dear to him were now—because of that other career—at risk. Being Jawbreaker was no longer just a dangerous game or action-filled pastime. It had become his primary reason for living. And it had become personal.

Moving like a human automaton, Dave Andrews walked back towards the living room, the rudiments of a plan already forming in his brain.

CHAPTER TEN: A HERO'S DEATH

In accordance with his instructions from Fulton, Andrews said nothing of Barbara's kidnapping to anyone. Approximately twenty-four hours later, the telephones in the Van Aaron mansion rang again.

Once more, Stanford, the Van Aaron butler, began his dignified stride across the living room floor to answer, as was one his duties, the main telephone. By the time he reached the phone, however, it had stopped ringing. Pausing, the butler cleared his throat, then marched off to pursue other tasks. Actually, the phone had already been answered.

For over an hour he focused upon two topics — most importantly, the fate of the woman he loved, and then how he could possibly kill, in front of witnesses, his other identity. If he could accomplish the latter — and that was a colossal "if" — would Barbara, as Fulton had promised, be let go, considering all that she must, by now, have learned about him and his brother and their illicit activities? Perhaps, he thought, she even had some inclination as to how all of the Fultons' crimes, unrelated as they seemed to be, tied together into some kind of crazy "master plan."

Andrews knew that the Fulton brothers were no better than terrorists who had already employed murder, sabotage, robbery and kidnapping in their shopping list of crimes. There was no reason to believe now that these cutthroats would, in fact, release Barbara if and when he performed the impossible task he had been ordered to perform.

Nevertheless, on the slim possibility that Theodore Fulton was speaking the truth and that Barbara might go free, Andrews had to take the risk—risk everything, his own life included. Now, the receiver of the kitchen phone pressed hard against his ear, Andrews was ready to tell Theodore Fulton what he planned to do. "Andrews," he declared into the mouthpiece.

The voice that issued from the earpiece was familiar. "You know who this is, Mr. Stuntman. So—tell me your clever plan for disposing of that masked fool."

"In exactly two hours, Jawbreaker will die," replied Andrews in a cold and quiet voice. "And you and your brother will have the pleasure of witnessing his death."

"Where?" snapped Fulton. "And how?"

"Remember the old Henderson Ranch out in Chatsworth?"

"You mean where Democracy used to do location shooting?"

"That's the place," Andrews affirmed. "Not much left of it now, except for a lot of land . . . and the old barn. That's where it will happen."

"The barn," said Fulton, sounding almost nostalgic. "How well I remember that. Howard and I must have blown it up in miniature at least a half dozen times. So—how will it happen?"

"Remember how the sixth episode of *Riders of Ghost Canyon* ended? Remember what almost happened to Dawson on that show?" Andrews could picture Fulton smiling.

After a thoughtful pause, Fulton replied, "Yes! I remember handling the pyro on that gag. Yes, I think my brother will be pleased, also. Howard is *so* fond of such destructive spectacle."

"I think you'll both enjoy this little spectacle."

"And you've made all the arrangements?"

"Yes," answered the former stuntman, "I've already made contact with Jawbreaker. He believes that he and I are to discuss some 'top secret' caper involving national security. I convinced him that he's the only person who can save the world from some newly arising subversive threat—real James Bond stuff."

"And he doesn't suspect a trap?" asked Fulton.

"He suspects nothing," replied Andrews. "I guess when you put on a mask and fight crime, you also become overly gullible."

"Splendid!" said Fulton, excitement in his voice. "What next?"

"Meet us there in precisely three hours, no sooner, as I don't want to give anything away prematurely and maybe jeopardize what I plan to do. And no later. I'll meet you in front of the old Henderson barn. If he's as punctual as he usually is, Jawbreaker will show up fifteen minutes later. That will give you time to hide—and then watch the action."

"All right then," returned Fulton. The enthusiasm, by now, had left his voice, supplanted by a tone of grim warning. "But I warn you, Andrews. Try to put anything over on us and, well . . . just remember that we still have your girlfriend. And the more I keep looking at her, the more tempting she becomes."

"And once Jawbreaker is deceased, Barbara goes free?" asked Andrews, his delivery sounding as much like a demand as a question.

"You have my word," said Fulton. Saying that, Fulton terminated the telephone call.

Quickly replacing the receiver of the kitchen phone, Andrews frowned. He suspected now, more than ever and no doubt correctly, that the Fultons had no intention of ever releasing Barbara. Still, he had to play out this scenario to its completion. There was, after all, no other option open to him. He was dealing not only with evil men, but also—of this he was certain—with madmen. *They* were in control of the situation and, no matter the outcome, Andrews had to play his intended drama out *their* way.

* * *

Dave Andrews arrived at the Henderson barn a good two hours before the time the Fulton brothers were scheduled to arrive—ample time, he thought, to put the plan he had concocted early that morning into operation.

The Henderson Ranch had been built during the late Eighteenth Century in the Santa Susanna Mountains, in the northern part of Chatsworth, nestled away in Southern California's San Fernando Valley. Originally the spread had been a working ranch, giving employment to numerous cowboys who had traveled West, seeking their fortunes and destinies. During the early part of the next century, the Henderson family found it more lucrative to rent out their property to the motion picture studios. At the same time, many of the people who had been employed at the ranch found new fortunes and a modicum of fame either appearing in the movies as stuntmen, "heavies" or both.

The ranch continued to be used by the studios through, mostly for TV Westerns, the middle 1950s, until the last member of the Henderson family died and the property fell into a condition of disrepair.

Tonight, the only reminder of the ranch's former glory, the barn—location for myriad celluloid action scenes—seemed almost invisible against the enveloping cloak of night. No artificial lights illuminated the area; indeed, it was that very absence of light that Dave Andrews intended to utilize in his plan to "murder" his alter ego and, he hoped, save his beloved Barbara in the process. Additionally, if Howard and Theodore Fulton were indeed determined to witness the death of their ebony-hooded foe, his plan should bring them here, "out in the open," where he might confront them one on one.

Andrews had selected the former Henderson location for two reasons—first, the irony of staging a masked hero's death at a place where so many fictional heroes had escaped death; second, because the barn was situated by itself atop a hill mostly barren of vegetation. Acres of empty space, most of it comprising only dirt and rock, enveloped the abandoned barn. Like so many other parts of Southern California, Chatsworth was a fire-hazard area, and, given the plan he had devised, he did not want to risk starting burning down the entire surrounding community.

Actually, Andrews had come to the Henderson farm early that afternoon, slipping away in the Cadillac just following his usual lunch at the mansion with Aaron Van Aaron. During that earlier visit, Andrews had checked out all the possibilities that the barn had to offer and worked out the logistics. Thankfully the old wooden structure seemed basically unchanged since he had performed his last stunt fight here, and fortunately he had remembered its basic layout after so many years.

In Andrews' estimation, the barn was ideally constructed for the plan he had concocted. The front and only doors faced the only road that led up the hill to the ranch property. These doors, he predicted, would be what the Fulton brothers saw once they arrived on the scene in just about two hours. He knew that the brothers, having made their own scale models of this building, must be aware of the fact that it had no back or side doors. Most likely they remembered that detail.

Jawbreaker was scheduled to appear just a quarter of an hour after their arrival, if the brothers showed up on time. Fifteen minutes was not long to wait, which was part of Andrews' plan. The Fultons would not, therefore, have much — if any — time to investigate the premises, searching for telltale signs of deception. Consequently, the brothers would be compelled, as per his instructions, to take concealment almost upon their arrival, thereby not giving their presence away to the one they were coming to see perish.

The road that led up the hill did not continue all the way to the barn. It terminated several hundred feet away from the old structure, an area where sparse patches of uncut vegetation continued to grow. That would be the spot from which the Fultons must become the audience to observe the show he would soon present to them. From there, the brothers could only see the front wall of the barn.

What the Fultons would *not* see or know is that, upon his afternoon visit to the barn, Andrews had entirely removed the glass of one of its back windows. Behind that wall, which would remain out of the Fultons' range of vision, the hill sloped downward. Andrews would use this open space, the darkness, plus his own skills, coupled with the imagination and gullibility of his audience, to carry out his ruse. He would also require a sizeable helping of good luck.

Now, as Andrews awaited the arrival of the men who held Barbara hostage, he completed his final preparations. Parking the Van Aaron limousine some hundred feet away from the barn, he opened the vehicle's spacious trunk, eyeing the objects he earlier had concealed there, unobserved by either his employer or the butler.

First he removed his black mask and gloves. These he hid beneath a rock that he placed strategically outside the broken window. From sport-jacket pockets he drew out his two matching revolvers. These he set down just inches away from the rock now hiding the mask and gloves.

Then, he took from the trunk his boss' battery-operated tape-recorder that he "borrowed," upon which he had already recorded the sounds that would also figure into his plot. This he placed inside the barn close to the front doors, its speaker directed outwards.

Finally, returning to the limousine, he removed from the trunk, one after the other, three heavy metal canisters. On the rounded sides of each of these containers, stenciled in white capital letters, were the words:

GASOLINE! DANGER!

One at a time, Andrews rolled the three canisters up to the barn. When two of the containers were inside the barn, he unscrewed the caps, then splashed the strong-smelling contents on the floor . . . along the walls . . . over the torn sheets of scripts and other artifacts of Democracy's former presence there, converting the place into a deathtrap. Just one spark from a match, he thought, and the barn would erupt into an inescapable inferno. The third canister he emptied outside the barn, drenching the doors and part of the outer wall.

Leaving all three canisters inside the barn, Andrews dusted off his hands, then exited and returned to his car. He drove it down the road and, as he had done before, parked it far enough away so as not to be associated with the action that was to come.

He took his time walking back up the hill and to the Henderson barn. There he would wait out the remaining time for the arrival of the Fultons, replaying in his mind the script and non-dance-related choreography he would soon be compelled to perform, and also thinking about Barbara.

* * *

Just a few minutes before the designated hour, a Bonneville drove up the road leading to what was left of the Henderson

Ranch. Illuminated by the beams of the car's headlights, Andrews was already standing in the middle of the road — the precise spot that he had planned for his arrivals to stop. He waved his arms to get the driver's attention.

The black automobile came to an abrupt stop, just inches away from hitting Andrews. He could see that three men were inside the car, two in the front seat and one in back. "Right on time, I see," said Andrews approvingly.

He looked into the front seat area of the Bonneville, recognizing both of its occupants. In the driver's seat was the red-haired man whom he had first encountered at the Count Franz Lojos fiasco. Seated next to him was a man Andrews had not seen since his employment at Democracy Pictures, but whom he instantly recognized as Theodore Fulton. Andrews was not familiar with the man in back; just another hired thug, he assumed.

"Matson and I are always on time," boasted Fulton. He looked out the side window and towards the barn. "Where's your car, Mr. Stuntman? Or did you come by taxi?"

"I parked someplace else and hiked up the hill. Considering what I've planned, I don't want my boss' car to be found nearby and him implicated, in case something goes wrong."

"Nothing better," threatened Fulton.

"It shouldn't, if all goes according to my plan. I don't see your brother," Andrews observed. "I thought he wanted to be a witness here tonight, too."

"Howard will believe me when I report to him what happens here tonight," he said. "And I will take pictures. Besides that, someone had to stay behind to baby-sit your girlfriend. Now — have you made all the preparations?"

"Three drums of gasoline," said Andrews. "The place is thoroughly soaked with every drop of the stuff. The place is so old, the wood so dry, it should go up like the proverbial tinderbox."

Fulton cleared his throat. "It would probably look a lot better if done in miniature. But if it does the job, I'm not going to play the role of critic."

"Everything's set to go like clockwork," said Andrews, "as long as you don't interfere in any way."

"And what about our 'guest'?" asked Fulton, looking away from the barn, then back at Andrews.

The ex-stuntman walked around the front of the car and stepped up to the passenger side window. He checked the time on his wristwatch.

"He should be here within the next ten or fifteen minutes," he answered. He pointed at some of the foliage alongside the road. "Now I suggest that you park your car over there and take cover. He'll know something's wrong if he sees you three out here spying on him. And you don't want this pretty car accidentally damaged by what I have in store."

"Agreed," said Fulton, a smile contorting the side of his face. "But first. . . ." Fulton snapped his fingers and the other two men immediately responded.

"What . . . ?" said Andrews, reacting and tensing up as two of the Bonneville's doors rapidly opened.

"Don't need to go into a panic," said Matson, as he and the man from the back seat proceeded to "frisk" him. "Just want to make sure you're not planning to try anything 'clever'." He felt Andrews's chest and sides, finding nothing out of the ordinary. "Clean," said the other man, patting the sides of Andrews' hips and legs.

Remembering where he had hidden his weapons, Andrews suppressed a smile.

"Just being careful," said Fulton.

"I know what you mean," agreed Andrews, this time letting his smile materialize. "I try to be careful, too. Now you'd all better hurry and make yourselves as invisible as you can."

"And you . . . ?" asked Fulton.

"I'm going to keep my meeting with Jawbreaker."

The Pontiac turned around, its lights fading to black. Three dark-suited men exited the car to take their concealment behind vegetation. At the same time, Dave Andrews walked nonchalantly back to the barn, vanishing inside.

* * *

Inside the barn again, Andrews temporized, but only for several minutes. Twice he stepped back out of the barn and looked around, hoping to convince the three men observing him from down below that he was indeed awaiting the masked man's arrival. Upon his last return to the barn, Andrews no longer delayed.

Slipping outside through the open back window, he quickly removed his sports jacket and tossed it into a clump of bushes. Then he reached down and removed the rock, and slipped on the disguise of Jawbreaker. Moments later, the two .38 snub-nosed pistols were stuck under his waistband.

Again in the guise of Jawbreaker, he dashed into the darkness behind the barn, then, moving with the speed of a champion track runner, he continued on a route that Andrews had mapped out earlier that day. Silently and swiftly, he bolted through the underbrush, arching his body forward so that there was less likelihood of his being noticed, all the while doing his best to blend into the darkness.

Within minutes he had run in a wide semicircle that brought him to the front of the building and within fifty or less feet behind the parked Bonneville. Now, if only Fulton and his cronies did not question his arrival here on foot. . . . But Jawbreaker had appeared at other scenes before, with no visible means of transportation.

Taking in a deep draft of night air, whipping out his snub-nosed guns, Jawbreaker walked with confidence up the hill, passing and not looking back at the darkness-concealed black car, and towards the barn.

Jawbreaker played his part well, his true identity having once been something of a bit actor in addition to performing stunts. He walked with stealth and confidence up to the closed barn doors, revolvers held at the ready. Stopping at the doors, he looked around, as if trying to find someone.

Turning his head away from view of the men watching him, he spoke in Andrews' natural voice, "Jawbreaker—in here!" Then, reacting as though the voice he apparently just heard originated from within the barn, the masked man stepped inside, shutting the door behind him.

Once inside, he switched on the tape recorder, its volume already turned up high. From the speaker issued the familiar sound of tape hiss. Via an earlier rehearsal at the scene, he knew exactly how much time would elapse before the revolving reels brought the prerecorded voice to the recorder's playback heads, and approximately how many minutes would pass as he played out his greatest performance.

So far, everything pertaining to his own "master plan" seemed to be working perfectly, on schedule and according to his unwritten script, including both picture and sound.

* * *

Theodore Fulton and his two underlings, the latter gripping pistols, watched the old barn from their hiding place. Matson, holding his .45 semiautomatic, looked at his wristwatch. "He's been in there with Andrews for five minutes." He spoke in a voice barely louder than a whisper. "Maybe we should forget this plan of his, just go inside there and finish both of the creeps off."

Fulton shook his head. He looked over at the man with the red hair. "My brother wants Jawbreaker's death to be inventive and spectacular. We'll give them a few more minutes. Then, if nothing happens, maybe. . . ."

"Wait, boss," said the third man softly, his .38 snub-nosed weapon directed towards the barn. Eyes focusing again on the building, Fulton saw that its door was opening. Immediately Matson and the other man raised their weapons.

"If that's Jawbreaker, and he gets close enough," commanded the man in the continental suit, "might as well grab the opportunity and kill him."

However, the man now slipping out of the barn was plainly not the same man who had so recently entered. This man was wearing a sports jacket and his features were not disguised by a black mask.

"It's Andrews," whispered Matson. The criminal started to take aim at the figure in front of the barn. "And he seems to be alone. Should I . . . ?"

"No, wait," replied Fulton, grasping his wrist and forcing down the weapon, "he's doing something. We'll wait and see. . . ." The three men watched.

Even in the darkness they could see what Andrews was

doing. They saw him take something from his pocket, something that suddenly ignited into a small but potentially deadly flame. They saw him toss this match against the barn doors, which suddenly erupted into a growing wall of fire. Saw him turn and bolt away from the barn and down the hill, as the almost century-old structure quickly went up into a crackling holocaust.

Suddenly, behind Andrews, filled with terror and pain, sounded the shrill voice of a man — Jawbreaker, it could only be, obviously revived by the sudden rush of heat — yelling pitifully for his annoying life.

"Splendid, splendid!" exclaimed Fulton as his eyes watched the ever-increasing flames. "I'd say that's 'cut and print.' Like Andrews said, it's just like that chapter of the *Riders* serial. Howard and I could hardly have done it better. Come on, there's no longer any reason for us to keep getting scratched up in these bushes." Fulton pointed towards the black Bonneville.

"We've got to get the hell out of here fast, Andrews," he said. "Those flames are sure to bring the fire department — and probably the cops, too — and I don't want to be here when they arrive. You know how the feel about arson."

With no more words being spoken, the four men rushed into the Bonneville, with Matson again taking the driver's position. The red-haired gunman started the engine, revved up the engine, and made a fast ninety-degree turn. Wheels skidding along the earthy road, the car, with its four occupants, screeched down the hill.

Fulton turned around to address the occupants of the back seat. He saw Andrews, sitting beside his other gunman, gaze out through the rear window. A look of disappointment crept onto Andrews' face as he observed the retreating image that attested to his handiwork — the last artifact of the Henderson Ranch going up one immense holocaust.

"So . . ." began Fulton, "how'd you do it? I mean, how did you manage to keep Jawbreaker inside there long enough to start that fire?"

"Actually, it was easy," replied Andrews, sounding depressed. "Jawbreaker was my friend. He trusted me. It didn't take much for me to catch him off guard — with a wrench. God, but I never felt so low in my life. Some friend I turned out to be!"

"Jawbreaker really better have died in those flames," warned Fulton. "If I find out that he somehow managed to escape. . . "

"I tell you, he was out cold when I lit that match," said Andrews. "There's no way he could have revived in time to get out. And even if he did revive, there were no other doors in that barn. If you don't believe me, you can always go back and . . ."

"Never mind," said Theodore Fulton. He looked straight ahead again. "Matson, keep driving along this road." Already the black automobile had lost itself among the curving roads of Chatsworth. From somewhere in the distance, the baleful sirens of approaching fire engines could be heard.

* * *

Barbara squirmed in her chair, but could not stand up. The ropes that bound her to the chair had been securely tied around her chest, waist and ankles. Her hands, bound at the wrists, were snugly forced behind the chair's back.

And although she had tried at least a dozen times to break those bonds and wriggle her lithe body free of them, she always failed.

Even if she could get free, getting out of this dark room alive would be another problem and probably an impossible one to solve. At the far end of the large room, one posted at the closed door and another at a window, were two sinister-appearing men in dark business suits. Although they stood empty-handed with arms folded, Barbara was keenly aware of the fact that these guards were armed.

Worse than the guards was the madman who commanded them, Howard Fulton, the former special-effects genius and now master criminal who had assumed the guise and persona of the fictional Scarlet Skull.

Viewed in the flickering light, the monstrous crimson Death's head loomed over Barbara, much of its grotesque appearance hidden by the shadows cast by the red monk's cowl. Fulton pulled a pocket watch from under his crimson tunic and checked the time. It was probably just an optical illusion caused by the candlelight, Barbara thought, but that skeletal countenance seemed to move, its toothy mouth widening into an even more hideous grin.

"If all has gone according to your boyfriend's schedule," Howard Fulton said with a slight cackle lacing his voice, "Jawbreaker should be dead by now—having suffered a demise worthy of the original Scarlet Skull himself."

"No!" shouted Barbara with a fierce shake of her head. "I still refuse to believe Dave would do anything like that. He wouldn't kill anyone in cold blood, especially someone you say is his friend, even if it meant saving my life."

"Is that so?" he returned. "It's surprising to what extents a man will go, just to save a pretty face like yours—and you'd better pray that Andrews fits that clichéd mold."

"I . . . don't get it," Barbara said, shaking her head slowly. "What are you after? What are you trying to accomplish that had this Jawbreaker risking his life to stop you? Revenge, because of that accident that happened so long ago, or something else?"

"Revenge, yes," he said, "that's part of it, my dear. "But I have something else in mind. A 'master plan,' if you prefer. One that, so far, no one else in my organization—not even my brother Theodore—yet suspects. A very *big* plan . . . that's just about ready to be launched!"

Throwing back his head, Fulton laughed, the sound of his maddened voice filling the big room.

"You're crazy!" exclaimed Barbara. "Crazy as a loon!"

Then, eyes seemingly burning in their dark sockets, he stared down at his beautiful captive. He slammed a fist down onto the table, the sudden impact prompting her to twitch.

"That may be true," he agreed, "but who on this planet has more of a right to be a little mad than I? But you—and everyone else, my brother included—will soon see just *how* crazy I really am. Can a crazy man have created what I have in store for this country . . . perhaps even the world? We'll see about that, my dear . . .and it won't be long. And my brother, of everyone, should be the most surprised of all!"

Again Howard Fulton laughed, this time more boisterously, more insanely than before.

Barbara, helpless under the ropes that bound her to the chair, shuddered, pitying this dangerous lunatic as much as fearing him.

* * *

Dave Andrews sat impatiently in the back seat of the cruising Bonneville. Pleased with the presumed success of his deception, he wanted to smile. Restraining himself, however, he remained stone-faced.

Ahead of him, Matson kept the car at the prescribed thirty-five mile per hour speed limit, no doubt not wanting to attract police attention, while Theodore Fulton continued to look towards the road ahead. Next to Andrews, a sullen look on his craggy face, sat Fulton's other henchman. For the past ten minutes no one had spoken a word, the silent void filled by the soothing jazz music playing from an FM station over the car radio.

Pressing his arms close to his body, Andrews felt the comforting bulges of the revolvers he had retrieved from behind the barn. Those weapons, plus the mask and gloves of his other identity, were again concealed on his person. So far, he had been lucky—Fulton had not thought to search him again since the original frisking back at the Henderson Ranch.

Finally Matson spoke. "I gotta admit that was one beautiful fire. I wonder how ours will compare tomorrow night, once we cook that museum."

"Quiet, you idiot!" Theodore Fulton.

"But what's it matter what Andrews hears, now that . . . ?"

"I said shut up! Anyone tell you that you talk too much, Matson?" Snapping his head to the side, Fulton glared at the driver, and a chill rushed along Andrews' spine at the implication of Matson's reply. Andrews pretended ignorance to Matson's blurted-out revelation. "So . . ?" he asked the man in the front passenger seat.

"So?" repeated Theodore Fulton. "So . . . .what?"

"What about Barbara?"

"What about her?"

Andrews leaned forward, stopping just inches away from

the back of the front seat. Instinctively, it seemed, the thug sitting beside him thrust a hand beneath his suit coat, a look of warning in his eyes. Undaunted by the man, Andrews continued, "You said you'd let Barbara go once I did away with Jawbreaker. My end of the bargain's been fulfilled. Now it's your turn."

Without looking back, Theodore Fulton laughed. "Come now, Andrews. You didn't really think we were that naïve . . . that stupid, did you?"

"I . . . guess not."

"Whether or not you got rid of Jawbreaker," he said, coldly, "is a moot point. Either way, Miss Foster knows way too much about my brother and me and our operation. Since I left her with Howard, she probably knows even more."

"You're going to . . . kill her?" Andrews asked, his voice betraying emotion.

"Maybe not just yet," said Fulton. He finally turned to look at Andrews, flashing him a suggestive smile. "I've kind of taken a fancy to her. Howard, you see, has not had much if any interest in women since his unfortunate accident. I, on the other hand . . ."

Andrews felt his body angrily tense up, and it was difficult to remain calm. "And what about me?" he asked, still fighting to control his temper.

"That should be obvious," said Fulton, again directing his attention to the road. "As they used to say in all those old gangster movies, we're taking you for a ride."

"Isn't that kind of old hat?" smirked Andrews.

"Undoubtedly," he replied, "but sometimes the oldest, most clichéd things work the best."

But Dave Andrews was not dead yet. Glancing out the side window, he took note of the passing terrain as the car continued on its way, rolling at a steady thirty-five miles per hour along the winding mountain road. A plan was already forming in his mind, one that might get him out of his present situation. But he needed time to make that plan work. If he could only stall his captors for a minute or so, unbalance them, get them to relax their guard . . . .

"Then once Barbara and I are eliminated, you and your

brother will just go on your merry way—killing people, robbing, blowing things up?"

"Something like that."

"And all for what?" asked the former stuntman. "All of these crimes must be leading to something. Come on, Fulton, tell me what that is. What have you got to lose? Like all those movie villains used to say, as long as I'm going to die anyway . . . "

"That, Mr. Stuntman," replied Fulton, is my brother's and my secret."

"Then tell me this? How much farther before this little 'ride' comes to an end?"

"Not much farther, that I can tell you. Nice thing about these hills and winding roads. They make ideal places for disposing of enemies. It could be days later before a body is found—although the coyotes usually find them first."

Soon, Andrews knew, the car would stop, and he would be marched at gunpoint out into the underbrush, never to return. Not only would Dave Andrews perish, but also Jawbreaker, perhaps the only person that could save Barbara. He had to act now, do something before Matson drove the Bonneville to the spot where Fulton intended to have him killed. Andrews's eyes shifted in the direction of the side window, again noting the passing, darkness-shrouded scenery.

This was it, the moment of decision! There was no other choice to make, no turning back. The slightest error on his part, the tiniest miscalculation, and there would no longer be a Dave Andrews . . . or Jawbreaker . . . or, worse, Barbara Foster.

Now!

It all occurred within seconds. Andrews turned, slamming a rock-hard fist into the man sitting next to him, stunning him into unconsciousness. At the same time his other hand unlocked, then opened, the side door.

"What...?" he heard Fulton say.

By that time, however, Andrews had flung himself from the car and was bouncing off the road and off the edge of the hillside. He had escaped the car and its three murderous occupants. All that concerned him now was the several hundred feet of space and the jagged rocks of the canyon awaiting him below.

CHAPTER ELEVEN: MUSEUM OF HORROR

Never before had Dave Andrews' perfect physical condition and so many of his sharply honed skills come into play at the same time. His reflexes shifting into automatic functioning mode, the former stuntman rolled . . . somersaulted . . . leaped . . . slid . . . did whatever he had to in order to make his way down the rugged slope of the hill. By the time he reached the end of his descending journey — a ravine, mostly hidden from overhead view by thick growths of unkempt vegetation — his body ached incredibly and his lungs gasped for air. But he was alive — and out of the clutches of his three captors.

Keeping hidden in the dark brush, Andrews waited and looked back up towards the spot from which he had made his daring jump. The black automobile from which he leaped was already parked at the edge of the rode, with the three occupants of that vehicle looking down towards his hiding spot.

One of the men — the person Andrews recognized, even at this distance, as Matson — held a flashlight, the beam of which the crook was flashing about the shrubbery that served as his hiding spot.

Voices carried well in these hills and valleys, and Andrews was able to hear, albeit faintly, the conversation taking place above him.

"You think he could have lived through that?" asked Matson, continuing to manipulate the flashlight. "That's a pretty long drop."

"I don't know." Andrews recognized the voice as that of Theodore Fulton. "Remember, Andrews was trained as a stuntman. He's taken high falls before. Only this time he didn't have a mattress waiting for him at the bottom."

"I don't see nothin' down there, boss," said the other man. He switched off the flashlight.

"You're right, Matson. Besides, Andrews wasn't our main concern tonight. Jawbreaker's dead and that was our top priority. Come on. We've got a lot to do before tomorrow night."

Tomorrow night, Andrews thought. He remembered Matson saying something about a fire scheduled at some museum on the following night. Definitely a nocturnal event that Jawbreaker, even without an invitation, should attend. But what museum? Los Angeles had plenty of them. And what time?

Right now was not the time to worry about that. Andrews had to get back to the limousine, and then return to the mansion. There, not only would he try to figure out what that talk of some museum was all about, he had to try and devise some way to find and then rescue Barbara.

He waited until Theodore Fulton and his two cronies returned to their automobile and drove off.

Once certain that he was alone, Andrews climbed back up the slope of the hill and stepped onto the road. Dusting himself off, he waited again, within ten minutes spotting a pair of headlights approaching from the opposite direction. His hands ready to grab his revolvers in the event this was the Fulton gang returning for a second inspection of the ravine, he waved down the car, finding to his satisfaction that its sole occupant was no criminal but just an average Chatsworth resident.

Thus, following an hour's worth of hitchhiking coupled with a fair amount of walking, Andrews returned to Van Aaron's parked limousine. There was nothing more the ex-stuntman could do that night but work out, in his mind, a plan of attack for the following night . . . and, of course, to worry about Barbara, whose fate remained in the hands of a madman and his beyond unscrupulous brother.

* * *

The Langley Storage Company was even more of an eyesore in the morning sunlight. Inside the supposedly abandoned old building, Theodore Fulton continued to search the many rooms for his brother. Howard was not, apparently, in any of the rooms where he could generally be found, particularly the small back room where Barbara Foster continued her existence as hostage.

Barbara was still in the chair where Theodore had last seen her, bound securely with the ropes he had tied himself the day before. Matson and another hired crook were guarding the helpless beauty. Noting the discomfort the woman was obviously enduring, Fulton said, "How're you feeling today, Miss Foster? Are you getting enough to eat?"

"I won't die of starvation, if that's what you mean," Barbara said to him, making a face. "But I'd bet it would taste a lot better if I didn't have to be fed like a baby."

Nodding to Matson, Fulton said, "Untie her. Let her freshen up, too, if she wants to. I'm sure you and the other boys won't let her escape. Just keep an eye on here."

Grinning, Matson said, "That won't be hard to do." He began to untie Barbara's ropes.

"By the way, Matson. Have you seen my brother? I've checked all the rooms and he seems to have disappeared." "He went out," replied Matson, removing the last of Barbara's bonds.

Free again from the ropes, Barbara stretched her limbs, performing an almost sensuous movement of her body that was not unnoticed by Fulton.

"Out?" replied Fulton, his attention back on his main hired gunman. "But Howard never goes out."

"Don't believe me then," said Matson. "Maybe it's somebody else out there all dolled up in that Scarlet Skull getup."

Hearing those words, Theodore Fulton turned to exit the Langley building. As he had told Matson, his brother Howard never ventured outside these haunts during the day. Like some Hammer Films vampire, he preferred the darkness that the building afforded him, especially at night. For some reason, undisclosed even to Theodore, he apparently did not relish being seen in bright light. The way Theodore reasoned the situation, Howard had become so immersed in this Scarlet Skull impersonation that the darkness only enhanced the aura of mystery he was attempting to convey.

As Matson had informed him, Theodore found his brother outside the Langley building. His crimson-frocked back to Theodore, Howard seemed to be gazing off the edge of the hillside. Below him, in the distance, was the smog-enveloped city of Los Angeles, with its familiar buildings and winding freeways.

"Howard?" said Theodore as he walked slowly up to his brother. "What are you doing out here?"

"Just looking, brother," said Howard, his attention still directed toward the metropolis, "at the city . . . while I still can."

"Still can?" asked Theodore, stepping up beside his brother. "Are you going blind? I don't understand."

"You will understand . . . soon . . . after you and the men complete tonight's assignment."

"Then . . . you're finally going to reveal to me this great 'master plan' of yours . . . and tell me the damned *real* reason we've been committing all these crimes?"

Nodding, then clenching a fist, Howard said, "The fictional Scarlet Skull wanted to rule the world, a noble if not impractical ambition. I, his living incarnation, have a similar yet less lofty ambition — one that will pay back everyone responsible for my . . . accident."

"Everyone? It was just one person who caused the explosion that destroyed your face. Seriously, Howard, don't you think that you've been carrying this Scarlet Skull act a bit too far?"

As he spoke, Theodore Fulton looked more directly towards his brother's countenance. Strangely, Howard turned away, as if self-consciously trying to hide what Theodore had already viewed countless times before. Yet in that those brief moments, when the sunlight had caught that red, bony visage, details — horrible ones — were revealed that must have been beyond the powers of candlelight to expose. In the daylight, Howard looked somewhat . . . different, in a way that Theodore could not yet fathom.

His interest aroused now, Theodore, even as he continued speaking to his brother, persisted in getting a better look at his crimson face. "But why do we have to destroy this museum?" he temporized. "Isn't robbing it sufficient?"

"You know how I like to destroy things, Theodore. Accuse me of being nostalgic, but I miss the work we once did before my . . ."

"But you won't even be there to experience it. You're never present when we burn something down or blow something up. And a fire like that only puts us all—*me*—that much more at risk."

"I'll experience the museum's burning vicariously," said the other brother, "just as I did all the other acts of destruction . . . and as I did, last night, the death of Jawbreaker. And be honest with me, brother. You also miss the work we used to do."

But, even though he knew his brother's words rang true, Theodore did not answer.

Slowly, almost imperceptibly so, he was reaching out towards the cowl that cast most of Howard's face into shadow. Then, moving swiftly, his fingers finally grasped the edge of the concealing hood, exposing the red face to the direct rays of the sun.

"No!" snarled Howard through his teeth, at the same time jerking his head away from Theodore's hand.

"What's wrong, Howard?" he interrogated sternly.

Without another word, Theodore Fulton touched the cheek beneath the cowl. Although traces of the red greasepaint came off on his fingers, the feel of that cheek was unlike that of any putty or rubber make-up appliance he had ever touched before. The surface of that face was warm and had the consistency of real flesh—flesh that barely covered the other soft tissues and bone that lay beneath, real flesh that had suffered the ravages of an explosion!

"My God!" gasped Theodore, as he stepped back away from his brother, a sickening feeling stabbing at his abdomen.

Lowering his head, Howard replied. "Yes, Theodore, now you know the truth. Indeed, those quack doctors tried to restore my face after that explosion. But they bungled the job, made me look even more like the character in that movie serial. So—I decided to pretend to be that character. No, I would *be* the Scarlet Skull. All that was missing was the red flesh—a feature easily added with theatrical greasepaint.

"As far as you and anyone else were concerned, I was simply wearing a disguise. For how could I bear anyone knowing that this ghastly face was neither make-up nor mask?"

Theodore Fulton continued to stare incredulously at this... this creature that was his brother. There was, for the first time in so very long, a genuine sadness . . . even shame . . . in the voice that had just issued from the lipless mouth of this ersatz "Scarlet Skull." Indeed, Theodore empathized with that voice, sympathized with this fiend who had once been a normal man... and sibling.

"We'll do what you want tonight," he said, "as we've always done. And this time Jawbreaker won't be there to interfere."

"Perfect," replied the man with the face of a corpse. "Now, my brother—we are finally nearing the climax of our journey. And it's about time that you learned what I've been planning all these months. . . ."

* * *

Andrews spent much of the day at the Van Aaron mansion performing the tasks of a detective. Although no Sherlock Holmes—not even a Stu Bailey or Amos Burke—the former stuntman prided himself on possessing some, if only minor, detective skills.

As far as his foes were concerned, Jawbreaker was dead, killed according to the instructions from Theodore Fulton. At least Andrews was reasonably certain that Fulton had fallen for and still believed his deception. Given Fulton's stated interest in Barbara, she was probably still alive and perhaps even safe, at least for the present. That afforded the young man additional— although, not much—time to concentrate his attention mostly upon the crime that was scheduled to be perpetrated this very night.

Matson had blurted out the fact that the next target of the Fulton gang was to be a museum—a robbery and a torching. He had not, unfortunately, stated what museum or what time the crime , whatever that might be, was to take place.

Assuming that a break-in of such a place could be best executed late at night, Andrews focused his attention on the location of the impending crime. Los Angeles had its fair share museums—the natural history and science museums in Exposition Park, the brand new art museum on Wilshire Boulevard, not to mention all the many smaller and usually private cultural and art museums located throughout the city.

Because the Fulton gang's crimes included robberies as well as acts of destruction, Andrews presumed that their target might be a museum that had recently acquired some items of substantial monetary value. A telephone call to the reference desk of *The Sentinel*, within less than fifteen minutes, turned up the information that, just a week ago, a temporary exhibit of priceless Egyptian artifacts on loan from the much larger Marshall Natural History Museums Group—most of them made of gold, thousands of years ago having belonged to long-dead Egyptians with names like Im-Kha-Ra, Ra-Ka-Tep and Hor-Shep-Sut—had gone on display at the Spevack Museum of Culture and History, located just outside and west of downtown Los Angeles. Significantly, Andrews was informed, no other new or temporary exhibits had opened in the past few months in any of Los Angeles' bigger County museums.

Although Andrews had no certain knowledge that Fulton and his cronies would strike at the Spevack Museum, he had no other options. Working on his personal hunch as much as his deductions, taking a chance, he determined to be on the premises that night and wait there until dawn, if necessary, for the criminals to arrive.

There was only one problem with Andrews making his nocturnal vigil.

* * *

Aaron Van Aaron grimaced, the reflection of his homely face showing clearly in the limousine's rear-view mirror.

"I still want to know where my new tape recorder isn't where it's supposed to be," he said. "You've been using it again to tape Top 40 tunes off the radio, instead of buying the records, haven't you? And why are you driving so fast? This isn't one of your old movie car chases, you know. It doesn't start until nine o'clock. It just a little past eight thirty and you know how I hate being the first one there."

Dave Andrews, his hands firmly clutching the Cadillac's steering wheel, continued to look straight ahead as he drove the vehicle through the Hollywood Hills. He was not happy about having to work this night. It was already dark and he wanted to spend as much time, taking advantage of that darkness, waiting hopefully for his enemies to arrive at the museum. And while he should be maintaining his vigil, wearing the mask and gloves of his other identity, here he was, driving his spoiled employer to yet another stuff-shirt soiree.

In truth, he had done his best to get out of his chores tonight, used every excuse he could invent, including a trumped up stomach ache, to stay home. Of course, nothing — short of physical violence to his wealthy boss — worked. Van Aaron was determined to attend this get-together and remained adamant that Andrews drive him there.

"The quicker we get there," answered Andrews, "the sooner we can leave."

"Leave? What in hell are you talking about, you over-muscled orangutan? We're going to be there for the duration. This is one of the most important society bashes of the year. You should be honored that I've even let you drive me there tonight."

"You can always hire yourself another driver," said Andrews. He was speaking to his employer almost without thinking — by rote — his thoughts being on what he believed was to happen this night, and also on trying to concoct a believable means of extricating himself from this current situation. Andrews noted something else in the rear-view mirror, something that might prove to be a more welcomed sight than Van Aaron's unsightly reflection. A taxicab was cruising behind the limousine, in Andrews' estimation less than a few hundred feet away. More guests on their way to the soiree, he presumed, as there was no other main road in this area, and this one led directly to the event's address. Taking a gamble and hoping to get the cab driver's attention, Andrews flashed the Cadillac's emergency lights as if in some gibberish Morse Code.

"Andrews! What the hell are you...?"

Before Van Aaron could finish what he was saying, Andrews was slamming down the break pedal, the momentum of the limousine's fast stop sending the multimillionaire slamming forward against the back of the front seat. Recovering quickly, Van Aaron yelled, "Have you going completely nuts? Are you trying to get me killed?"

"Enjoy the party, boss man," said Andrews. He flung the driver's door open and bolted out of the car, waving his arms at the cab. "I just remembered. I've got a big date."

"A date?" said Van Aaron with a laugh. "I thought that girlfriend of yours dropped you."

Ignoring his employer's remark, Andrews turned away, saying, "You know how to drive this baby? Good—you can dock me a day's pay."

"What . . . ?" Van Aaron fumed. "You want me to . . . where are you. . . ? And what about my tape recorder?"

As Van Aaron continued to rave, the other vehicle slowed to a stop. Andrews rushed up to the open driver's side window. He looked into the taxicab, noting the formally dressed elderly couple sitting in the back seat. Behind him he could hear Van Aaron shouting threats and obscenities at him.

"Sorry for the inconvenience," Andrews told the three people inside the taxicab, "but I'm commandeering this vehicle. Police business. You two folks can ride in style—in that limo. Once you get out and its owner calms down, you'll find him to be a fairly nice man. But one of you will have to do the driving."

"See here, now. . . " complained the man in back.

"Listen, buddy," said the taxicab driver. "I need to see some identification, if. . . ."

Unseen by the people in the back seat, Andrews flashed the driver his "identification" —the handle of one of his .38 revolvers.

"Where to, officer?"

"I need to get to the Spevack Museum just east of downtown. Know the address?"

"Hell, I'm a cab driver. Get in. Not a major tourist stop, but. .

. ."

Ignoring the driver, opening one of the rear doors, Andrews motioned for the two people seated in back to get out and over to the limousine. The taxicab having been vacated, he hurried inside and shut the door.

"Get there as fast as you can, if possible without breaking any laws. And don't try any fancy routes. I know all the shortcuts."

"And who's gonna pay me for this little joyride?" asked the driver, smirking. "The LAPD?"

"You can send the bill to Mr. Aaron Van Aaron," replied Andrews. "He's in the phone book."

Even as the taxicab made a U-turn and started to drive away from the limousine, Andrews could see that the man now sitting at the wheel of the big Cadillac was still ranting.

* * *

Andrews had the taxicab driver drop him off a block away from the Spevack Museum of Culture and History, an obviously old building that might have been built during the early Twenties. Upon exiting the vehicle, Andrews slipped into the shadows and looked down the street towards the darkened building. Nothing about the place looked suspicious, at least from the front. Once the taxicab had sped off and away from the scene, he made his first move, surreptitiously hurrying to the alley behind the museum.

It was already past nine o'clock and, it seemed, he had arrived at a most opportune time. Moreover, both his deduction and his hunch seemed to be hitting their targets dead center. Two vehicles, illuminated by beams from the half moon, were parked in the alley behind the museum, for all appearances innocently making a delivery. But Andrews recognized both of them—a canvass-topped truck, like the one he had already pursued, and those he had seen at the Jackson dealership, and Theodore Fulton's by now very familiar black Bonneville.

Crouching behind a dumpster, Andrews instantly underwent a dramatic transformation, taking from his pockets and then donning the three component items of his disguise—

the black hood-like mask and black gloves. He took out both revolvers, one after the other, confirming that each held six bullets. Replacing the guns, he felt that surge of power and excitement that always accompanied his metamorphosis from ex-stuntman to masked crimefighter. Once again he was no longer Dave Andrews -- but Jawbreaker!

Taking three steps at a time, it required but seconds for Jawbreaker to reach the rear entrance of the museum. Something was lying just outside the back door, haphazardly hidden behind some crates bearing the museum's name — the body of a man, a caretaker's probably, a dagger imbedded deeply in his bloody chest.

Jawbreaker frowned. The sight of this dead man sickened him, made him feel like a failure. If he had been able to get away sooner, maybe he could have prevented this needless waste. For he knew that he was changing, realizing that the reasons for Jawbreaker's existence were progressively becoming more and more salient.

He looked away from the corpse and to the back door. No doubt Theodore Fulton was confident that the work to be done here this night would be accomplished quickly and efficiently, with no interference from the police. They had conveniently left the door open.

Slipping into the museum, Jawbreaker found it easy to blend into the shadows. Only a few lights were on inside the building, just enough, he fancied, for Fulton and his men to accomplish their unlawful and destructive work. The place basically comprised several rooms displaying various ancient artifacts, including weapons and armor possibly dating back to the chivalrous days of King Arthur and his Knights of the Round Table.

In addition to the exhibits, the very interior of the place suggested a Los Angeles of almost a century ago, with much wooden paneling, some rather old-fashioned light fixtures and other telltale signs betraying of the museum's age. From a nearby room, almost echoing through the large chambers, he could hear voices, including those of Theodore Fulton and the gunman named Matson. Fulton's voice, however, sounded strangely different than it had before, somewhat fainter, almost uncertain.

"Get those items out . . . as fast as you can," he heard Fulton say.

"Are you sure you don't want any of this other stuff?" asked Matson.

"Just the Egyptian gold," Fulton insisted. "The gold . . . we can melt it down. The other items . . . well, we can't and are too tough to fence. Besides, we want to get out of here fast. Yes, fast. And as . . . as quietly as possible. We're in the heart of the city now where the police are ubiquitous."

"Where they're what?"

"Never mind. Just . . . load those items into the truck. Then . . . then torch the place."

"Say, boss—are you sure you're okay?" asked Matson, plainly concerned.

"I'm . . . fine."

"You don't sound so good, boss. And you're lookin' to me a bit on the pale side."

"Don't be concerned about me," Fulton said, this time with his usual force. "Just be concerned about getting this job done."

"Okay, boss, no need to get all riled up. I promise you, when this place goes up, your brother's gonna be real happy."

Remembering what Fulton had said, Jawbreaker likewise did not want to attract the attention of the police. Deciding that he would resort to gunfire only if there were no other options, he, with a mighty yank, removed one of the Medieval broadswords from its fastenings on the wall. He tested the heavy weapon's balance in his hands, feeling somewhat like a brave knight of old.

In years past, Dave Andrews had performed well in fencing matches and had often put his swordsmanship skills to good use, doubling the phony swashbuckling heroes of the screen. He had never, however, wielded a broadsword before, especially not in real combat. Fortunately the former stuntman had been conditioned to learn fast. Armed now like Sir Galahad, Jawbreaker stealthily made his way towards the room from which the voices were emanating, then peered around the corner.

There was much activity in the adjoining room. While a

clearly nervous Fulton gave orders, four men—one of them Matson—proceeded to grab up various exquisitely formed Egyptian artifacts, all of them made of gold that glittered in the meager illumination. A pharaoh's ransom, Jawbreaker thought, priceless relics of the past that would soon, if this activity were not stopped, be melted down for their basic scrap value. None of the items being purloined had been placed – at least not yet -- in glass cases, making their theft relatively easy. Resting against one wall of the room were four devices that Jawbreaker recognized as flamethrowers, reserved for the *coup de grace* of the night's activities. Jawbreaker had to put a stop to those activities now, he knew, before a single golden artifact left the building.

Taking a deep breath and clutching the sword tightly, he stepped into the room, the blade of his borrowed weapon glinting in the light. "All right!" he said in a fearless and commanding voice. "Drop those artifacts!"

"Jawbreaker!" Matson stated the obvious, clasping a golden Egyptian mask, as the other three men set down the items they had been trying to steal.

"Just like in the movies," said Jawbreaker, grinning. "Why do the crooks always feel this compulsion to say the hero's name whenever he shows up?"

"I thought he was supposed to be dead!" exclaimed Matson.

"It wouldn't be the first time, Matson," returned Jawbreaker with a chuckle. "Probably not the last, either."

"So—Andrews tricked us! So what? We'll kill you now!" ordered Fulton, his men instantly reaching for their weapons, "but using a quicker method."

"Uh, uh," mocked the man in the hood, "wouldn't do that if I were you. One shot and this place will be swarming with LAPD."

"No guns!" agreed Fulton. "Anyway, he's just . . . just one against all of you."

Matson, still holding the shiny mask, was the first to move, bolting at Jawbreaker like an onrushing locomotive. Savagely he swung the mask at Jawbreaker's head, the crimefighter ducking in time to avoid being struck. Still holding the broadsword in both hands, the hooded man elbow-jabbed his dark-suited foe in the jaw, sending him toppling over, semi-conscious, the golden artifact clanging against the floor. But there were still three other men—plus Fulton—with whom to contend.

Two more of them, one armed with an ancient battle-axe and the other brandishing a more modern switchblade, were now charging towards the masked man at full speed. The crooks' faces were twisted into expressions of hate and rage. Curses issued from their mouths.

Swinging with all his might, Jawbreaker made his broadsword dance through the air. With the skill and speed of an expert he slashed at his foes, the weapon twice performing the grim work for which it had been designed. Moments later, two men, their dark suits stained by rapidly expanding rivers of blood, dropped moaning to the museum floor.

"Forget the artifacts!"

Jawbreaker, the bloodied broadsword held ready, if necessary, for a third strike, turned in the direction of Fulton's voice. "Just torch the place . . . then get the hell out of here!"

Matson, fully revived again, and other hired man were already rushing towards the four flamethrowers. As they ran they reached into their pockets, taking out protective face masks that they affixed to the lower areas of their faces, covering their noses and mouths.

Aware that the weighty sword would now only slow him down, Jawbreaker dropped it and started to move towards Matson. But, fast though the masked man was, he was not fast enough, and the act of disposing of his weapon took up valuable seconds. Already Matson was switching on the device in his hands, releasing a deadly stream of fire in Jawbreaker's direction.

The other man, too, turned on his flame-throwing device, streaming incendiary power across the room to ignite the nearest wall.

"Stay here until you're certain the fire will do its work," said Fulton, his voice wavering, through the sound of crackling flames. "I'll . . . I'll meet you back at the hideout!"

Having given his commands, Fulton dashed out of the room in the direction of the back door.

"You see?" hollered Matson, aiming his flamethrower at his hooded adversary. "You're not the only one who can wear a mask. Except ours does something that yours can't—lets us breathe!"

Seemingly Jawbreaker was powerless to do anything. Already Fulton was making good his escape and would soon be driving his Bonneville back to his headquarters, probably the same place that Barbara was being help a prisoner, wherever that might be. Stalking towards him now was a man armed with a weapon against which even one of good King Arthur's swords was useless, a man determined to transform him into a human torch. And off to one side, yet another of Fulton's thugs was spreading fire throughout the museum, setting ablaze every combustible item in sight. Obviously, with all of its draperies and exhibits, many of the latter made of wood, the museum was a veritable firetrap. The fire was already a raging conflagration, growing bigger and hotter by the moment. In very little time the entire place would go up in a Hell from which even a man of Jawbreaker's talents could escape.

Already the fire and smoke were affecting Jawbreaker's respiration, his lungs aching as they filled with the hot atmosphere of the place. Just breathing was becoming more difficult for him by the seconds. He coughed, still fighting off the stifling heat, battling to remain conscious...just to stay alive.

"What's wrong, Mr. Jawbreaker?" Matson taunted, the fire stream from his weapon eating through the floor towards Jawbreaker's feet. He laughed as he continued, "Looks to me like you got a little respiratory problem there. Maybe you should see a doctor . . . but at the rate you're goin', you'll be seeing the coroner first!"

Jawbreaker replied only with a cough.

"Funny, ain't it," continued Matson, "the death you faked at the barn is happening now again—only this time for real. What would Fulton call that . . . ironic, is that the right word?"

Even as Matson taunted him, his weapon still spewing out its flaming death, Jawbreaker remembered what he still harbored inside his sports jacket. Gagging from the smoke inhalation, he took out one of his guns and tried his best to aim. But not only was it difficult breathing, it was also hard to see.

His eyes smarted painfully from the smoky air and the heat made his gun hand feel like it was already on fire.

All the while, Matson—stalking Jawbreaker like some jungle cat ready to pounce on his prey—came towards him, wielding his flame-hurling weapon.

"We gotta split this joint, Matson," said the other man. "If we don't get out now, we're gonna be cremated."

"We have to make sure he goes down in the fire," said Matson.

"No problem there!"

With his peripheral vision, Jawbreaker glimpsed the other man making his way across the room, his flamethrower still doing its work. He was making his was ambling around the place, carefully trying to avoid the spots already burning, at the same time trying to get behind the ebony-masked man. Also, he shut off his flamethrower, then raised it high over his head. . . .

What happened next, not even Jawbreaker really knew. Fighting the heat and the flames, trying to aim his gun and at the same time evade the fire that Matson continued to shoot at him, he felt something hard and metallic strike hard the back of his head. Then, only darkness and oblivion.

Jawbreaker never saw Matson and the other man drop their fire-shooting weapons and bolt through the building, escaping the scene toward the rear exit. And he never saw the inferno continue to grow around his inert form, their dancing fiery tongue eating their way ever closer.

CHAPTER TWELVE: THE MASTER PLAN

Jawbreaker's eyes slowly fluttered open, his consciousness returning beneath what at first felt like rain. Looking up, he saw that the museum's sprinkler system—as archaic, it appeared, as some of the artifacts on exhibit—had finally kicked into operation. Accompanying the downpour was a loud alarm bell. Soon, he knew, the place would be crowded with members of the Los Angeles Fire Department.

Whether or not the sprinkler system was powerful enough to dowse the flames and save what was left of the building and the collections it housed was irrelevant. All that was important to the masked man now was that he was alive. And alive, he might still be able to catch up with Theodore Fulton and his arsons and, inevitably, save Barbara Foster.

He had to get out of this inferno before the firemen—and with them, probably the police—arrived on the scene. Detainment now could mean doom for Barbara. Also, he did not relish having arson added to Jawbreaker's already sizable list of alleged crimes.

Coughing again from the flames, Jawbreaker forced himself to stand. Flames were erupting virtually everywhere he looked and breathing was difficult. If he was to escape the fire he had to move *now*, before the conflagration grew any larger. Again his quick thinking and superbly trained body were called to action.

Spotting a fire-extinguisher on one wall, he rushed through

the flames and tore the device down. Switching the cylindrical gadget on, he shot a spray of flame-eating chemicals towards the floor. Then, rushing forward, he used the fire extinguisher to create in front of him a flameless path. Onward the masked man made his way through the blazing museum, leaving behind the now-melting Egyptian artifacts and passing the soon-to-be-consumed medieval relics.

As he approached the open back door, he heard the roar of a mighty engine approaching. It sounded like a motorcycle— specifically, a Harley-Davidson 74 Electra Glide —the model Dave Andrews knew well, having ridden that bike in one of his movies. It was also the brand and model favored by the Los Angeles Police Department.

He had no choice but to continue his flight outside and into the open air. His only other option was to allow his body to feed the raging flames. Tossing aside the fire extinguisher, he stepped outside boldly, ready to face the armed might of the LAPD.

Luck on his side again, he found not a policeman but someone else astride the brand new Harley-Davidson that slowed to a stop just yards away from the museum's rear entrance. The rider was huge and burly, sporting long wind-blown hair and a frizzy beard, and wearing a leather vest worn over his all-black outfit.

"Whoa, man! What's happenin' here?" He slurred his words, a sign to Jawbreaker that this biker was not in complete control of his faculties. Then he reacted broadly to the man wearing the mask. "Hey, cool outfit, man. That mask is, like, far out."

Breathing deeply the restorative night air, Jawbreaker quickly assessed his present situation. The masked man had no idea how much time had elapsed during his period of unconsciousness. Perhaps it was only minutes, maybe even seconds before the sprinkler system returned him to awareness. If that were true, perhaps Matson and his partner did not have too much of a head start. Trucks like the ones the Fulton gang used were not, after all, built for speed.

Taking advantage of the burly man's apparent condition, Jawbreaker stepped up to him. On a hunch, he asked, "Hey, friend. By any chance did you happen to see a big, canvass-topped truck?"

"Big canvass-top?" the biker said, his gaze shifting back and forth between Jawbreaker and the fire. "Sure, I seen one . . . just as I drove up. Going onto the freeway. Headed north."

"Thanks." Painfully aware that there was no time to run back to the limousine, if he were to catch up to the truck, Jawbreaker eyed the motorcycle. "Nice bike."

The bearded man beamed proudly. "Brand new. It'll look better when I chop it."

"Gas tank full?"

"Just about. Why?"

Jawbreaker's answer was in the form of a powerful fist slamming with all the force it could muster into the big biker's jaw, knocking him into near-unconsciousness. Shoving the groaning man off the motorcycle and onto the pavement of the alley, he climbed onto the motorcycle and grasped firmly both handlebars. His right hand turned the throttle and revved up the mighty engine. He depressed the clutch and, with a depression of his right foot, engaged the first gear.

Moments later, the Harley-Davidson, with its masked rider, was roaring toward the onramp of the Harbor Freeway, heading north.

* * *

Jawbreaker had to assume that the canvass-topped vehicle seen by the biker was, in fact, the same one that Fulton and his men had used in their raid on the museum. Such trucks were rarely used anymore, he knew, although they were popular in earlier decades, and also were mainstays in so many of the serials made during the Thirties, Forties and early Fifties by Democracy Pictures as well as other studios. He wondered if the Fultons continued to use these vehicles, outmoded though they may have been in some ways, to satisfy some deep-set yearnings to return to their more pleasant days spent at Democracy.

Presuming that the Fulton brothers' base of operations was hidden somewhere beyond the more metropolitan areas of the city, and therefore had not yet exited the freeway, Jawbreaker continued heading north on his borrowed motorcycle, always maintaining a speed of fifteen miles per hour above the posted speed limit of sixty-five. Traffic was mild this night and moving nicely, and he had the bonus advantage of being able to weave the Harley-Davidson between the freeway's lanes.

Again Jawbreaker's prediction proved accurate. Within minutes of joining the flow of traffic, he spotted his quarry — probably the only canvass-topped truck in the vicinity — in the right lane, and moving slightly slower than most of the other vehicles on the freeway tonight. Reducing the motorcycle's speed, Jawbreaker followed at a safe distance of approximately seventy-five feet, always careful not to betray the fact that he was in pursuit.

He followed truck as it merged onto the Hollywood Freeway, again in a northerly direction. Passing the popular exits for Hollywood and then Sunset boulevards, the truck finally turned off at Highland Avenue. Jawbreaker maintained his carefully distanced pursuit of the truck as it eventually turned off Highland, continued at slower speeds along various connecting side roads, eventually to make its ascent into the darkness of the Hollywood Hills.

* * *

Both hand- and foot-braking the motorcycle to a stop, Jawbreaker gazed towards the old building, situated in a clearing several hundred yards up the hill. Even in the darkness and at that distance, he recognized the place, outside of which both the canvass-topped vehicle and Theodore Fulton's Bonneville were parked. A smile came to the face exposed below the mask. Jawbreaker knew well this building — home to the former Langley Storage Company that once housed and preserved original negatives and prints of so many of Democracy Pictures films. This place would indeed make a fitting and even ironic headquarters for the Fulton brothers. Imagine, he thought, Howard especially hiding out in a place that had once preserved the product made at the studio where both his face and his sanity were destroyed!

Now the old Langley building might also be the prison in

which Barbara was being held. The time for acting clandestinely
. . . for careful planning and being subtle was over. Jawbreaker
might never again have such an opportunity to free Barbara,
and, at the same time, put an end to the Fultons' seemingly
unrelated albeit illicit operations. He checked his guns, making
sure that each contained six bullets.

Then he gunned the Harley-Davidson and, like a human
torpedo, roared up the hill on a direct collision course with the
Langley building's front door.

Fortunately the door was as old and decrepit as the rest of
the structure. Its warped and brittle surface easily gave way to
the impact of the motorcycle, as Jawbreaker crashed through it
head-on, sending wooden shards of all sizes flying through the
air. Moments later, the motorcycle was approximately in the
middle of a large room, its wheels skidding, spinning around in
a forty-five-degree arc as the hooded man worked fast the hand
and foot brakes, finally bringing his mechanical steed to a
screeching stop.

"Jawbreaker!" Several voices shouted his name, almost
simultaneously, like in a chorus.

The voice was familiar—Matson's. Looking around furtively,
at the same time setting the motorcycle down on its kickstand
while leaving the engine running, Jawbreaker quickly spotted
six hoodlums in addition to Matson. Three of them, plus
Matson, were stationed at ground level, making their way
towards wooden crates or any other place of concealment.
Three more were above on a catwalk. All seven of the thugs
were already drawing their pistols.

There was no sign of Barbara, nor either of the Fultons
anywhere; right now, however, Jawbreaker's main concern
were these seven gunmen. "Kill the creep!" shouted Matson.
"And this time make sure he stays dead!"

Seconds later, the sound of bullets reverberated through the
large room, deadly points whizzing precariously close to the
man in the mask. There was no place to run or hide. Other than
the people occupying it, the room was mostly empty and
Jawbreaker was in the center of it. In desperation, while trying
to avoid his enemies' gunfire, he ducked behind his only shield,
the motorcycle, and drew his own weapons.

Aiming high, he fired twice, one bullet from each .38 simultaneously striking the chests of two of the men on the catwalk. The masked man heard them groan, then, their chests bleeding, the men crumpled forward, falling off the catwalk to strike the floor with matching sounds of impact.

Five men left, Jawbreaker thought, with ten bullets remaining before he had to reload. So far, the odds were working on his side. "You can't get us all!" It was Matson talking again, firing twice again from behind a pile of crates, obviously trying to intimidate Jawbreaker with words as well as bullets. "You can't be that dumb . . . or foolish!"

The bullets ricocheted off the Harley-Davidson, nicking its highly polished chrome. Almost at the same time, gunfire erupted from another direction—two gang members shooting from behind wooden boxes—several bullets missing the masked man's back by mere inches.

He was trapped, caught between Matson firing from one direction and these other two men from behind. If he could eliminate the firepower from one of these directions . . . A plan!

"You brag a lot, Matson," he shouted, firing three rounds at the man behind the crates, pretending to ignore the two lesser hirelings behind him. "But you haven't killed me yet!"

Turning slightly, Jawbreaker saw, with his peripheral vision, movement from the direction of the other two foes. He was banking on their assumption that, for the moment at least, his attention was exclusively on Matson. Now, he predicted, they would think him to be at his most vulnerable, his back an easy target, reducing their need for caution.

In that moment Jawbreaker spun around, instantly spotting the two men who, guns ready to fire, were already standing in full view from behind their places of concealment. A wry grin on his face, the masked man again fired both revolvers.

Blood erupted from each of the thugs' heads. They faces frozen into expressions of surprise and bewilderment, the men fell forward, disrupting the boxes that had once protected them.

Just two men left, Jawbreaker thought, and not yet one bullet wasted. But time was fleeting, and every moment that passed would make rescuing Barbara more difficult, if not impossible. If Barbara were on these premises, the Fultons undoubtedly would be aware already of the in-progress gun battle, and would act upon her accordingly. He had to end this fight now, quickly and efficiently, and proceed to his next task — saving the woman he loved.

Bullets — fired by Matson as well as the remaining man on the catwalk — continued to fly by the masked crimefighter. At this distance he was a difficult target to hit, and his foes were probably more adept at shooting things at closer range. That gave Jawbreaker an idea. If they were having problems hitting a relatively distant target, how much more difficult would it be for them to shoot at a moving one?

Shoving both guns into his belt, Jawbreaker swiftly climbed back onto the motorcycle, revved up the engine with several turns of the right handle, then proceeded to zoom around the parameters of the room. "What's he doing?" shouted the man on the catwalk, uselessly firing his gun at the man speeding around the room below him. "Is that guy flipped?"

"Don't ask dumb questions!" Matson holler back. "Just shoot!"

By the third go-round, easily ducking the bullets being fired at him from both ground level and above, Jawbreaker, his right hand maintaining the motorcycle's speed, withdrew one of his revolvers. Aiming at this speed was no easy feat, especially with his left hand. He fired four times, at least one of the bullets ripping through the neck of the target, emptying the .38.

As the motorcycle completed making another circle, the overhead gunman collapsed. Gurgling, uselessly clutching his throat, he became a bloody heap atop the catwalk. That left only Matson. If he could take the red-haired thug alive, make him tell where Barbara was being held. . . .

Making one last ride around of the room, Jawbreaker aimed the motorcycle directly towards the man still firing at him from behind the crates. Instinctively ducking, the masked man crashed the bike through the piled-up boxes, sending Matson, his .45 still held tightly in one hand, flying off to one side. At the same time, Jawbreaker leaped from the motorcycle and onto his adversary, struggling to restrain his gun hand.

"Where is she?" Jawbreaker demanded. "Where's Barbara? Better talk, or I'll . . ."

"You'll what, masked man?" Matson retorted, straining to maintain mastery of his weapon, inching it ever so slowly towards his enemy's chest. Although he wanted desperately to live, the criminal seemed adamant on not surrendering. Indeed, as Jawbreaker struggled to restrain him, the red-haired crook—a man of considerable physical strength—fought even harder, exerted more strength, to force his gun in the masked man's direction.

Jawbreaker, however, was equally strong, if not moreso, and also better trained for one-on-one battle. He knew now that it was senseless to try simply subduing Matson. Barbara's fate now depended exclusively on his own survival. Matson had to be eliminated—and, before he could fire that weapons into Jawbreaker's body, as quickly as possible.

Grunting, muscles exerting themselves to their extremes, Jawbreaker slowly yet gradually turned the muzzle of the .45 in the direction of its owner. Two right index fingers—one Jawbreaker's, the other Matson's—struggled over mastery of the weapon's trigger. One of them—Jawbreaker was not certain of which one—jerked the trigger back. A deafening roar exploded between the two men and Matson, giving out a gasp, folded forward at the waist and dropped.

No chance remained for questioning Matson.

After shutting off the motorcycle's engine, the empty .38 snub-nosed pistol still in his left hand, Jawbreaker strode into the middle of the room. For the first time he noticed that the room was lit by a series of lamps, each hooked up to a small generator. All of the windows had been painted black, probably to conceal the light and the fact that the building was currently being used.

Seven bleeding corpses now littered the place and the air still smelled of gunpowder. His heart still beating rapidly following his most recent ordeal, Jawbreaker studied his surroundings. There must be many rooms in the Langley building, he realized; and from where he was now standing, he could see doors that led to at least a dozen of them. One of those doors, he prayed, would take him to Barbara.

* * *

Guns reloaded again and drawn, Jawbreaker spent almost an hour searching the myriad halls and rooms before coming upon a small room located in the rear of the building. Like the other parts of the building already searched by the masked man, this one did not contain Barbara Foster.

The only illumination in the room came from the moon. The room, seen mostly in darkness, was spartanly furnished—just a simple table and a few chairs. Lying on one of the chairs were several lengths of rope. The ropes had been neatly cut, suggesting to Jawbreaker that someone had indeed been held captive here and then freed, that "someone" most likely being Barbara.

A burnt-out candle rested on the table's top, most of its wax having melted away. Also on the table were the stubby remains of other extinguished candles. Striking a match, he re-lit candle and continued to scrutinize the room.

Most curious was something hanging on a wall of the little room—a large "one-sheet" poster for an old Democracy Pictures movie serial, coincidentally among Dave Andrews's favorites. "*The Scarlet Skull*," Jawbreaker read aloud the title, his memory briefly and nostalgically recalling the Saturday afternoons of his youth, spent with countless other children in the darkness of his local movie theater.

"Yes, Andrews—*The Scarlet Skull*."

Instinctively snapping up his revolvers, Jawbreaker spun around, the short barrels of his weapons directed towards the familiar figure now stepping boldly into the room. "No need to point . . . those at me," said the man wearing the continental suit. "I'm not going to . . . try to harm you or even run away. Not anymore." Having said that, Theodore Fulton slumped into a chair, brushing aside the ropes.

"You're . . . giving up?" asked the man behind the mask, incredulous at what he had just heard from this man who had already spent so much time trying to kill him. "This better not be some trick."

"No . . . trick." Fulton shook his head slowly as he spoke, giving the appearance of a genuinely tired individual. Not just tired, Jawbreaker observed, but depressed and defeated. There was a kind of pallor about the man's face and a look of hopelessness in his eyes. And when he talked, his voice wavered slightly, sounding completely bereft of all its past confidence and arrogance.

"Don't worry . . . I'm not armed."

Taking no chances, Jawbreaker searched Fulton for weapons. Finding none, he reluctantly returned his own guns to the pockets of his jacket. Then he walked up to the seated man, placing his fists on his hips, looming over Fulton in a threateningly dominant pose.

Wasting no more time, he emphatically asked, "Where's Barbara?"

"With Howard," replied Theodore Fulton. "For the present she's still safe."

"And where's Howard?"

"I'll tell you where she is . . . tell you everything. But first, I have to tell you about Howard . . . the truth about my brother."

"I'm listening," said Jawbreaker. His eyes narrowed coldly behind the slanted holes cut into his black mask. "But talk fast."

"My brother . . . he's mad. Totally insane!"

"So tell me something I don't already know."

"You don't understand," said Fulton, grabbing the standing man's sleeve as if in an act of desperation. "It's what he plans to do. Jawbreaker, or whoever you are beneath that hood, you've got to stop him!"

"Right now, I'm only interested in saving Barbara."

"No, you don't understand! This is all much bigger than you realize . . . more than I even knew, until my brother finally told me. Yes, I knew Howard's mind had snapped following his accident. And I'm guilty of going along with his psychoses, so I accept equal guilt for all those killings . . . the robberies . . . the sabotage . . . But now, what he's planning, his 'master plan,' is so immense, so monstrous that, even for me . . ." Then this man, who had commanded criminals like Matson and presided over so many acts of violence and sabotage, wept like an infant.

Jawbreaker realized, then, that to best save Barbara, he would first have to know all that he could concerning Howard Fulton's so-called "master plan."

"What is this big 'master plan.'? And how do all those crimes relate to one another, if, in fact, they do? I could never see any connection."

"There are indeed . . . connections," said Fulton, at last bringing his tears under control. "The robberies are the most simple to explain. There were materials that needed to be purchased for Howard to realize his big scheme. And people to be hired . . . and bought off. Howard needed money . . . lots of it . . . to accomplish what he secretly had set out to do.

"The murders? Some of the people paid to acquire Howard's materials . . . to do his clandestine work, perform experiments, assemble items, even smuggle things out of their respective countries . . . instantly became security threats. A few of them — like that foppish count with his habit of becoming... overly loquacious after downing a few drinks, had to be dealt with sooner than others, which is why... the overt assassination at which you were present. Once the services of such hirelings were... completed, they had to be silenced. Again, a simple ...explanation."

"All the destruction?"

"Just slightly more...complicated," explained Fulton. "Some of the places robbed were destroyed to conceal evidence. Some were the working places of... people that Howard had hired and then needed to dispose of — scientists, and so forth."

"And what about that museum?" asked the masked man. "You went there to rob the place, right? Why also burn it down?"

"You don't yet completely understand the way Howard... thinks. He'd made his living creating movie effects, his specialty being scenes of... destruction. He's always loved huge fires and explosions. He... still does."

Jawbreaker grunted, trying to take what Theodore Fulton had just told him and to make some sense of it all. "And now," he demanded. "This 'master plan' of his."

"Howard wants revenge... against the movie industry because of what happened to him in the explosion. As you know, there are three... major hubs of film production in this country — Los Angeles, of course, then New York, and to a lesser extent, probably... because of taxes and all the handouts, Chicago. Howard plans to destroy... all three cities, starting with our own, then perhaps move on to yet more... targets, any place where movies are even shown."

The masked man chuckled. "And how the hell does he plan to do that? With a couple canvass-topped trucks and a handful of heavies in dark suits?"

"With what all these robberies and killings and acts of sabotage have been... leading up to," Fulton blurted out, getting out of his chair and grabbing the other man by his jacket's lapels. "Howard's managed... to acquire three... nuclear bombs . . . built by the people he'd hired to his own... deluded specifications."

"Atom bombs?" gasped Jawbreaker. "Three of them? You're kidding, right?"

"I wish...to God I was!" he replied. "If those bombs are detonated, millions of people will die, people whose lives ...I don't want on my conscience. More than that, this could be the beginning of the end of the world, Jawbreaker . . . and I, quite frankly, don't want to die!"

"Frankly, I don't believe your story," said the masked man. "It's just too far-fetched."

"I... believe it," Theodore Fulton affirmed, his expression intensely serious.

"Then you're as loony as your brother."

"Whether or not you do believe me, just remember . . . Miss Foster is *with* my brother."

"Where is he?" he exclaimed, violently grabbing Fulton's shirt and pulling him to just inches away from his masked face. "Tell me now, or I swear I'll . . ."

"He's . . . he's on a strip of desert out near Victorville. I took him and Miss Foster this afternoon. I can give you exact... directions.'

"And what's he doing there?"

"He's got a plane hidden out there . . . one of the items those robberies financed. He plans to wait until daybreak, when he... has visibility, then take off — with Miss Foster in tow — and then drop the first bomb on L.A. But there's still... time for you to reach Howard before he... takes off! Still time for you to save Miss Foster . . . and, if you believe what I've told you is the truth, also save us . . . save this country from destruction . . .

maybe even the world!"

In that moment the weight of what Fulton was telling him nearly crushed Jawbreaker's spirit. What had started out as the whim of a bored chauffeur and bodyguard, and then had metamorphosed into the task of rescuing a kidnapped young woman, could now also be a chore of incalculable proportions. If Theodore Fulton's crazy story about his brother and three A-bombs was correct, then Jawbreaker was being called upon to prevent the destruction of a major city . . . three cities, and after that. . . .

"It looks like I've no choice," Jawbreaker said in a somber voice.

Reaching into his pocket, Fulton removed a piece of paper and a fountain pen. "I'll draw... you a map."

"Don't waste your time," said Jawbreaker, grasping Fulton's wrist.

A look of shock appeared on the ex-special effects man's face. "You're not suggesting. . . ?"

Again the two revolvers were in the masked man's gloved hands. "I'm suggesting nothing. I'm telling you. You're going to drive — and I'll be sitting next to you with *these* . . . all the way."

LAST CHAPTER: UNMASKED

The first hint of dawn was showing over the flat horizon, as the Pontiac Bonneville roared across the desert beyond Palmdale. Dust and dirt billowed about the four black-wall tires as the vehicle sped along the dry flatland on its northerly course, racing against the rising of the sun. Theodore Fulton, pale and trembling with fear, was at the steering wheel. Although his attention was focused mostly on the barren land stretching for miles before him, his eyes sometimes shifted to the vehicle's only other occupant.

The man sitting beside Fulton wore a tight-fitting black hood and black gloves. The eyes that stared out from the mask's slanted holes were cold and determined. The twin .38 revolvers in the masked man's hands were pointed directly at the driver.

"Can't you get this crate going any faster?" inquired Jawbreaker sternly.

"I've got it floored now," replied Fulton, his voice cracking. "Maybe . . . maybe we should have taken that motorcycle."

Jawbreaker shook his head. "It'd have gotten us there faster. But it wouldn't figure into what I've got planned for when we get to our destination."

"And what's . . . that?"

"You'll find out soon enough. In the meantime, you're going to do some talking. For starters, what's this weird hang-up your brother has over the Scarlet Skull?"

"Yes, the Scarlet Skull . . . the masked serial villain who tried to kill that movie hero for a dozen chapters straight," related Theodore Fulton. "Well, following the special-effects accident that destroyed Howard's face, my brother could not handle his new appearance. His mind . . . began to slip. You see, the face he was burdened to keep for the rest of his life, even after some failed plastic surgery operations, looked very much like . . . like the red mask worn by the Scarlet Skull. With a little make-up, Howard easily transformed himself into a real-life counterpart for that character. We all . . . I, too, until just yesterday . . . believed that Howard was just wearing a costume. I never dreamed that he really. . . ."

"Go on."

"Anyway, as Howard's sanity continued to deteriorate . . . he began to identify more and more with the Scarlet Skull . . . even acting like the character right down to... speech patterns. And like that character, he eventually devised a 'master plot' by which he could have revenge upon those he considered ...responsible for his accident."

"I was under the impression that it was one person — a prop man — who was responsible for that miniature building blowing up in his face," said Jawbreaker.

"That's correct," answered Fulton. "But Howard's demented mind held . . . not just that careless prop man . . . but the entire motion picture industry responsible for his horrendous disfigurement. As a result, Howard set out... to destroy that industry. At first, when he told me told me he was out for revenge, he gave me no... hint as to the magnitude of his plan."

"So you went along with it," the masked man stated.

At last Fulton began to relax. "I did. For when Howard lost his face and his... mind, he lost his status... in the movie business also. Howard's loss of employment included . . . my own. I must admit, without Howard's genius, I was . . . nothing. And I, too, wanted to get even with the people I would no longer be... working for."

"Amazing," said Jawbreaker with a shake of his head, "assuming, of course, that all you've told me isn't a lie or some concocted plot of yours. Tell me more . . . about this plane you said your brother bought."

"It's an old World War Two-vintage DC-3, also known as... a

C-47. War surplus and not in the best of shape, but it will take Howard and Miss Foster to... his three targeted destinations. Howard chose the DC-3 because he could afford it, because it would do the job he needed it to do, and for some historical... significance. It must have turned up in dozens of serials and movies since the war."

"I know the model," said Jawbreaker, an angry tone creeping into his voice. "And I also know it's not big enough to hold three even low-end atom bombs. In fact, I doubt you could fit *one* A-bomb through the entrance of a DC-3."

"Remember that I said Howard had these bombs built to his... own specifications? Again influenced by the old chapterplays, he had them made smaller . . . somewhat rocket-shaped . . . like the super-bombs the Scarlet Skull exploded in the serial. Why, he's gone so far as to equip them with... those old-fashioned timing devices you always saw in the serials — you remember, the kind with the arrow... that ticks off from 'start' to 'detonation' before the bomb... blows up."

"My God!" said Jawbreaker. "Your brother's even loonier than I ever expected. But I still don't know if I believe he actually possesses three A bombs."

"Are you willing to take... the risk that he doesn't?"

The eyes looking out from the ebony mask replied more saliently than their owner ever could in words.

Finally, after a long pause, Jawbreaker instructed him, "When we reach the plane, here's what we're going to do. . . ."

* * *

The silence of the lone stretch of desert was interrupted by the whirring sound of airplane engines. The sky was rapidly getting brighter, the first rays of morning glinting off the battered silver-gray hull of the decades-old DC-3. The airplane's propellers, one on each wing, were rapidly building up speed.

Inside the cockpit of the vintage aircraft, the pilot — possessing the face and wearing the garb of an old movie villain called the Scarlet Skull — laughed as he made a final check of the airplane's gauges. Once satisfied that everything was in order, he turned his hideous visage in the direction of the shapely brunette sitting beside him. Her make-up had long worn off and her luxurious hair was unkempt, but she remained a strikingly beautiful young woman.

Fulton smiled, although he realized that his skeletal expression was virtually the same when he frowned. Barbara continued to squirm, trying without success to push her trim form through the ropes that kept her a prisoner of the co-pilot's chair.

"There's nothing accomplished by wasting your energy, Miss Foster," Fulton told her. "I'm almost as good at tying knots as I am blowing things up."

"Please . . ." Barbara pleaded, relaxing. "Think about what you're about to do. It's insane!"

"That's where you're wrong, Miss Foster. It may be the sanest act anyone's ever done on this planet."

Frowning at Fulton, Barbara made another futile attempt to break her bonds.

"No need to be so impatient, Miss Foster," he said. "We'll be taking off in just a few minutes, as soon as it gets a little lighter out there. That leaves me just enough time to take care of one small — but important — detail."

Getting out of his chair, leaving Barbara where she helplessly sat, Fulton exited the cockpit, leaving the door open. He stepped into the airplane's cabin and then paused, pleased at what he was now seeing.

There were no seats in the cabin. In the past aircraft such as this had been used primarily to transport supplies and equipment, not passengers. To accommodate the loading and unloading of larger items, the hull of this particular airplane had been customized with double doors in the aft section of the cabin.

Feelings of pride, elation and satisfaction rushed through the man with the skull face as he beheld the fruits of so many months of planning and spending and labor — three rocket-shaped bombs, each about four feet in length, resting silently and ominously on the cabin floor. Each device was equipped with one of those quaint timing attachments Howard was so fond of, reminding him of the fake bombs the Democracy Pictures prop department used to create during the heydays of the serials.

Howard knew what he had to do next. His mind had already gone over the schedule many times. Initially he would activate just one of these devices—the one that would reduce Los Angeles, the hub of the industry he was determined to destroy, to rubble and nuclear dust. Once that city—along with the Hollywood film industry it contained—was obliterated, he would then fly east to the city of New York, where he would activate the second device. The third device, the one that would destroy Chicago, would be switched on last.

As he admired his three bombs, something sleek and black, moving outside the airplane, caught Fulton's attention. Turning to a side window, he observed his brother's Bonneville slowing to a stop about a hundred feet away from the plane. Waiting and watching, he saw his brother exit the automobile and hurry towards the airplane's aft doors.

There were only two reasons his brother would have come here, Howard knew—either to stop him from carrying out his mission or join him on it. Remembering the effect the revelation of his plan had had on Theodore the previous day, he suspected the former reason. Either way, however, he would be ready to greet his younger sibling.

Howard Fulton rushed up to the bomb that was closest to the double doors. His heart beginning to pound fiercely, he noted its arrow-like timer device, then pressed the activation button just to the side of that feature. A weird combination of humming and whining sound issued from the rocket-like device, ever so slowly elevating in pitch, as the arrow began its crawl forward from left to right.

A loud pounding on the outer surfaces of the double doors broke through the sounds emanating from the bomb. The smile on Howard Fulton's Death's head face widened grotesquely and the eyes in their cavernous sockets almost glowed in the light coming in from the cabin's side windows. His device—the thing he had acquired at the cost of so much money, time and trouble, so many lives—had been successfully activated. Now, if brother Theodore had, in fact, come to thwart his "master plan," it was already too late.

Confident that his plan could not fail, Howard Fulton

breathed a sigh of relief, opened the doors and leered out towards the man standing outside. "So, Theodore," the skull-headed man said, "have you finally decided to join me?"

"Yes. . . ." said the other man, speaking the word Howard had not expected to hear. "We are, after all, still... brothers." He reacted to the strange sounds coming from the cabin, his eyes shifting towards the first of the three devices. "I see you've already activated the first of the three bombs."

"Indeed I have," replied Howard, proudly. He motioned politely for Theodore to enter the aircraft. "And the way these bombs have been designed and built, nothing can turn them off once they've been activated. The moment that metal arrow reaches its destination, it's all over . . . but by that time it will be falling over Los Angeles."

"I . . . see," said Theodore, gazing down at the activated device. "Then I guess it's a good thing that I finally decided to... join you, isn't it?"

"I wish I could offer you a more comfortable ride. The co-pilot seat is already occupied."

"Miss Foster?"

The skull-like head nodded. "You'll have to stand or sit on the floor during the trip. But I'll try to make the trip as smooth as possible."

"Thanks, Howard, I appreciate... your concern."

"Oh," commented the red-garbed man, "from this moment on, you will stop calling me by that name. Howard Fulton is officially dead. He died on that fateful day at the studio when that miniature building exploded.

"Today, and very much alive, I *am* the Scarlet Skull."

* * *

Barbara Foster glanced once more at the skull-faced man seated next to her again. Howard Fulton—or rather the "Scarlet Skull," as he insisted on her calling him, enthusiastically worked the controls of the DC-3. The cockpit of the old aircraft vibrated slightly as the airplane rolled forward along its makeshift runway, proceeding on a southerly direction. Then, right on schedule, the aircraft rose into the early morning sky.

197

Barbara knew that it was useless to attempt further reasoning with this lunatic. He was determined to carry out his mad and murderous plan regardless of the consequences. Among those consequences, on a personal matter, was the death of the one person in this world that she cared about most. Somewhere down below, in the city that the man now claiming to be the real Scarlet Skull was about to destroy, was Dave Andrews. Dave—like that mysterious character Jawbreaker, whom Howard Fulton hated most—would soon, along with the rest of Los Angeles' vast population, go up in a cloud of radioactive destruction. Barbara's lithe body pushed back against the seat, as the old aircraft continued its ascent.

Howard Fulton—or the "Scarlet Skull"—did not speak again until the airplane had attained sufficient altitude. "We can relax for a little while," he told her, leveling off the aircraft, and then working more controls, "before we reach the target area, Democracy Pictures. I may as well see how little brother is doing back there. Hope the ride isn't too bumpy for him. Don't worry, my dear, you'll be safe while I'm gone. I've switched on the autopilot."

"Don't hurry back on my account," Barbara said, as the crimson-garbed man arose again from the pilot's chair, vanishing from her view as he left the cockpit while again leaving open the door. Silently she prayed that something would go wrong, interfering with Fulton's cleverly worked out scheme. What that "something" might be, however, she could not even imagine. It would require a veritable miracle for any force to stop Howard Fulton now that he was in the air and on the way to his first of the three doomed targets, one bomb already activated.

Yes, she thought, a miracle was needed . . . and it had to happen fast.

That was when she heard the shrill voice of the self-christened "Scarlet Skull" exclaim from the cabin: *"You!"* Listening, Barbara heard a lot more suggesting that her prayers might indeed be answered.

* * *

Eyes—peering coldly from behind holes cut into an ebony hood—looked up towards the cockpit's now-open door. They shifted briefly, observing within the cockpit a long and nicely tanned female leg, one that was immediately familiar. Barbara was sitting in the co-pilot's chair, Jawbreaker was now certain, probably tied there. The masked man was down on one knee, his gloved hands running over the first of the three bullet-shaped devices—the one from which the weird sounds were emanating—frantically searching for some switch or button that might shut the thing off.

Howard Fulton, posing threateningly in his guise of the Scarlet Skull, the character Jawbreaker remembered from the old movie serial, stood at the fore end of the DC-3's cabin, just outside the cockpit. His face appeared frozen into a look combining shock with horror, and his eyes seemed to blaze with almost godlike power within their dark sockets.

"Howard Fulton, I presume?" said Jawbreaker in a mocking voice.

"Howard is dead!" insisted the man with the Grim Reaper face. "But the Scarlet Skull lives!"

"Is that so? I thought you were that Nazi from the 'Captain America' comic books. Only he had better luck than you. He was just wearing a mask."

A sensation of nausea suddenly attacked the masked man's stomach, as he beheld the skull-faced man up close and "in person." Indeed, Theodore Fulton, during their drive across the desert, had already described this fiend in the most gruesome details. Yet actually seeing him, in color and three dimensions, made him feel as if he had suddenly been thrust into a horror movie.

"You!" Howard Fulton emphatically declared again, grinding his exposed uneven teeth and glaring down at the man now hunched over the first bomb, "I thought you were. . . !"

"Don't say it, please!" said Jawbreaker, still looking up at the man in scarlet. Wincing at what he saw, he returned his attention to the more pressing matter of the purported nuclear bomb. "I'm really getting tired of hearing that line," Jawbreaker grumbled, "although finally seeing you, I might say the same thing. In fact, you look like you've been rotting in a grave for several months."

"And *you* . . . !" Howard's head snapped to his right, noting the third man inside the cabin, leaning against the inner wall of the cabin. "When my back was turned, you betrayed me! Brought aboard my worst enemy!"

"I'm . . . sorry, Howard," said Theodore Fulton, "really I... am."

"I told you — *I'm the Scarlet Skull!*"

"All right then, 'Scarlet Skull.' But I did everything you told me to do, at the studio, even lighting the fuses during our early pyro tests, and then did all those other things afterwards . . . except this. Here I had to draw the line. I *had* to bring Jawbreaker here . . . to stop you before you had the chance to use any of . . . those." He reached forward, indicating the three bombs.

Naturally, Jawbreaker could not determine if the device in front of him was or was not an authentic nuclear bomb. The only such devices he had ever seen — all of them made by the United States Government, rather than some crazed private citizen obsessed with old films on which he had worked — were in photographs published years ago by *Life* and other magazines. And this thing, with its much smaller size and streamlined rocket-type shape, along with the detonation gadget, certainly bore no resemblance to the nuclear devices shown in those pictures.

Jawbreaker wondered: Had Howard Fulton, in his delirious attempts to emulate the celluloid screen's Scarlet Skull, merely convinced himself that these three metallic things were the genuine articles?

He could not take the chance. Even if these were not authentic hydrogen bombs, they could, at the very least, be *some* kind of explosive devices, and very powerful ones at that.

"You're wasting your time," the "Scarlet Skull" said to the man with the black hood and gloves. "There's no way to shut the bomb off once it's been activated. And once that arrow hits its mark, it's all over. And unless I drop that device overboard when we reach the target, we will all die with it."

"Is that so, Mr. Bones? Then I'll just have to make certain that the arrow *doesn't* reach that mark."

Promising that, Jawbreaker grasped the metal arrow with both gloved hands, exerting all of his considerable physical might in an attempt to pull it back in the opposite direction. But, despite his greatest efforts, the detonation device—albeit slowly—continued to advance.

"Damn!" he said, straining, grunting, fighting in vain against the ever-advancing attachment.

"Like I said, masked man, there's nothing you can do to stop that bomb from exploding—and I assure you, it's going to explode over its intended target, and not here."

Again looking up from the bomb, Jawbreaker saw that one of his adversary's hands now clutched a pistol—a weapon he recognized as a World War Two German military Luger—its polished black barrel aimed in his direction. "Now you really remind me of that comic-book Nazi." Knowing what to do without being told, Jawbreaker raised his hands, at the same time stepping back away from the bomb.

"Theodore," the "Scarlet Skull" stated in a commanding voice, "open those doors. Before our masked friend here can cause me any more grief, he's going for a little trip. Unfortunately I won't be able to spare him a parachute." The eyes in the sunken sockets indicated the folded parachutes lying on the floor. There were only two of them.

"No!" Theodore vehemently protested, sounding to Jawbreaker as if the man had regained some of the confidence he had formerly commanded when addressing Matson and the Fultons' other hirelings. "I'm finished helping you . . . doing the work of some underling! The dirty work! You won't involve me in anymore of this madness!"

"Won't I?" returned Howard Fulton, casually aiming the Luger at his brother's shoulder and firing, a blazing spike erupting in the airplane's cabin.

Gutturally, Theodore moaned. He grasped his wounded shoulder, cupping his hand over the flowing blood.

From the cockpit, the familiar voice of Barbara Foster cried out, "What's happening back there?"

Ignoring the woman in the co-pilot's chair, the "Scarlet Skull" warned his sibling, "This gun holds eight more cartridges—more than enough to keep whittling away at your body until you do as I've told you. Where shall I fire next, Theodore? Your leg, or . . . ?"

Raising his blood-spattered hand imploringly, Theodore made his way to the double doors. Still groaning from the pain of the bullet lodged in his shoulder, he managed to open the doors, letting inside a tremendous, ongoing rush of air.

"But first, Mr. Jawbreaker," said the scarlet-garbed madman with a slight wave of his pistol, "before you make your dramatic exit, I want to see who it is that's been such a thorn in my side," he said. "Now . . . *Take off that mask!*"

"Seems like I've got little choice," replied the crimefighter. "Okay, 'Scarlet Skull,' you win this round . . . but the bout's not over yet." With a broad and deliberate action, Jawbreaker grasped his ebony hood, and then dramatically yanked it off his head. There was a crooked smile on the countenance that was now exposed. "There," he said, dropping the mask to the floor. "Happy?"

"That face!" exclaimed Howard Fulton. "I recognize it from somewhere . . . years ago . . . but I can't seem to. . . ."

"Andrews!" blurted out the other Fulton Brother, appearing stunned. "Mr. Stuntman. So it *was* Dave Andrews all along."

"I must admit I'm perplexed," said the fiend who had been Howard Fulton. "Why would someone do what you've done . . . risk his life like you've been doing? What's in it for you? Did someone hire you to put on that mask?"

"Did someone pay you to put on that Halloween costume?"

That stated, now exposed and taking advantage of the "Scarlet Skull's" surprise, Andrews moved again—leaping forward with blinding speed, launching himself off through the air. In just seconds he was already landing on the man with the Luger, forcing him down against the floor. His adversary's fingers relaxing, the German-made weapon flew from the "Scarlet Skull's" hand and slid.

"Theodore!" shouted Andrews, struggling to pin down the other man. "Can you fly this rust bucket?"

"I . . . I think so," said the wounded man, still groaning from his pain. "Hope...so!"

"Then pick up that gun . . . change course for due west

getting us as far out as you can over the ocean . . . and then free Barbara . . . !"

Andrews glimpsed Theodore Fulton, fighting to keep standing amid the incoming wind, nodding and then retrieving his brother's Luger, then making his way across the cabin towards the aircraft's cockpit.

The "Scarlet Skull" — that is, the person he had been — was a man of advanced years, a man neither physically fit nor trained in the arts of combat. Nevertheless, he fought back his younger and physically superior foe with a strength augmented by madness. Thus, while Andrews fought to restrain him, the lunatic went for his neck, seizing his throat as if in the jaws of a human vise.

The taste of blood surfaced hotly in Andrews' throat, as the two men — each one determined to end the existence of the other — slipped and jerked each other about the cabin. Just inches away from Andrews' face, the skull-like visage grimaced, the dark-encircled eyes almost burning as they stared intently into his own.

The proximity of that ghastly Death's head was all that Andrews required to get his heart and blood racing — that, plus the ominous sound that issued ominously and relentlessly from the first of the three bombs. With a powerful burst of energy, Andrews punched the raw face of his enemy, knocking him back against the wall. At the same time, Andrews heard the whining sound of the airplane's engines and felt the floor tip to one side, upsetting his balance and toppling him over. Obviously Theodore Fulton was executing his second task, making the prescribed turn in the airplane's course.

Already the "Scarlet Skull" was reviving and starting to get up again.

Quickly regaining his stance, Andrews leaped back atop his opponent and pressed his body tightly against the floor. He saw his foe, desperately struggling to flee, intentionally — or maybe accidentally — kick out with one foot, colliding with one of the plane's only two parachutes, jettisoning it out the open double doors. Managing to get in another punch, Andrews sent the older man falling backwards, his body relaxing in a heap on the floor. Already too much critical time had already been wasted.

Glancing out through the open doors, Andrews noted the expanse of water moving into view. Theodore Fulton was performing the second of his tasks quite admirably. The airplane was presently cruising over the Pacific Ocean, the only place he knew where he might safely dump the three bombs — atomic or not — *if*, that is, he could somehow first prevent one of them from detonating.

"Dave . . . !"

As instructed, the younger Fulton brother had performed his last assignment. Glancing towards the cockpit again, Andrews saw Barbara rushing up to him. Presently not in her usual glamour mode, she did, in that moment, appear to him more beautiful and alluring than she ever had before. She was, indeed, the proverbial sight for Dave Andrews' sore eyes.

"My God, Barbara!" he exclaimed, as she ran towards him, being careful not to make contact with any of the three menacing-looking devices. "I never thought I'd see you again," she said, sobbing and embracing him. "I thought you were going to die along with the rest of LA, and I . . . "

He saw her notice his gloves, then the black mask lying on the floor. "Dave, you're . . . Jawbreaker?"

"We'll talk about that later, sweetie...when we have more time."

In that moment Andrews wanted nothing more than to crush Barbara against him, kiss this woman whom he had so missed and who had become such an integral element of his existence. He wanted to make love to her on the spot and then never let her go. But for now the only thing that could rightly matter was bomb number one. In the past few minutes the arrow indicator had advanced a significant distance. Already it was but inches away from its final destination.

"Right now I've got to figure out how to deactivate this damned thing," he replied to her after a silent pause. He crouched down and again moved close to the bomb. "As to how, I don't have a damn clue."

As Andrews' mind worked to solve his problem, he turned his head slightly, reacting to movement elsewhere in the cabin. He glimpsed the would-be "Scarlet Skull" staggering back to his feet, then slowly make his way back towards the cockpit.

"Dave . . ." said Barbara, reacting towards the skull-headed man.

"No time to worry about him now. This baby's got top priority."

Hearing the cockpit door slam shut, Andrews once again directed his full attention to the bomb.

"Can you turn it off?" asked Barbara, her voice filled with emotion. She bent her knees, joining Andrews beside the device.

In frustration, he shook his head. "Somehow — and I don't have the foggiest notion how — I've got to stop that arrow from moving forward and reaching its mark. But I'm not strong enough to physically force it back...and this gadget doesn't seem to have come with an 'off' switch." For another full minute Andrews pondered his dilemma. Once that arrow completed its journey, the bomb should explode. If the device was still on board the aircraft when that occurred, everyone inside the aircraft, Barbara included, would be blown to dust. Moreover, the explosion would probably also set off the other two bombs, resulting in even greater and near-instantaneous devastation. Yet if he shoved the thing outside, even over the Pacific Ocean, the bomb — if, as the Fultons claimed, was a nuclear device — would destroy millions of lives. Either way, the situation — and the fate of Los Angeles — seemed hopeless.

Suddenly the DC-3 lurched . . . violently, knocking both Andrews and Barbara away from the first bomb and against the cabin wall. From the cockpit came sounds of struggling . . . objects banging against its inside walls . . . noises accompanied by angry masculine voices. The Fulton siblings had to be fighting within the cramped confines of the cockpit, battling perhaps over mastery of the airplane's controls, or over trying to end each other's life. Andrews knew that, if Howard won that unseen battle, the airplane would soon be leaving behind the vicinity of the Pacific Ocean and heading back towards his intended target area.

Absolutely no more time remained to deliberate the situation. The mechanical arrow was now mere inches . . . seconds . . . away from its detonation mark.

The airplane continued to lurch, its wings tipping from one

side to the other. The air from outside continued to shoot into the cabin. It was difficult for Andrews just to keep his footing, let alone deal with the bomb. But he was not giving up. . . . "Maybe if I had something small . . . very solid . . . to block that arrow. . . ." Andrews mumbled, loud enough for Barbara to hear him, while struggling to maintain his footing. In desperation, perspiring, he looked around the shaking and tipping cabin, hoping to find something . . . a tool . . . *anything* of the appropriate strength that he might wedge between the arrow and the place where it would finally come to rest, and upon making contact with that point, set off the bomb. Nothing!

Then, something occurred to him. Almost simultaneously, he and Barbara looked with wide eyes at each other, and then towards the pocket area of his sports jacket. Why, he wondered, had he not thought of this possible solution earlier? And right now it seemed so obvious . . . Smiling, Andrews reached below his jacket, extracting one of his prized revolvers . . . cracked it open . . . removed from its cylinder a single .38 bullet. Then, his heart racing as the arrow — too fast — closed in towards its mark, he carefully moved his arm towards the arrow, all the while fighting to keep his hand steady as the cabin did its best to shake him down. Carefully he managed to set the bullet between the arrow and its destination.

The arrow — jammed — stopped moving, barred from fulfilling its deadly duty by the cartridge. The whining sound that had been issuing from the device suddenly wound down in pitch, and then faded away. "I think we did it, Barbie!" said Andrews, gasping. "Imagine . . . stopping one explosive by using another."

"Will it . . . hold?" she asked, as the cabin continued to shiver around her.

"It'd *better* hold, baby," he replied, trying his best to believe what he was telling her. "Because if it doesn't, we're going to be in for one hell of a surprise."

"So, now what do we do with it?"

"We're going to drop these that little horror — along with its two friends over there — where, with luck on our side, no one will ever find them. But we've got to do it fast, before we're back again over dry land."

Working together, each one taking an end, Andrews and Barbara yanked and shoved the first bomb towards the open double doors. Accomplishing their intended feat was difficult; for the bomb was heavy, and the jerky movements of the aircraft made movements of any kind all the more difficult and precarious.

Fortunately they were still flying over the ocean. Apparently Theodore, even as he continued to struggle with his crazed brother in the closed cockpit, was maintaining at least a modicum of control over the DC-3's course. But that control, Andrews predicted, would not last for long.

Careful not to disrupt the saving bullet, Andrews and Barbara, exerting all of their combined strength, managed to edge the first bomb out through the open double doors and off into space. Taking only a moment to catch their breaths, they proceeded to eject the second bomb . . . then the third. To their relief, no explosions occurred.

Presumably the three devices were now safely descending to the bottom of the Pacific, the .38 cartridge permanently wedged into the timing mechanism of the first. Again the plane lunged, this time more severely, violently jostling the two people in the now-empty cabin.

Moments later, from behind the closed cockpit door, sounded the blast of a gun being fired — Howard's Luger.

"One of the Fulton brothers may have been shot," stated Barbara.

"Maybe," said Andrews, as the DC-3 continued to lurch from one side to the other. "But which one?"

Another gunshot . . . "No time to find out which," Andrews said, at the same time reaching for the airplane's only parachute. "The plane's out of control and I never took flying lessons. And look out there — we're already over the Santa Monica Mountains."

"Then how. . ." she started, "are we going to get down?"

Moving fast, Andrews slipped on the parachute. Shock registered on Barbara's face. "You're not...leaving me up here?"

Andrews laughed. "What do you think, Barbie?"

His arm shot around her bare waist and held her snugly. "Now, no matter what, don't let go."

Then, Barbara clinging to him with both arms, Dave Andrews jumped out of the airplane.

* * *

The parachute opened, safely catching the air. Andrews, still holding onto the woman he loved, felt his body jerk strongly as the parachute broke their fall, retarding their descent. Looking down, Andrews could see solid earth gradually rushing up towards them. The plane had been diverted east—away from the Pacific Ocean—in a mostly unpopulated area that he identified as probably either Santa Monica or, more likely, Malibu.

Overhead he saw the erratically flying DC-13 as it continued, wings tipping, on its course, the two brothers possibly still entangled their battle. He witnessed the aircraft wobbling from side to side, its trajectory now sending the plane directly towards the mountains' peaks. Whether or not Theodore or Howard Fulton remained alive in the airplane's cockpit—and if both were alive, if either sibling happened to be winning his battle—were now moot points. Moments later, the DC-3—an aircraft whose cargo might have meant doom for three major United States cities and their millions of occupants—collided against one of the mountaintops, erupting in a colossal ball of cascading flame and black smoke.

Wryly, Andrews had to smile, as he and his precious burden alighted on the ground just yards away from a bicycle trail. The explosion, he thought, perhaps had an ironic implication. For, indeed, it was a spectacular blast—an act of destruction of which both Fulton brothers could be proud.

Waiting for Andrews to slip off the parachute, Barbara moved close to him, grasped his wrists and gazed soulfully into his eyes. "We have to tell everyone that you . . . you saved the world!" she told him with pride and excitement.

"Tell who what? Any proof we might have had just went up in that fireball. Besides, if the world really did just get saved," he said, moving closer to her, "we both saved it . . . working together."

"There's lots we can do together," she said, just before

kissing him. Andrews had missed that kiss for too long a time.

* * *

Late that same day, Dave Andrews and Barbara Foster, both wearing swimsuits, sat stretched out on patio chairs beside Aaron Van Aaron's swimming pool. Stanford, the multimillionaire's British butler, was smiling and cocking an eyebrow as he served them iced tea.

"What about . . . you know, 'him'?" asked Barbara. "Are you going to . . . you know . . . put on the . . . you know, again?"

Andrews placed a finger against his lips and slowly shook his head. "That, Barbie baby, must remain our little secret. Remember, he's – and me too, if his true ID were to be revealed – is a much-wanted man. Let's just assume he died in that plane crash."

"There you are, Mr. Andrews, my own special brew," Stanford stated with his very English accent, seemingly oblivious to the meaning of their brief dialogue. "I brought it back with me from London, my Mum's very own recipe. For you also, Miss Foster. You know, Miss, it's been far too long since you last graced us with your presence."

"Don't lay it on so thick, Stanford!" came a rather venomous voice from across the patio. "Well, *Miss* Foster, I was under the impression that you dumped that loser. Obviously I was wrong and misjudged you. No accounting for taste, I suppose."

Turning as he sipped his cold drink, Andrews saw his employer—his poor excuse for a physique revealed by his boxer-style bathing suit—exit the house and walk towards the pool.

"Did I detect a little hostility in those remarks, *Mister* Van Aaron?" grumbled Andrews.

"More than just a little, *Mister* Andrews?" replied the other man. "Do you mind telling me where the hell you've been all this time . . . and with my limo?"

Andrews took another sip of his iced tea. "I mind. And your car's back where it should be—in its carport—safe and sound, and with a full tank of gas."

Aaron Van Aaron paused for a few moments, as if trying to

think of what next to say, before speaking again. "You know, *Mister* Andrews," continued Van Aaron, "if you weren't so damned good at what you do—driving me around and providing me with much needed protection—I'd fire you on the spot. Then what would you do? Go back to working as a dumb stuntman . . . making less than half what I've been paying you? Well, *Mister* Andrews . . . what have you got to say to that? Are you going to threaten to quit again, is that what you're going to do?" Aaron Van Aaron laughed. "Oh yes, and where's my tape recorder?

But Dave Andrews, for once, did not threaten to leave this relatively easy job, nor did he reveal the fate of Van Aaron's tape recorder. This time he said nothing in reply. Rather, he arose from his chair, clasping Barbara's hand and flashing her a warm smile, then walked across the patio and into the mansion. Determinedly he walked into the kitchen, stepped up to the telephone and dialed a number that he knew from memory. After three rings a receptionist's voice greeted him.

"Democracy Pictures?" Dave Andrews began. "Could you please put me through to Dale Steele, if he's working today? Thanks."

He waited a little more, less than a minute, before another voice spoke over the phone. "Dale? Hi. It's Dave. Say, pal, life's been kind of dull lately, and I was just wondering . . . "

AUTHOR'S AFTERWORD

After more than half a century, Jawbreaker is back!

But, in reality, he was never really gone.

Jawbreaker (AKA Dave Andrews) is a super-hero in the sense that other famous, bigger-than-life champions of justice — *e.g.*, Zorro, the Scarlet Pimpernel, Tarzan, the Spirit, the Lone Ranger, Santo, the Phantom, etc., some of them wearing masks and having dual identities — can also be so labeled. Traditionally, super-heroes have what are called "origins" and Jawbreaker is no exception. Not gifted with actual super-*powers*, as possessed by Superman or Captain Marvel, Jawbreaker was a so-called mystery man who wore a black hood with matching gloves. Thanks to his athletic prowess and superb fighting skills, he excelled when it came to battling bad guys ranging from common crooks to evil, megalomaniacal criminal masterminds. Like most super-heroes, Jawbreaker's actual origin was — at least *almost* — in a comic-book.

In the late 1960s, I was just starting my professional writing career, having written three articles that were bought by publisher Jim Matthews for the third issue of his Hollywood-based magazine *Modern Monsters,* then gearing up for that issue. Jim's company Prestige Publications was based in what was then the Playboy Building on the Sunset Strip. I had looked up the company's telephone number, called Matthews and scheduled a meeting. That meeting included my artist friend Larry M. Byrd. While I succeeded in selling Matthews those three articles, Larry got work for the magazine doing cover

211

paintings and art direction.

At that initial meeting, Larry and I also pitched to Matthews two new magazines—the first, *Movie Marvels*, somewhat like Warren Publishing Company's *Screen Thrills Illustrated*, but with less emphasis on Westerns; the other, *Ka-Pow! Comics*, a black and white illustrated magazine not unlike Warren's *Creepy*, but featuring, instead of stand-alone horror stories, the adventures of offbeat super-heroes that probably would not, for various reasons, get approved in a regular color comic book that had to be approved back then by the restrictive Comics Code Authority. This was when "Batmania" and "camp" were at their peaks, thanks largely to the phenomenal success of the *Batman* television series.

After some weeks of consideration, Kable News, *Modern Monsters'* newsstand distributor, passed on *Movie Marvels*, despite the potential magazine's emphasis on movie serials, *Batman*, *The Crimson Ghost*, *Atom Man vs. Superman* and the like. But *Ka-Pow! Comics* seemed like a natural, a winner right out of the starting gate.

I had assembled for the premiere a group of atypical "super heroes," whose non-Comics Code-approved exploits would fill out each issue. One of these heroes, intended for the magazine's second issue, was Jawbreaker, whom I named after a hard candy I remembered liking from my younger days.

I mentioned that the *Ka-Pow!* heroes were offbeat. Jawbreaker was a masked crimefighter. Unlike such characters as Superman, Captain America and the Flash, Jawbreaker did not wear a colorful skin-tight costume. And *why* would an adult man—a *sane* man, even one existing in the fantasy realm of pulp fiction—put on a hood or mask and risk his life fighting criminals? Jawbreaker didn't fight crime because of some traumatic childhood experience, as did Batman. He wasn't ultra-altruistic, nor did he need any reward money; his day job paid well, he had a beautiful girlfriend and he lived comfortably.

Frankly, Dave Andrews battled evildoers because he was *bored*. A successful movie stuntman, in the 1960s, his film career was suffering thanks to do-gooders campaigning against on-screen violence. Now he worked as a bodyguard for a somewhat paranoid multimillionaire who, as things turned out, never really required protection. And action was something Andrews needed, craved; it was in his blood, it was his life. Therefore, he decided to engage in real life the thrilling kind of activity a film studio once paid him to perform on screen in "reel" life.

I named Jawbreaker—his real identity, *sans* mask and gloves—after both my stuntman friend Bart Andrews, who had appeared in some of my amateur and USC student films, plus his personal hero and role model, stunt ace David Sharpe.

Mostly through Larry Byrd's efforts and connections, we had been able to find, prior to our initial meeting with Jim Matthews, a number of artists who would do—"on spec," as neither of us could afford to pay them—sample "splash pages" for the various features. We were mildly successful in this venture, among the submitting comics artists being Landon Chesney, who, although the strip was scheduled for issue number two, promptly submitted a "splash page" for the intended first "Jawbreaker" feature. Alas, the *Ka-Pow!* project, "Batmania" notwithstanding, was not accepted by Kable News, and the new publication's planned premiere issue was literally a dead issue.

Almost dead, anyway.

It's long been a policy of mine not to allow anything I do to perish—*if* I believe that project has merit but may require some revising. So it was with my Jawbreaker character and his story. I decided to go from sequential artwork to prose fiction and transform the project into a *novel* written in the style of the old pulp magazines, *i.e.*, periodicals that featured such masked and mysterious crime-fighting characters as the Spider, the Black Bat, Doc Savage and The Shadow.

Back then I was a Big Fan of comic books, old-time radio drama and, as was Bart Andrews, movie serials, particularly those made by Republic Pictures. I thought it would be fun to base the novel, then titled *Jawbreaker, the Hooded Hunter*, on those old chapterplay adventures from previous decades. Jawbreaker, who wore only a hood with eyeholes to conceal his true identity, was based upon such masked movie-serial good guys as the Black Commando (played by actor Paul Kelly), whose secret identity was a police lieutenant, in *The Secret Code* (Columbia, 1942), also on comic-book heroes like the cop-turned-vigilante Black Hood, whose exploits appeared not only on the four-color pages but also in pulp magazines and on a short-lived radio series, and Joe Simon and Jack Kirby's Stuntman, a costumed circus performer who doubled as a crime-fighter. Mostly, however, Jawbreaker was patterned after the dynamic Copperhead, a man who donned a masked to avenge the murder of his guardian, in Republic's excellent 1940 movie serial *Mysterious Dr. Satan,* wherein David Sharpe handled star Robert Wilcox's more rigorous action scenes.

But what is a masked hero without an evil arch enemy?

A traditional character type in stories of this nature, regardless of format, is the mystery arch-villain. My novel's equivalent of such a nemesis, the Scarlet Skull, had, like Jawbreaker, several influences. One inspiration, no surprise, was the similarly named Red Skull, Captain America's main Nazi (later, for a while, turning Commie) opponent, aside from Hitler of course, in myriad Timely (now Marvel) comic books. There was also some facial inspiration from the fire-scarred antagonists in movies like *Mystery of the Wax Museum* (1933) and *House of Wax* (1953), both from Warner Bros.; and from various filmed versions of *The Phantom of the Opera*. There was also the aptly named Skull, a top bad guy in the 1940 Columbia Western serial *Deadwood Dick*. But the main inspiration for my Scarlet Skull, however, came from the megalomaniacal Grim Reaper-like villain in a 1946 serial from Republic, *The Crimson Ghost* (whose image would later be appropriated by a punk rock band, the Misfits).

As to the true identity of the Scarlet Skull, I combined the names of both Howard and Theodore Lydecker, who created all those great (often exploding) miniatures at Republic, with John P. Fulton, whose special optical effects enriched so many movies at Universal.

Rather than setting some locations of my novel at Republic, I used Democracy Pictures, a fictional studio I've featured, over the years, in my other novels, comic-book stories and even credits of some of my old amateur movies. Although my novel would have numerous references to the movie serials of past decades, I made my story contemporary, setting it in the era with which I was then most familiar (during the time I wrote it), the 1960s.

I wrote the novel on standard *i.e.* manual, non-electric typewriters, in my Hollywood apartment and while on vacation in my home town of Chicago, then sent it off to a few publishers, and — nothing happened. No one was interested in publishing it. Therefore, into a drawer it went — where, after approximately half a century, it remained. More recently, recalling that novel's merits, I decided to resurrect it. The plot, I believed, still held together, although the text would benefit from some rewriting, as any writer's work tends to improve over time. I wrote a new draft, this time putting the text through a computer instead of a typewriter, fine-tuning it, giving it the new title *Jawbreaker vs. the Scarlet Skull* (which sounded more like the title of an old movie serial), subsequently shortening it to the punchier Jawbreaker, even injecting some continuity with *Brother Blood* (a vampire novel published in 2010 by Pulp 2.0 Press), which was also set during the 1960s, and, among other of my writings, the science fiction novel *Spawn* and horror novel *Bugged*.

Trivia note: The character Dale Steele, named after famous movie stuntmen Dale Van Sickle and Tom Steele, was also a pen name I'd used in one of my *Modern Monsters* articles, a name I used for myself in the credits of an amateur movie *Rocketman Flies Again* (1966), which featured Bart Andrews, and as the same character in *Brother Blood*, wherein he was killed by a vampire.

After all these years, Jawbreaker's story is finally being told in print, although his adventures occurred some 50 years ago.

* *

A special thanks to legendary artist, author, all-around Renaissance man — and professional escape artist — Jim Steranko, without whose help, via a 2:00 AM telephone call, my masked hero would never have broken out of that locked vault. (Dave Andrews, aka Jawbreaker, thanks you, too, Jim!)

216

KA-POW COMICS: The Magazine that Never Was!

The following original (and very dated) article was published in the fifth issue (summer, 1969) of GUTS... The Magazine of Intestinal Fortitude! *published by Rob and Jeff Gluckson. The opinions expressed therein were those of the author at the time of its writing, and are not necessarily held by the writer today. The article, despite any grammatical, punctuation, spelling, consistency, all-around awkward early writing or other problems, has not, to preserve its original spirit, flavor and integrity, been in any way further edited (except for some minor spacing issues). This is its first and only reprinting – DFG.*

A wave of monster movie magazines, spawned in the mid-1960s, encompassed short-lived titles such as MONSTER MANIA, the British SHRIEK, and MODERN MONSTERS. Warren's SCREEN THRILLS ILLUSTRATED had already met extinction. His comics format magazine CREEPY had toppled from its peak and was devolving toward mundane mediocrity. These magazines, however, influenced future publications.

The beginning of 1966 also brought BATMAN to television, an event which gave birth to a craze that was to almost totally snuff out the dwindling monster and secret agent fads. James Bond was becoming familiar, routine, less exciting and fresh than he appeared in the film DR. NO. Fantastic powers and abilities were steadily replacing suave and gimmicked agents in popularity. The true costumed superhero was "in."

The market seemed obviously right for two new quality magazines.

The first of these was of the SCREEN THRILLS type, but the way I felt the book should be done. Originally titled MOVIE MARVELS, then through a progression of working titles including THRILLERAMA, the film magazine was to be completely devoted to serials, super-heroes, and the like.

The second book was a magazine-sized, black and white publication, similar to CREEPY in format, but presenting super-heroes so way-out, so out-of-the-ordinary, that the COMICS CODE would not allow them to appear in the conventional comic book size. I do not mean to imply that these heroes would be in bad taste or be gory for the sake of uncensored thrills. Rather, these new costumed characters would be well founded and hopefully believable. However, the very fact that their personalities would be dramatically human would result in some questionable actions. In other words, despite the absence of color, I wanted to give the readers something they couldn't get in a 12¢ comic book. This article deals with this second type of magazine.

I was to edit both magazines; Larry Byrd, familiar to the pages of most quality monster magazines, was to be art director. We presented both packages to Jim Matthews, publisher of MODERN MONSTERS, who in turn attempted to convince the distributor, Kable, that we had a couple hits in the works. MOVIE MARVELS reached the stage of completed layouts, accompanied with photostats of all photographs to be used. Unfortunately, that was as far as the project went. The magazine was turned down because of the failure of another Kable publication that came out several years premature— SCREEN THRILLS; turned down, despite the unbelievable success of BATMAN, the reinterest in comic book heroes, and the revival of serials. The camp craze was not enough to deviate from the status quo. All was not totally lost, however, for at least some of the material eventually saw print in MODERN MONSTERS and is scheduled for future issues of CASTLE OF FRANKENSTEIN. The complete history of MOVIE MARVELS and the true fate of MODERN MONSTERS, including the fifth issue that has been confiscated by the printer since the fall of '66, is another story.

The second magazine, called <u>KAPOW!</u>, though theoretically a good idea was almost doomed from the outset. Kable was extremely interested in the venture and fully realized its newsstand and subscription potential. Our main problem involved the sample package we were to send to their New York office for final decision—a package that was to include a <u>substantial</u> amount of finished artwork. When one is attempting to get professional artists or even professional-looking fan artists to meet deadlines on speculation, this is indeed a difficult task. We had at least part of the issue ready to show the men with decisive power at Kable—but not enough. Therefore, after I had written most of the scripts, Larry Byrd had broken them down, and Bill Spicer had lettered the flats, and some of the scheduled artists had penciled and inked a few splash pages, the magazine, along with the super hero fads, gradually vanished in a state of disinterest.

KAPOW! COMICS, as it was first entitled, was changed by Kable's representative to simply KAPOW! The exclusion of the word "COMICS" was a precaution against any possible friction from the Comics Code Authority, placing it on the racks" with other "picto-fiction" magazines. And as CREEPY and EERIE have their Uncle and Cousin, our magazine was to have a costumed personality introducing each of the strips— KAPTAIN KAPOW, drawn by Larry Byrd. Since the magazine will doubtless never see print and distribution, I'll break down the contents of the first issue, strip by strip:

KAPTAIN KAPOW — editorial, later to become the letters page.

MAN-LIZARD, STONE AGE AVENGER — This ten-page strip as [sic] to appear in every issue as a serial, telling the story of Boran, a caveman in love with Lona, daughter of the aged tribal chief. However, the beautiful blonde girl is also desired by the evil, lecherous Graggu, leader of the hunt who, despite his gruff mannerisms & frightening appearance, is a coward. One night Graggu brutally murders the chief, planting enough evidence to reveal Boran as the guilty one. In the morning, Graggu's plan reaches materialization. Without chance for explanation, Boran is branded a killer, and by tribal law must be executed on the spot. Leaving a disbelieving Lona, Boran acts like a Wildman and axes his way through the wall of screaming vigilantes. He then dives off the skyscraping cliff towards waters plagued with crushing rocks and hungry sea monsters. Believed to be guilty and dead, Boran's own hatred and will to survive push him to a nearby body of land. There, half-drowned, he vows never to have anything to do with humanity — for if his loved ones have rejected him, what else can he do? Suddenly, he hears a familiar rumbling — a stampede of gigantic prehistoric monsters! Overhead, a glowing meteor crashes down. After the confusion has settled, Boran notices that the weird magnetic rock from the sky is resting, sizzling. Curious, he touches the giant lodestone meteorite; it instantly explodes, bathing the caveman in its radiation. Boran does not die; but later realizes that he has absorbed the powers of that lodestone. And by utilizing the attracting and repelling forces now within him, he can simulate flight, acts of super-strength and so forth. His method of revenge is almost complete. Finding the remains of a mammoth and a Ceratosaurus killed in the stampede, he fashions a costume of hair and skin and returns to his former people. He would make them pay!

In further episodes, Man-Lizard was to kill Graggu and to be accepted by the tribe as a hero. However, his love for Lona, his inability to ever prove his innocence, his hatred for everyone else present problems. He does not want to be a hero but likewise does not want to lose Lona entirely. Never able to show his true face even to her, the main substance of the strip was the manifestation of his own conflicts in trying to find himself and relate his existence to the primitive world about him.

Jeff Jones was to illustrate MAN-LIZARD, STONE AGE AVENGER. The splash page sample was drawn in the days between the fanzine and professional Jeff Jones. And I believe that his work on MAN-LIZARD surpassed anything he did for professional comic-format magazines. One thing which entirely turned me on to Jeff's sample page was the fact that he followed my demand that his Pteranodon be original and not copied from a Charles R. Knight painting or something. I suppose it is a fetish of mine against dinosaur swipes in comics and text books. In a letter from Jeff to Larry Byrd was the line, "I think it is original enough not to resemble any other artists' work. The poses are mine. Hope it is suitable." It sure was!

MAN-LIZARD, STONE AGE AVENGER went through many phases; a completed comic script written in various styles, depending on where it was submitted after KAPOW!, with different degrees of violence and gore; a feature-length motion picture script with the addition of a Triceratops "pet" and mount; and the first chapter of a tentative full-sized novel. MAN-LIZARD started out as quite an original concept — a prehistoric super-doer. It was interesting to later view the television cartoon hero slanted for a much younger audience, The Mighty Mightor [sic], although the similarities were purely superficial.

SKY ALTITUDE — This was a one-pager to appear in each issue, a character created many years before by Ron Haydock when he was editing and writing for fanzines. Sky Altitude was a Captain-Midnight-type hero who flew around in an old dilapitated [sic] bi-plane. Readers of Larry Byrd's defunct fanzine TERROR might still have their identification cards to the SKY ALTITUDE FAN CLUB. The scheduled artist was Charlie Scarborough, familiar to Ron's FANTASTIC MONSTERS OF THE FILMS MAGAZINE.

LEGENDARY SUPER-HEROES — Every issue of KAPOW was to have this single page feature, presenting the obvious. George BARR [sic] consented to do the series. Scripted for the first was biblical strongman SAMSON.

COMMANDER BIRDMAN — Created and to be written by Larry Byrd, the Commander had been adapted to the pages of TERROR, to FAMOUS MONSTERS OF FILMLAND, to Ray Steckler's feature film THE LEMON GROVE KIDS, and even appeared with Rat Pfink in Hollywood's Christmas Parade some years ago. No relation to the BIRDMAN television show, this one-pager to appear in every issue of KAPOW! had Charlie Scarborough scheduled as artist. The strip was to be humorous; "almost" a takeoff on HAWKMAN.

RAT PFINK AND BOO BOO — No artist had been scheduled for this ten-page take-off on Batman and Robin created years before the advent of the BATMAN TV program. The strip was based on a feature-length movie starring Ron (Lonnie Lord) Haydock as Rat Pfink, a rock singer moonlighting as a super-hero. The film, involving a gorilla, fights, chases, et cetera, was produced and directed by Ray Steckler. It was originally titled MURDER A GO GO and ended up simply as RAT PFINK. The strip was never scripted, but was to be an adaptation of the film story. Again, Ron Haydock was to write the adventures.

STEELMASK — Created and written by Jim Harmon, author of the best-selling book THE GREAT RADIO HEROES, this was a character in the tradition of the pulp magazines, similar to THE SHADOW and THE SPIDER. STEELMAS\K wore standard pulp hero attire — a trenchcoat [sic] and a black hat. His face was entirely covered by a metal mask, but not merely to conceal his identity. STEELMASK wore his disguise for a more profound reason — his face had been totally erased by acid. In short, he had none! The character originally appeared in a novel titled TWILIGHT GIRLS, written by ""Judson Grey," the collaborative pen name of Jim Harmon and Ron Haydock. The avenger also starred in the short story "Steelmask meets the Zombie Master" in FANTASTIC MONSTERS, an item which drew the most fan mail in the magazine's history. The character was never completely scripted for KAPOW!, but is tentatively scheduled for adaptation as a new dramatic radio fighter.

COUNT NOCTILIO — Ten pages long, this was to be another running, serialized character that never went beyond Jim Tutweiler's first draft penciling stage. Count Noctilio, originally conceived as Vampire-Man, might have emerged as the most bizarre super-hero of them all. He was a genuine, actual, real vampire, hundreds of years old, but after centuries of evil enactments, he has decided to reform. To make ammends [sic] for his vampiric crimes, he wants to use his Un-Dead powers to battle crime. Taking a noted psychiatrist and his pretty secretary into his confidence, the Count relates his Slavic origins and past atrocities. He explains that he possesses vast powers, yet can still be defeated by conventional limitations — garlic, daylight, the stake, etc. And he must still consume human blood, which he purchases from blood banks

— not the fresh stuff used for transfusions, naturally; but outdated blood, normally just thrown away. Operating out of a crypt in a virtually unused graveyard, Count Noctilio dons a bizarre costume and sets out to bring to justice a maniacle [sic] axe murdered. The first script ended with the axeman, aware of Noctilio's true nature, holding him against a wall with a Crucifix. Grinning like a ghoul, the killer cackles that both of them will just wait around for the sun to rise. That cliffhanger would never get by the Comics Code!

Realizing the potential in sales of gothic romance novels, I considerably diluted the story as far as horror and super-heroics were concerned, and wrote four chapters plus an outline for a novel entitled THE MYSTERIOUS COUNT NOCTILIO, still unsold. The vampire's flashy costume had been reduced to a simpler and more logical black outfit including a hood, cape, and a turtle-neck sweater without the big and bold "N" chest emblem. And his morbid but secret headquarters were [sic] moved to a more liveable [sic] sanctuary of an abandoned mansion. Count Noctilio's main enemies, however, were not criminals. The general population, when learning of his vampiric condition, wanted only to destroy him. That was his major hangup.

Thus, we reach the back cover of this forty-eight page magazine.

Future issues were to remain basically the same, but with substitutions made for some of the strips. In KAPOW! #2, NIN-JITSU, written and illustrated by Jiro Tomiyama of FANTASTIC MONSTERS, would replace RAT PFINK, and JAWBREAKER would appear in place of STEELMASK.

NIN-JITSU was at first only a costumed judo/karate expert named the Black Belt, his skill of the ultimate degree. However, Jiro took my original creation and developed it into NIN-JITSU, which was the name of an actual masked and gimmicky mystery character of ancient Japan—a true, historical, factual super-hero (or villain) in the strictest sense of the term. Unfortunately, the strip did not reach the scripting stage.

JAWBREAKER had no real powers or spectacular costume. In reality he was Dave Andrews, a retired movie stuntman, now working for multi-millionaire Aaron von Aaron. The playboy is afraid that someone will someday attack him for his money and hires Dave as a bodyguard. His pay is good, so Dave will not quit. However, the two men hate each other tremendously, their personalities clashing to the nth degree. And since no one ever bothers to attack Aaron, Dave Andrews really has nothing to do more than just sit around. He'd quit— except for that pay. But being a man of action, he has to do something . . . spectacular. So Dave Andrews, experienced fighter and stuntman, dons a mask and becomes known for obvious reasons as Jawbreaker, battling crooks for kicks. Unfortunately, JAWBREAKER is not a Code-approved orthodox hero. In order to pursue a criminal he thinks nothing of first slugging a cop and stealing his motorcycle as a chase vehicle. In the first story, never fully scripted, JAWBREAKER was pitted against Howard and Theodore Fulton, a brother team of mad special effects experts using their knowledge of explosives to destroy everything in sight. The splash page was done by Landon Chesney. You may have caught his "in joke" in the sixth issue of Bill Spicer's FANTASY ILLUSTRATED fan-magazine.

The character and story were later expanded into a full-length, still unsold novel entitled JAWBREAKER: THE HOODED HUNTER, presented as a satire of the old Republic Pictures' movie serials.

KAPOW! and the various creations within its pages have been shelved; however, it is not completely dead. Perhaps Man-Lizard, Steelmask, Jawbreaker and the rest will materialize in other media. Better still, perhaps some publisher reading this will recognize potential in a magazine that would give the comic fan something besides a wishy-washy do-gooder that always has a sweat-free costume and only drinks milk. And perhaps, if that transpires, KAPOW! may someday become the magazine that IS.

ABOUT THE AUTHOR

DONALD F. GLUT has been professionally active in both the entertainment and publishing media since 1966.

Although he may best be known for his novelization of the movie *The Empire Strikes Back* (A Number One Best Seller for almost two months, having sold millions of copies, still in print – and read — today), Glut had a long and varied career. He has been a musician, actor, film director, executive producer, photographer, magazine editor, proofreader and (briefly, for an advertising agency) copywriter, but is mostly known for his long career as a freelance writer. He has authored approximately 80 fiction and non-fiction books (none self-published), also motion-picture scripts, TV scripts (live action and animation, network and syndicated), comic-book scripts, short stories, articles, music and theatre. As a novelist, television and comic book writer, Glut has been involved with popular franchises such as *The Monkees, Tarzan, Spider-Man, Star Wars, Transformers, Captain America, G.I. Joe, Vampirella, Masters of the Universe, The Flintstones, Johnny Quest* and others. An Inkpot Award winner for his comic book work, he has written for many of Gold Key, Marvel and DC's most famous comics and also created original comic-book characters for all three, including Doctor Spector. Currently he pens horror-comics scripts for *The Creeps* and

Vampiress Carmilla magazines (and is their Associate Editor).

In addition to all these efforts, the prolific Mr. Glut has also carved a niche in the film world as an executive-producer, writer and director of "traditional-style" horror movies featuring iconic monsters, among the most recent *Tales of Frankenstein, Dances with Werewolves* and *The Mummy's Kiss.*

For updates on his endeavors visit his website at www.donaldfgflutl.com/

Printed in Great Britain
by Amazon

29112694R00132